THE BANGOVER

LILI VALENTE

❀ Created with Vellum

THE BANGOVER

By Lili Valente

ABOUT THE BOOK

Dear Self—Do not pass Go, do not bang your oldest friend in the limo on the way to the swanky Vegas hotel. Just get back on the plane, fly home, and forget you almost had co-ed naked best buddy fun time with the one man who is completely off limits.

I give myself very good advice.
Too bad I suck at taking it.

Not that Colin Donovan, my bad boy rock star best friend, is any help. Walking around looking ridiculously sexy, telling me I'm beautiful and fun and perfect the way I am and somehow making me believe it.

If only we hadn't drunk so much whiskey that first night, if only I'd kept that red bikini in my suitcase, if only his evil ex-girlfriend hadn't come sniffing around making me feel all territorial and protective.

And if only I hadn't been secretly in love with Colin for

years before this Friends with Bennies Vacation got started.

Who knows? Maybe the high will be worth the fall. Either way, there's no way I'm leaving Vegas without one heck of a Bangover.

The Bangover is a red-hot, laugh out loud rom-com featuring two best friends on a collision course with Vegas-flavored disaster—and each other. It stands alone. No cheating or cliffhangers.

ALSO BY LILI VALENTE

Red HOT Laugh-out-Loud Rom Coms
The Bangover
Bang Theory

The Hunter Brothers
The Baby Maker
The Troublemaker
The Heartbreaker
The Panty Melter

The Bad Motherpuckers Series (Standalones)
Hot as Puck
Sexy Motherpucker
Puck-Aholic
Puck me Baby
Pucked Up Love
Puck Buddies

Sexy Flirty Dirty Romantic Comedies
(Standalones)

Magnificent Bastard
Spectacular Rascal
Incredible You
Meant for You

The Master Me Series

(Red HOT erotic Standalone novellas)
Snowbound with the Billionaire
Snowed in with the Boss
Masquerade with the Master

Bought by the Billionaire Series

(HOT novellas, must be read in order)
Dark Domination
Deep Domination
Desperate Domination
Divine Domination

Kidnapped by the Billionaire Series

(HOT novellas, must be read in order)
Filthy Wicked Love
Crazy Beautiful Love
One More Shameless Night

Under His Command Series

(HOT novellas, must be read in order)
Controlling her Pleasure
Commanding her Trust
Claiming her Heart

To the Bone Series

(Sexy Romantic Suspense, must be read in order)

A Love so Dangerous
A Love so Deadly
A Love so Deep

Fight for You Series

(Emotional New Adult Romantic Suspense.
Must be read in order.)
Run with Me
Fight for You

Lover's Leap Series

A Naughty Little Christmas
The Bad Boy's Temptation

The Lonesome Point Series

(Sexy Cowboys written with Jessie Evans)
Leather and Lace
Saddles and Sin
Diamonds and Dust
12 Dates of Christmas
Glitter and Grit
Sunny with a Chance of True Love
Chaps and Chance
Ropes and Revenge
8 Second Angel

Co-written Standalones

The V Card (co-written with Lauren Blakely)
Falling for the Boss (co-written with Sylvia Pierce)

The Happy Cat Series

(co-written with Pippa Grant)

Hosed
Hammered
Hitched
Humbugged

To Lauren Blakely again. Mwuah!

CHAPTER ONE

Colin

"So let me get this straight..." My best friend Kirby's voice is husky and soft in the darkness beneath her back porch, where we've been hiding for the past thirty minutes, preparing for our favorite post-hometown concert tradition—the pranking of Shep, my drummer. "You're swearing off sex so you can write songs."

"Correct. Not fun, but it has to be done."

"Does it?" She sounds bemused. "Really?"

"It does." There's a skittering sound on the planks overhead, and we both fall silent, but after a moment a plaintive *meow?* makes it clear we're not in danger of being attacked by trash-raiding raccoons.

It's just Murder, the evil ring leader of Kirby's collection of misfit cats.

"I'll be in soon, baby," Kirby calls softly. "Go inside."

I grunt. "He's probably out here looking for me. Fangs bared. Ready to take his pound of flesh."

"Probably," Kirby agrees with a chuckle. "He hates you so much." She nudges my shoulder with her smaller, pointier one. "But don't take it personally. He's just jealous that there's another creature on earth I like nearly as much as him."

"Nearly, huh? Thanks," I say, a smile in my voice. But I've been smiling pretty much nonstop since we took the stage earlier tonight.

There's nothing like a hometown show—the energy, the excitement, the noise, and best of all, a crowd packed with people who dreamed an impossible dream with you until the dream came true.

A lot of the greater Bangor, Maine area fans have been with us from the beginning, when Lips on Fire was just a bunch of high school kids playing all-ages venues on weekends—when Cutter wasn't grounded for getting caught smoking pot and Shepherd didn't have to babysit his herd of little siblings. In other words, they knew us way before our lips had ever set a girl on fire.

The people around here are more than fans. They're family, tribe, and I refuse to let them down. The new album is going to come out on schedule, even if it means I won't be coming.

At all.

Not a single orgasm until the songs are written, recorded, and in the bag.

Fuck...just thinking about it is enough to drive me to drink.

I take the flask from Kirby. Her skin is so white it's easy to find her hand, even in the midnight shadows. "When was the last time you were out in the sun, Larry? You're glowing in the dark."

"Don't call me that," she says in a tone that makes it clear she still loves it when I call her that. I might only see my best girl a few times a year, but we talk on the phone almost every night. I know her better than anyone, including her snot-nosed whiner of an ex-boyfriend, Peter, who I can't say I'm sorry is no longer in the picture.

The dude was a dud. If personalities had colors, his would be puce.

"I've been on deadline," she adds with a sigh. "And the sun stifles my spooky muse."

"Maybe you should write a children's book, instead," I tease.

Kirby Lawrence, KJ Lawrence to her legions of horror-loving fans, is about as child-friendly as a rusty razor blade. Sure, with her pale blond hair, bright blue eyes, and permanently pink cheeks, she looks sweet, but Kirby is a dark horse. Emancipated from her crap-tastic mother at seventeen and supporting herself and her little sister, Bridget, purely with her fiction skills two years later, she's a legend around Hidden Kill Bay. If it weren't for the phenomenon that is Lips on Fire—at last count, we've sold eight million records world-wide—she'd be our Bangor suburb's most famous export.

But Kirby doesn't care about fame. She plies her trade for the sick and twisted thrill of scaring people to death and the cash to support her cat adoption habit. At last count, she had four of her own and was footing the vet bills for at least a dozen other local felines.

I used to tease her about having Early Onset Cat Lady disease, but then she went down to the DMV and got a tragically dorky vanity plate that reads MEOWU-DOIN, and I stopped. I didn't know what she'd do if I continued to yank her chain. She threatened to have whiskers tattooed on her cheeks, and even though I was

95 percent sure she was kidding, I wasn't willing to risk that 5 percent.

Kirby's too cute to go full-on weirdo just yet. We have to get her hooked up with a non-snot-nosed dude who will worship at her love altar, first. She can be a prickly pear sometimes, but beneath her Wednesday Adams demeanor beats the heart of a sweet lady any dude would be lucky to call his own.

"And maybe *you* should pass the flask before you break the two-sip rule," she says, invoking one of our many adolescent rules of honor. Never hang on to the flask for more than ten minutes, and never, ever take more than one sip at a time. "And maybe you can explain to me why you can't bang and write at the same time?"

"I'm a man. I'm bad at multitasking." I pass the flask, adding in my 70s porn star voice, "And when I'm focused on my lady, that's all that's on my mind, baby."

Kirby snorts. "So focus on your lady for two minutes, or however long it takes rock stars these days, and then get back to writing songs. I'm pretty sure that still leaves several hours of your day free."

"You wound me, Larry. I'm a ten-minute man. Sometimes twelve, if I've eaten my Wheaties and think of my grandmother's underwear."

She snorts again, and I feel unreasonably proud of myself for making her laugh twice. Kirby isn't an easy mark. Either I'm getting funnier, or the whiskey is starting to make her feel as fuzzy around the edges as it's made me, a fact for which I'm grateful.

Having a killer case of writer's block is less scary after the buzz sets in.

Though, pretty soon, that's going on the shelf, too—

no alcohol, no sex, no nothing that might mute the muse.

"But seriously," I add in a softer voice. Kirby had her place reinsulated last year, but it's still an old cottage with thin walls, and I don't want any of my bandmates knowing how far behind I am. "I've got to do something. We're going into the studio in August to record, and I've got one song, dude. One. After a hundred hours in the writing cave."

"Fuck," she says, clearly feeling my pain. But she would. As a fellow career creative, she knows all about the strain of making art on demand.

"Yes. That. So I'm going to quit fucking before I'm any more fucked."

"You seriously think it will help?" She shifts my way, passing over the flask. "I thought only meathead jocks believed their power seeped out of them with their seed. Remember when Coach Brewer made the wrestling team stop jerking off senior year, and they all kept getting hard-ons during the meets?"

"I do remember," I say with a laugh-shudder. "It's not like that for me. It's just..." I shrug. "My best song-writing years were before we blew up, back when I was a kid right out of high school, writing songs and dreaming of a day when getting laid would be something that happened to me more than once or twice a year."

It's her turn to shudder. "Sounds torturous."

"It was pretty miserable," I agree, "but great for the creative muscles. Yes, I've written good songs since then, but never so quickly or with such consistent quality. You know?"

Kirby hums beneath her breath. "Okay. I can see your point. But what if it was a timing thing? I mean, maybe back then you were just full of that early fire. I used to write a lot faster, too. Five thousand-word days used to happen all the time. Now I get two thousand, and I treat myself to ice cream."

I take a long swig of whiskey, chest burning as I swallow. "You could have a point. But I prefer to believe that I've been distracted and can course correct, not that I'm washed up at twenty-nine."

"Aw, there, there." Kirby's hand lands on my shoulder for a series of awkward pats. "Don't have a quarter-life crisis. It's going to be okay."

"You're such a dude," I say with a laugh.

"I'm not a dude." She sniffs. "I'm just bad at offering meaningless words of comfort. I'm better at action. What can I do to help? You want to stay here and write for a while, now that the tour is over? The Garret room over at the bed and breakfast is empty until August, when it goes on the rental calendar again. It's hot as balls up there on sunny days, but it's quiet."

"You're really going to rent it out?" I say, surprised. "I thought you loved being the mad woman at work in the attic."

"I did, but it's time for a change of scenery." She looks at the weathered boards above us. "I'm thinking of selling this place, too."

"What? Why?" Kirby bought this cottage just off the square with her first big royalty check. It's been a fixture in our lives since we were barely old enough to buy liquor to fill up our flask.

She's silent for a moment before she adds in a voice almost too soft to hear, "Peter is all over the place here."

I turn to her, squinting in the shadows, but it's too dark to know if she's wearing a "let's talk" expression or her "mention feelings and I'll cut you" face. But any mention of her ex is rare enough that I can't let it slide. "So how's that going? The getting-over-Peter project?"

"Shitty." She reaches over, her cool fingers brushing mine as she takes the flask. "I mean, ending it was absolutely the right thing to do. If he hadn't, I would have, but...I don't know. He was my longest relationship, the guy who knew me best in the whole world. And then he decided I was too much of a pain in the ass to stay in love with and left. It just...sucks."

"*He* was the pain in the ass. He was clearly threatened by your confidence and success. And that was his problem, not yours. You're a kick-ass lady, and that's a scientific fact."

"I don't think that was his problem. I think it was... other stuff," she says vaguely. "But thank you."

"No thanks needed. Facts are facts."

She hums, a little too dubiously. But before I can insist she own her awesome, she says, "I've dated a few guys since it ended, but nothing serious, and none of them got further than a goodnight kiss. No matter how hard I try, I can't get into anyone around here."

Now I'm grateful for the darkness hiding my shock. "Wow. So you mean..."

"I haven't had sex in nine months."

"Damn," I mutter. "And you're still alive?"

Kirby and I have only ever been friends—she's been in a relationship with one tragically pale douchebag or another since we met in our freshman year of high school—but we're *close* friends. We talk about everything, including our healthy sex drives, the ones that can apparently be overwhelming and/or irritating to people who don't enjoy banging as much as we do.

I'm dreading the month of celibacy it will take to get these songs written like a prison sentence. But a year of genital isolation?

The thought alone makes my cock play the world's tiniest violin.

"Yeah, I'm still alive," Kirby says, taking a swig and swiping her hand across her lips. "But just barely."

"Is it because you're still hung up on Peter?" I ask, trying to keep my distaste for Mr. Puce from my voice.

"No. I'm over him, I really am," she says. "It's more that I feel lost, unsure what comes next. I just know I don't want to settle for *meh*, and *meh* is all that's left around here. All the good guys are already coupled up and starting to make babies. I have to flip the script, find a new dating pool before my vagina shrivels up and blows away."

I shudder. "Yeah, don't let that happen. Twenty-nine's way too young to lose your vagina. So where are you moving?"

"I don't know. But somewhere. Soon. I'm taking a week off to binge watch all the TV I missed while I was on deadline and debate the options. Then I'm going."

"I'm taking a week off, too," I say. "But I was thinking of heading somewhere less family friendly. Like Atlantic City."

Kirby makes a gagging sound.

"I know, I know." I laugh. "But I can't go to Vegas unsupervised. You-know-who lives there, and you know what happened the last time."

"How could I forget?" she huffs. "I can't believe you married She-Who-Shall-Not-Be-Named. Thank God for annulments."

"Amen," I agree soberly. "And thank God for friends who mock your evil exes in their books."

"Any resemblance to anyone living or dead is purely coincidental," Kirby says, but there's a grin in her voice. "But you're welcome. Some people deserve to be turned into evil vampire clowns. And the answer is yes, by the way."

"The answer to what?" I pause with the flask an inch from my lips, wondering if I'm drunker than I think I am, 'cause I don't remember asking a question.

"Yes, I will go to Vegas with you." Her face is illuminated in the glow of her cell as she taps at the screen. "I'll message my assistant in California. She'll still be awake, and she'll get us a hotel and two tickets on an affordable flight."

If this were anyone but Kirby, I'd ask if she was joking, but I know her better than that. Kirby is *never* spontaneous. Until she is, and then, watch out, because she's the kind of crazy that will lead to just about anything.

It's one of the reasons I love her so damned much.

On impulse, I lean in, pressing a kiss to her cheek. "Tell her first class all the way. I'm paying."

Kirby's lips quirk as her eyes dart back and forth between the phone and me, making it clear I threw her with the kiss. "Shut up. You are not. We'll share, and we'll go coach. Only assholes fly first class."

"Well, I'm an asshole, and I can't fly coach without getting mobbed by fans," I say, kissing her cheek again, just for the fun of seeing her flustered. "First class."

"Coach. You can wear a hat. And stop kissing me, weirdo."

"Why? Because you like it so much?" I tease,

squeezing her thigh above the knee where her skirt ends, making her twitch and slap my fingers away with one hand as she hits send on her text with the other.

"Yes, you ass-wipe. I haven't been touched below the neck in nine months. My skin is starving. If you're not careful, you're going to make me want things I shouldn't."

The confession hits me and—*zot!*—I'm ice. I'm locked in carbonite. I'm thinking I'll spend my days as a gobsmacked objet d'art, when Kirby laughs and says, "Gotcha."

I suck in a breath and choke on whiskey fumes. "Shit, you had me. I thought you were serious."

"Of course not," she says, shutting off her phone and sticking it in her jacket pocket. "But now that I think about it..."

I narrow my eyes her way, heart zooming again, wishing she hadn't plunged us back into the dark. I can almost always get a read on Kirby's face, but without the visual clues, her dry delivery fools me every time. "But now that you think about what? Don't fuck with me again, Larry. I'm drunk. And fragile."

She hesitates. "Fragile in what sense?"

"Um, in the writer's block sense? I've got an entire album's worth of songs due in a month? I only have one written. Any of this ringing a bell?"

"Of course it is. But you're not hung up on a girl right now, right?" she asks. "There's nothing romantic going on in your life?"

"Hell, no. I mean, She-Who-Shall-Not-Be-Named is still cyberstalking me, even though it's been four months since we accidentally had sex again."

"I still can't believe you did that. You were doing so

well, and then you had to go and fall off the wagon, dick first."

"Well, that's why it's called accidental sex, Kirbs. Because it's accidental," I say, bristling even though I know she's right. "So that's a shit show. And then Kayla is writing a tell-all book about last summer in Barcelona, and Rhiannon texts me constantly. But I can't block her because she's threatened to set fire to the vintage Red Sox jersey I left at her place, so I have to play nice until I get it back." I sigh. "Yeah. So romance is pretty dead to me."

"Poor lamb."

"I am a poor lamb." I drag a hand through my too-shaggy-even-for-a-rock-star hair. "Feel sorry for me and make it easy for me to understand you." I cast a pointed glance up at the porch. "Where the fuck is Shep, anyway? He always calls his mom at midnight. Do you think he went out front instead?"

"No, he'll come out here. It's too loud by the road. And it's still a few minutes until midnight, which gives us just enough time to figure this out."

"Figure what out?"

"Figure out if we're going to Vegas as friends or... kissing friends."

Before I can call her bluff and remind her that a double "gotcha" is as off-limits as a double sip, her lips are on mine, soft, cool, and tasting of smoky-sweet whiskey. And for a moment, there's nothing but shock— sharp and head-clearing—and then electricity floods through me, lighting me up like the spots that drenched the stage tonight.

Damn, my girl's a good kisser.

A phenomenal kisser—assured, skilled, and a little

dirty, like she's fucking my mouth with her tongue, giving me a taste of what it would be like to be inside her.

It's exactly the kind of kissing I like. And then some.

"You're delicious," she whispers against my lips, making me even hotter, harder.

Shit. I've got a hard-on for Kirby, and though it isn't the first time—she's sexy as hell, and I've known her since I was too young to have much control over what got me hard—it's still a tricky situation. But *she's* the one who wanted to add kissing into the mix, and—fuck it—I want her on me. Now.

"Closer," I growl as I reach for her. "I want you closer."

"Yes," she agrees, breath hot on my lips. And then she's straddling me, and my hands are smoothing up her soft thighs beneath her skirt, and I know it should feel weird—this is *Kirby*, for God's sake—but it doesn't. It feels hot and good.

And...safe.

I know Kirby. I trust Kirby. She's not going to go crazy or clingy on me, and she'd never let something as trivial as seeing each other naked get in the way of our friendship.

We are forever. Rock solid.

So when she says, "I vote kissing friends," I answer, "Hell, yes, woman. I'm going to break your dry spell like spring on the Serengeti."

She laughs, kissing me harder as she says, "You'll taste the rains down in Africa?"

"Oh, I will definitely taste the rains, Larry. Just let me at 'em."

Kirby giggles—actually giggles, like a normal girl—

before covering my mouth with her hand and announcing in a too-loud whisper, "Shh, I think someone's on the porch."

"Someone is definitely on the porch," Shep's deep voice rumbles from overhead. "And someone isn't stupid enough to get pranked by you two assholes again. Come inside and quit being weird. Bridget's making crab dip."

"Oooo, crab dip. I love crab dip," Kirby says as the door closes overhead, signaling Shep has left the building. Or returned to the building, rather.

I am definitely drunk, but not too drunk to make decisions, and I know better than to question Kirby's judgment while she's inebriated. The last time I did that, she challenged me to a field sobriety test, which she passed with flying colors while I couldn't find my nose with my finger with my eyes closed.

"Should we eat crab dip and then pack?" she asks. "Or pack and then crab dip?"

I start to speak, but the sound is muffled. Kirby pulls her hands away with another giggle.

"I'd rather eat your pussy, please," I say. "Then pack. Crab dip optional."

She covers my mouth again with a scandalized gasp. "What's wrong with you?"

"I don't like crab dip," I mumble into her cold little hands, loving that she's still straddling me, rocking her hips against mine in an absent-minded way that gives me a clue how desperate she is to scratch that itch.

And I am getting equally desperate to oblige her.

"No, I mean the pussy talk," she whispers. "You just jumped straight to it. No warning, no verbal foreplay of any kind."

"So you want me to tell you how I'm going to lick your tits first? Bite your nipples and—"

Giggling harder, she orders, "Stop. Save it for Vegas, dude. And for real, what happens in Vegas stays in Vegas. We don't tell anyone about this, okay? Not even Shep and Bridget. This is our secret."

I hold up a hand in a solemn swear before circling her wrists and drawing her fingers away from my face. "Deal. But just so you know, what happens on my tongue also stays on my tongue. I don't eat pussy and tell. You can trust me, Larry. And I seriously don't know if I can wait for Vegas, I am so fucking turned on right now."

"Yeah," she whispers, rough and sexy. "I can tell." And then she rocks her hips, slowly, deliberately against my cock and says, "Hmmm...yes. That'll do, pig."

"Babe?" I ask with a disgusted shake of my head. "Seriously? You're on my cock, and you're quoting Babe?" She giggle-snorts in response, making me laugh as I slap her ass and say, "Get drunk; you're home, Larry."

"I am not. I am of sound body and mind, and I know what I want." She rolls off me onto the hard-packed earth beneath the porch. "Crab dip. Cat carrier. Suitcase. That order."

"Cat carrier?"

"Murder's coming, too."

My lips part to argue that we do not need a villainous overlord of a cat on our fuck-buddy safari, but Kirby cuts me off with a snap of her fingers and a firm, "Not up for debate. Let's move, Donovan. Move, move, move like you've never moved before!"

"I'm going to move *you* like you've never been moved

before," I grumble under my breath, standing to follow her out from under the steps.

"Oh, I hope so, Col," she says with a happy sigh. "I really do."

"Me, too," I agree, a smile stretching wide across my face.

Damn, this is going to be fun—the perfect way to get the last of the fucking out of my system before I straighten up, fly right, and crank out a bunch of beautiful music.

But until then, Kirby and I are going to have a fucking blast.

Literally.

CHAPTER TWO

Kirby

I wake up with no feeling in my right arm, my face smashed into an unfamiliar pillow, a case of cottonmouth any stuffed animal would be proud of, and the disturbing realization that I can't remember where I am or how I got here.

I can't remember, but I instantly know Colin is involved.

I am not a rock star.

I do not do rock-star things like stay up all night burning old love letters or go skinny-dipping in the ocean at midnight or drink so much whiskey after a show that building a pack of vampire snowmen in the town square at three a.m. sounds like a good idea. But under the influence of too much Colin Donovan, I have done all of these things and more.

And apparently, our latest case of shared insanity has landed me on a plane. There's no mistaking the lingering smell of jet fuel or the dull roar of the engines churning away on either side of this soaring death pellet.

I crack open my lids, and yes—there's the overhead

bin, dull gray and sad in the dim light of the darkened cabin. But instead of the usual packed sardine tin of people on either side of me, there's only a fully-reclined seat arranged head-to-toe with mine, a quaint swiveling bedside table, and gray plastic walls that grant this little cubby-for-two almost complete privacy.

There is, however, no sign of Colin.

But I wouldn't put it past him to talk me into buying a first-class ticket to somewhere and then drop me off at the airport before skipping off to do more exciting things. He knows I hate planes. I hate them so much that I usually have to be drunk, drugged, or both to force myself down the Jetway and into my assigned seat. But I've never booked a trip while under the influence. I make travel plans, arrange my life accordingly, and then I pop a Xanax like a civilized person twenty minutes before boarding.

This impulsive gallivanting is unacceptable. I don't usually do impulsive, not even in my work. I'm a plotter, not a seat-of-my-pants wordsmith. I know exactly how the vampire clowns became vampire clowns and who they're going to kill—and why—before I type a single word. And if I deviate from my outline, I feel anxious, unsettled, unmoored until I find my way back to the path and tie up any loose ends I've created.

I like the path.

I like knowing what's coming next.

I like waking up in my own bed with my own pillow and all my memories of the night before.

I like all of that...until I snap, decide I don't like it anymore, and do something fucking crazy. The last time I snapped, I moved to a yurt in Tibet for a month. The time before that I went cage-diving with sharks. And before that, I bought a bed and breakfast at a repo auction, without even seeing the inside. All of those things turned out okay in the end—I learned to meditate in Tibet, conquered my fear of sharks, and set my sister up as proprietor of a profitable business with only a few bumps along the way renovation-wise.

But I'm just waiting for the day when I do something impulsive that doesn't have a happy ending. And perhaps today is that day.

I have no idea what inspired me to drink such an inadvisable amount of whiskey. But as I reach for the water bottle on the table beside me, grateful my hangover doesn't appear to be too vicious, I vow never to do it again.

No more whiskey, no more pranks with Colin, no more...

"Pranks," I mutter as I twist off the cap and gulp down every drop of brain-restoring liquid. I remember hiding out under the back porch at my place for what seemed like forever, waiting for Shep to come outside so we could prank him. I remember Colin having an existential crisis about his inability to write songs, and then I remember...

I remember...

"Oh no. No, no." I sink farther down in my chair, tugging my blanket up to my chin to hide my flaming cheeks seconds before a shadow appears at the entrance to the swanky first-class cubby.

A shadow cast by the long, lanky, yet surprisingly well-muscled body of my best friend. A body I am well acquainted with seeing as I had my hands all over him last night. All over his chest, his biceps, his abs, his ass... The same lovely ass that moves across my field of vision as he climbs quietly over me to settle in his seat, clearly thinking I'm still asleep.

I squeeze my eyes shut and fight to keep my breath slow and even, but I'm a horrible actress, and Colin has superhero-like senses and reflexes. If he weren't a rock star, he could be a ninja assassin or a cat burglar or something more wholesome that involves a similar skill set, but which I can't think of at the moment because my mind is not naturally inclined to weave wholesome stories and because I am dying of shame.

Dying—my heart stuttering to a stop and my stomach turning to stone as Colin grabs a fistful of my blanket and tugs it down to reveal my face. "Hey there, sunshine," he says with a grin. "How you feeling this morning?"

I shake my head and tug the blanket back up.

"That good, huh?" He chuckles and pulls it back down. "Don't hide. Talk to me. How much do you remember?"

"Nothing," I lie, leaping at my one chance at salvation. "Nothing between going out to hide under the porch and waking up a few minutes ago. What happened? How did we get here?"

Colin's full lips purse, and his brown-and-amber-flecked eyes narrow. "Yeah? That's all?" He brushes a thoughtful thumb back and forth along the line of his jaw, the pad making a soft shushing sound as it disturbs his morning whiskers. He's rocking a seven-a.m. shadow that makes him look even more like a naughty rock star, but if memory serves, this time it isn't Colin who can't be trusted.

It's me.

The killer's call is coming from inside the house...

He leans closer. "So you don't remember kissing me last night?"

I shake my head, wide-eyed in what I hope looks like innocence mixed with utter shock.

"No? Really?" he murmurs, resting a hand on the curve of my hip, making my skin burn even through the covers and the long skirt I'm wearing beneath. "Then I guess you don't remember dragging me up to your room, stripping off all of your clothes, and riding me like the last roller coaster left standing?"

My eyeballs attempt to leap out of my skull, but thankfully there are muscles and ligaments in place to keep things like that from happening.

There are not, unfortunately, muscles in place to keep my tongue from flapping. "I did not, you dirty liar."

"So you do remember," he says, pointing a victorious finger at my face. "Now who's the dirty liar, Larry?"

"Don't call me that," I mutter automatically, even though I love it when he uses the old nickname. And I hate it, and love to hate it, just like I love to hate this Lost Boy who keeps tempting me off the beaten path and into the jungles of Neverland.

Though, *I'm* the one who did the tempting this time. I still can't quite wrap my head around what I did. Just... pouncing on him like that, with no consideration for the consequences or potential fallout. It's so out of character that there can be only one reasonable explanation.

"Sex deprivation," I whisper as he stretches out beside me, lying backward on his reclined chair so his head is close to mine. "It finally drove me over the edge of reason. I'm sorry."

His brows snap together as he exhales. "Why are you

sorry? You're a great kisser, and I think your plan is brilliant."

I bite my lip, but finally can't help but ask, "What plan is that again?"

"The Fuck Buddy Last Hoorah Sex-Cation in Vegas plan," he says in a tone that makes me suspect we must have officially named this plan sometime last night. "It's a win-win. You break your sex fast and get the orgasms you so richly deserve, I make the most of my last week before I put on my chastity belt without risking any messy romantic entanglements, and we both come home with stories we can never tell anyone else, further ensuring the longevity of our unique friend bond."

I smile weakly. "Sounds like a win, win, win."

"Exactly." He beams, his eyes glittering like dying stars. They always burn brightest right before they burn out—yet another reason I can't go through with this, even if I thought it was a good idea now that I'm sober.

Colin is at a critical time in his career. He needs to relax, focus, and believe that he can craft a third album as uniquely heartfelt, yet radio ready, as the first two. He doesn't need to complicate his relationship with the one person in his life he can trust not to blow smoke up his ass.

And I need...

Well, I need to get naked with Colin like I need my hands to fall off. Colin would wreck me; I just know it. He wouldn't mean to do it, not even a little bit, but it would happen all the same.

I have to undo this. Reel the line back in before I catch something way too big for my boat.

"But I hate Vegas," I say.

"You've never been to Vegas."

I wrinkle my nose, cursing his steel-trap of a memory. "Yeah, well, some things you know you're going to hate without having to experience them firsthand. Like bread pudding."

"The kind with rum is actually pretty good." Colin shifts onto his side, propping up on one arm as he draws my blanket over to cover him as well. "And Vegas can be a blast. You just have to know where to go, and I've already thought of at least five things I want to show you."

"Like what?" I ask, intrigued in spite of myself. Colin can be unpredictable, but he's also an excellent travel companion. He always finds the hidden gems the other tourists overlook.

"Like the Neon and Antique Sign Museum," he says, his brows bobbing up and down beneath his shaggy hair. "Four acres of vintage signage, including a giant neon clown rumored to be haunted."

A soft, hungry sound escapes my lips, and Colin scoots closer with a grin, "I could take your picture in front of it. It would be fucking sweet as hell for the Funhouse series page on your website..."

"I don't care about that. I just want to feel its energy up close and see if it feels spooky."

"I know this about you, but you can do both things." He brushes my bangs to one side, making me even more aware of how close he is and how lovely he smells, like soap and birthday candle smoke, while I'm sure I smell like something a drunk raccoon puked up on the porch. "And guess what else we could do while we're there?"

"What?" I ask, lifting a hand to hover in front of my lips.

"Why are you covering your mouth?"

"Because I have dragon breath."

"You don't," he says, leaning closer. "You insisted on brushing your teeth at the airport before we boarded."

I wince. "Should I be troubled by how little I remember about the journey to the airport and pretty much everything after?"

"Do you get blackout-drunk often?"

I shake my head. "Never. Well, almost never. There was that one time after the Fast Grass festival. Remember that weekend? When we fell asleep in what we thought was an empty field watching the stars come out and woke up to cars parked all around us."

He laughs. "We're lucky we weren't killed."

"Seriously. I'm never getting blackout-drunk again."

"I support this plan," he says, his fingers wrapping lightly around my wrist. "We don't even have to drink in Vegas if you don't want to. Now put your hand down."

"No." I resist the pressure as he tries to draw my fingers away from my lips. "Why?"

"So I can kiss you while you're sober and remind you why we decided this was the best idea we've ever had."

My eyeballs impersonate cliff divers again as I shake my head.

"Yes," he insists, lids drooping to half-mast as he shoots me a look I'm sure has singed the panties off many a groupie and supermodel. "Let me kiss you, Kirby. If you don't like it, I promise I'll stop."

"That's not what I'm worried about," I mutter.

"What are you worried about? Don't be worried."

"Breath. Bad breath," I lie, even though I'm pretty sure Colin is right, and my breath is just fine. But I can't very well tell him that the thought of kissing him while sober is terrifying to me. I can't let Colin in on the secret I've been keeping since the night of the vampire snowmen, the night we walked alone through the snow and it felt like we were the only two people left on earth.

Kissing him is the first step on a road that ends with my complete and utter mortification. And probably the end of our friendship, which would be even worse.

I need Colin in my life. As crazy as it sounds, this bad-boy rock star is the only adult I can count on when shit gets real. My mom is a hot mess who I haven't talked to since I was seventeen, my sister is a sweetheart, but far too anxious to turn to in times of trial, and my other friends—almost all of them artists of one kind or another—are even more socially awkward than I am. Gigi doesn't leave the house except on Sunday afternoons, when she goes to buy more paint, Nisha is physically incapable of making plans in advance or showing up anywhere on time, and Lars is so afraid to drive he has to have his boyfriend chauffer him everywhere. Theo, my surrogate little sister and Bridget's bestie, is the only semi-normal person in our group, and she talks so much she makes my ears bleed if I'm not careful to limit my exposure.

Colin is my safe place, the one person with whom I can let down my guard, and be my real, unfiltered self. He's the only one who knows why I'm so weird around loud noises and people who yell in public places. People who yell, period. Peter witnessed a Mortifying Meltdown a couple of times, but I refused to talk about the why of it all, even with the guy I'd been dating for almost two years.

Only Colin knows about my mom and how bad it was when I was really little, before I grew up enough to take care of myself and Bridget. Only he knows about

the shit show in the courtroom when I became emancipated and actually got guardianship of my sister at
seventeen because our mom was *that* much of a nightmare. He was there. He held my hand while we waited
for the judge to make her decision, and he hugged me
after when I cried so hard with relief it felt like I was
turning inside out.

If I lost him...

I can't even think about it.

I nod again, more emphatically. "It's bad. The breath.
I can tell."

"Okay, okay," Colin says, in a tone that makes it clear
he thinks I'm full of it. "Then I won't kiss you on the
lips."

Before I can say a word, he disappears under the
blanket, and my heart leaps into my throat. "Stop it," I
whisper, fumbling for his head but getting tangled up in
what has to be the world's largest, most luxurious plane
blankie. By the time I free my arms and locate the bulge
that is his head, he's pushed my T-shirt up and is kissing
my stomach—soft but firm kisses that make my breath
catch and my belly flip.

He murmurs something I can't make out, but that I
suspect is a request for me to relax, and shifts lower,
trailing kisses along the elastic waistband of my favorite
black peasant skirt. It's so comfortable I barely feel like
I'm wearing anything from the waist down, and it can be
up for an emergency pee break in two seconds flat.

It is also an easy-access garment for other things...

Things like Colin's mouth as he draws the elastic
down to my hip bones and then lower still until his
fingers catch on the sides of my panties and they join the
Coming Off on a Plane party.

Holy. Shit. This is really happening.

Colin is taking my panties off *on a plane*, while he presses increasingly hot kisses to the hollow by my hip, the top of the dark blond curls I haven't tamed in probably far too long, and then...

"Oh my God," I mouth almost silently as he kisses me *there*, his tongue teasing out to flick across my clit like he's done this a hundred times before.

And he probably has, but not *to me*. Until last night, the closest Colin and I had ever gotten physically was a friendly hug or holding hands at a crowded music festival so we didn't get separated in the crush of people.

But now I have kissed him, and it was completely fantastic, and now he's urging my thighs apart and shifting his head. And then his tongue is swirling around the top of me as his finger finds where I'm wet and pushes inside. And then he adds a second finger and more delicious friction and—

Oh.

Oh my—

Oh my yes there. That. Oh my—

I smash my fist into my mouth, stifling my groan as I join the mile-high club.

Does it count as the mile-high club if it's oral? I don't know, but it feels like it should count. And after nine long, lonely months, an orgasm brought about by another person instead of my own sad fingers is like waking up to learn they've decided Halloween should be celebrated twice a year.

So. Damned. Good. I feel wicked, wonderful, and so satisfied that when Colin emerges from the blanket, his cheeks flushed and his wild hair even crazier than usual, all I can do is let out a ragged sigh.

He grins. "See? It's going to be amazing." He leans in, kissing my forehead before adding in a whisper, "And your pussy is magically delicious."

My face goes hot, but I keep my tone casual as I ask, "Like Lucky Charms?"

"Nothing like Lucky Charms." His fingers slip back over my mound to push inside me, making me suck in a surprised breath. "Sugary cereal is for children, Kirby, and this pussy is full grown and capable of asking for what she wants."

"You have to stop," I say, moaning softly against his lips as he kisses me in that same barely-contained, starved-for-me way he kissed me last night. But this time, he tastes like me, an intimate flavor that is so sexy I want to let go and get lost in him again, but I can't, or we're going to get caught sex-handed. "Seriously. I hear the beverage cart. Someone's coming."

"You, I hope," he says, grinding the heel of his palm against my sensitized clit. "I want to make you come again. But first I want you to tell me what your pussy wants."

"Colin, please..." I fist my fingers in his soft T-shirt, holding on for dear life as he takes me to the edge.

"Tell me." His commanding tone isn't anything like the Colin I've known for over a decade. But I've never seen this side of him, the side that only comes out to play with his kissing friends. "Tell me, Kirby," he says again, "what does your pussy want?"

"You," I gasp against his mouth, rocking into his hand, shamelessly seeking what I need. "You. Making me come. Please."

"Good girl," he says, increasing the pressure on my clit until my eyes roll back in my head. "Now, come for me. That's it... Fuck, yes, I love feeling your pussy so tight and wet, Kirby. You're hot as hell when you come."

He keeps going, spilling out a stream of encouraging and complimentary filth until I dissolve into the seat beneath me, turning molten and sticky sweet with a cry he mutes with his lips on mine.

We pull ourselves together seconds before the beverage cart arrives. Lifting our seats to an upright position, Colin orders a coke with lime and I order a ginger ale with no ice.

And then we sit staring at each other, lips hidden behind the rims of our little plastic cups.

"You are bad," I say.

"But good at it," he says with a wink.

"Agreed." I nod. "So good that you deserve a reward. But I'm going home as soon as I return the favor. I can't stay an entire week in Vegas."

He shrugs. "We'll see."

"Return the favor, then home," I insist. "That's it."

He smiles smugly and takes a smug drink of his coke while his eyebrows do a smug dance of smugness over his smug eyes. He thinks he's got my number, but he doesn't. My will to maintain our friendship is stronger than my libido. And I'm going to prove it...

Right after I replay everything he just did to me about a hundred times in my mind.

Or maybe a thousand, if there's enough flight left.

CHAPTER THREE

Colin

Return the favor...
Who knew such an innocent phrase could inspire such an endless barrage of X-rated imagery? The naughtiness is still streaming nonstop on my mental screen as Kirby and I emerge from the Jetway into McCarren International Airport, her muttering into her open duffle bag and me busy imagining my best friend's lips wrapped around my cock.

It's scandalous, and maybe I should be ashamed of myself, but I'm not.

I'm just...excited. Excited to spend a week with one of my favorite people, excited to coax more sexy coming-sounds from her mouth, excited to find out if fucking Kirby is as amazing as I think it will be. I'm trying not to get my hopes—or anything else—up prematurely, but so far, the chemistry between us is intense.

Who would have thought?

That after all these years there were still stories left to tell about us?

"Stories left to tell about us," I murmur, my brain beginning to tingle as I whip out my phone to make a note. "I think I've got a song coming in, Larry." I nudge Kirby's arm with my elbow. "See? Vegas was a great idea."

"I'm glad someone has something. I've got three T-shirts, one pair of panties, and this..." Kirby pulls a pair of cat ears from her bag with an arched brow. "Are we attending a costume party I've forgotten about? One to which I was planning to wear nothing but panties, a T-shirt, and my cat ears?"

I laugh and nudge her again as the ears jog my memory. "No, but you did insist on bringing Murder along for the trip. You spent so much time making sure he had food and all the stuff he needed to travel as a checked pet, I don't think you gave yourself time to pack for yourself."

With a sigh, she lets her shoulders relax away from her ears. "Oh good. That's one thing I can mark off my list to text Bridget about. I'm glad we didn't leave him for her to watch with the rest of the kitty kids. She's so busy. Without me around to keep an eye on him, Murder would be an easy target."

I frown. "I can't believe someone threatened to kidnap your cat."

"Kidnap him and 'make him suffer the way I made them suffer,' whatever that means." She stuffs the cat ears back in her duffle and zips it up.

"And this just popped up in your email?"

"No, they sent the threat to my agent's office in New York. We took it to the police, but they didn't seem overly concerned, didn't even try to test the paper for prints. They said it's probably just a disgruntled fan venting their frustration about the end of the Funhouse series and nothing will come of it. But I'd rather not take any chances with my best friend."

"I thought I was your best friend."

"Nope." She sniffs as she hitches her bag higher on her shoulder. "You've been downgraded to kissing friend, at least until I fulfill my obligation to your penis and book a ticket home."

I grunt. "Several things I take issue with there, Larry. Firstly, a fuck buddy shouldn't be a downgrade. I'm still your best friend but now conferred with additional carnal benefits—an upgrade any way you look at it. Also, you are not obligated to my penis. My penis and I only want your attention if you're hot for us. If you can't imagine going to sleep tonight without experiencing how much harder I can make you come when I'm inside you, for example."

Kirby's eyes slide my way before completing a scan of our surroundings. "So you just...talk like that? No matter who might hear you?"

"Talk like what?" I glance over my shoulder. "And no one's close enough to hear me. I'm talking softly, using my bedroom voice so you'll find it impossible not to think about what it would be like to have me in your bedroom. And your pussy."

She exhales. "You're impossible."

"Irresistible, you mean." I loop my arm over her shoulder. "Now, let's go get your evil cat and grab an Uber to somewhere we can get food and clothing. As much as I hate to delay getting you behind closed doors, I'm starving. And you can't run around Vegas in nothing but panties and a T-shirt, as fetching as that would be."

"I'm hungry, too," she says. "And Murder isn't evil. He's territorial. There's a difference."

"Right," I agree, even as I silently congratulate myself for stealing Kirby's phone and ordering her assistant to book us a two-bedroom suite. Now the spawn of Satan can have his own sleep space and prowl around after hours, sitting on my chest and stealing my soul or whatever it is evil cats do in their spare time.

Murder is one of my least favorite furry things—he's hated me from the moment we met—but I still can't imagine doing anything to hurt the bastard. He's a creature ruled by instinct, who can't help being a complete asshole, and he's one-tenth my size. Anyone who threatens to hurt an animal should be locked in a dungeon and fed nothing but dung beetles until they grow a heart.

I don't like the fact that some freak figured out Kirby's agent's name and address, either. It's not common knowledge or easily found on the web. Whoever wrote that threatening letter did some digging to get it into the right hands, and who knows what else they found out along the way.

"What about security for you?" I ask as we head down to the pet claim area by the baggage carousels. "Until this person is caught?"

"They aren't going to get caught. I told you, the police blew me off." She shrugs. "But they're probably right. And it's not like I don't get threatening emails at least once a week."

A scowl sinks its claws into my forehead. "What? Seriously?"

"Seriously. A few of my readers are upset that I ended the Funhouse series. They want Beau and Amy back on the case, solving supernatural crimes and stabbing vampire clowns, and aren't afraid to call me a lazy piece of shit to make it happen."

"What the hell?" I shake my head, frowning even harder. "That's supposed to motivate you?"

"I have no idea, but I can't write any more Beau and Amy right now, or maybe ever. I need a break. New characters, a new world. And I can tell most of the people who tweet and email are just venting. They don't seriously want me to rot in hell. I probably wouldn't have worried about this threat, either. It's just the fact that they went to all the trouble to mail it the old-fashioned way, and that they threatened my cat instead of me, that made it stand out. I mean, you know how it is, right? I'm sure you get weird email."

I clear my throat. "Um, no. Not that kind of weird, anyway. I get people who want to have sex with me or paint me in the nude or send me their demo tape or collect a few strands of my hair so they can attempt to duplicate my rock god DNA."

She laughs as we duck into the tiny pet-claim office. "And you send it to them, don't you? Because you would secretly love to have a clone."

"You can't deny having a clone would be cool."

"I can and I will, at length, but first I need to see the prettiest, sweetest cat in the whole world." Her voice softens as she adds in a sexy purr, "Mister Murder, I see you back there. Mama's here to spring you from the clink, Big Boy."

"Just need your paperwork," the bored looking woman with tragically bleached hair behind the counter says, chomping her gum. "And ID."

"I've got it." I hand over my Driver's license and the form I tucked into my wallet, waiting until the woman glances at them and turns to collect Murder's carrier from the shelf behind her before I lean down to murmur in Kirby's ear, "Will you call me Big Boy, later? When we get to the room?"

"Behave yourself," she whispers back.

"Never," I vow with a passion that makes her lips quirk. "But I will go order a car to take us to the fancy mall. I'm pretty sure they have a stroller rental so we can rent a ride for Hell Cat and his carrier, grab food, and then get you a few fancy things to wear."

"I don't need fancy things to wear. I just need pants."

"No, you need fancy, my treat." I hold up a hand to silence her protest. "It's the least I can do to make amends for kidnapping you."

"He didn't really kidnap me," Kirby assures the counter attendant as she places Murder's carrier on the counter. "He's just joking."

"I figured," the woman says dryly. "And just FYI, you might want to get your cat checked out. The guy who carried him in thinks he might have rabies."

Murder meows menacingly in response, inspiring the woman to take a step back, away from the bars of his cage.

"That's demonic possession, not rabies. Isn't that right, Murder?" I ask, earning a hiss from the midnight-black hell beast. "Yeah, I'm glad you're here, too. We're going to have fun." I take Kirby's duffle bag and purse. "I'll get these. You get your jealous boyfriend."

Murder growls and Kirby clucks soothingly to him as we head out into a sparkling, sunny Vegas day that's just begging for two friends to get naked and sweaty in it.

CHAPTER FOUR

Kirby

"*I* can't pull this off." I turn to the side, amazed by how sexy I look. The dress is tinier than anything I've ever worn outside the bedroom—a clingy halter-top type thing with a puffy, sinfully soft, silk tulle skirt in midnight-blue with tiny vintage rhinestones that glitter tastefully in the dressing room light.

It's gorgeous.

And expensive.

Way too expensive for me to have taken it off the rack, but Colin insisted on bringing me a few more things to try on after we secured a pair of jeans, a black mini skirt, and a blouse with a dinosaur print and an oversize bow at the neck that should pad my wardrobe enough to make it through the week.

If I stay the week, which is still a *big* if and absolutely a bad idea.

If only Colin didn't make bad so much fun...

"You're already pulling it off. And we're getting it." His dark eyes rake up and down my body, lingering in the chest area in a way that makes my palms sweaty. I'm that girl—the one who gets damp hands every time she gets nervous or excited—and right now Colin is making me unusually nervous.

And excited.

But also nervous.

Jesus, I'm a hot mess, and the way he's staring at me isn't helping things. "Stop checking out my side boob," I hiss, tugging the sparkly fabric over a centimeter only for it to pop right back to where it was before.

"I can't. Your side boob is delicious," he says. "I want to bite it."

Murder, still trapped inside his carrier and wedged into a rental stroller beside Colin, yowls his disapproval, and I nod. "Exactly. Thank you. I couldn't agree more."

Colin arches a brow. "Translation?"

"Murder says friends shouldn't talk about friends' side boobs. Even friends with benefits. It's weird."

"This coming from the woman who thinks she speaks cat."

"I don't think, I *know*." I lift my nose higher as I look over my shoulder to check out the view from the back in the mirror—short, but maybe not too short. "Spend enough time listening and you'll understand just about anything."

I watch inspiration flicker across Colin's face in the reflection, and a moment later he's on his feet, pulling me into his arms and smacking a kiss to my temple. "You're brilliant, Larry. I'm going to write that down. And a few other things. Meet me outside. Have them add this and anything else you need to the bill. She already swiped my card."

"But I don't—"

"No. Stop. I'm paying, end of argument." He cuts a hand through the air before pointing a warning at me as he backs out of the dressing room area. "And if you don't get that dress, I'm coming back to get it myself, so you might as well buy it now and save me a trip."

He vanishes, and I turn back to my reflection, an increasingly familiar giddy sensation swelling in my chest. If I stay and allow myself to be sucked into the Colin Donovan Vortex at its most charming, I'm going to be sorry.

But maybe I should worry about that later, after the fun is over.

"He's right—you look incredible," the salesgirl says, poking her curly red head in through the archway leading into the changing rooms. "That dress is to die for and will sparkle like crazy on the dance floor. You guys going clubbing tonight?"

I shake my head, then pause and shrug. "I don't think so, but I don't really know for sure. This was kind of an impulsive trip."

"An impulsive getaway to Vegas." She sighs as she leans against one of the faux marble pillars framing the entrance. "You guys are going to have a blast. You know where you're staying yet?"

"The Legacy," I say, smiling when she squees softly and claps her hands.

"Oh, that's my favorite. I've only been once, but it's so swanky. You're going to love it." She leans down, lips puckering as she peers into Murder's kennel. "And you, too, buddy. It's so sweet of your mama and her boyfriend to bring you along on their vacation."

"Oh, he's not— I mean we're not—" I wave a dismissive hand through the air. "We're just friends."

Red stands, her brown eyes widening. "Oh, I'm sorry. I just assumed... Usually, friends don't buy friends two-thousand-dollar dresses."

"We're weird friends."

Her mouth curves. "Well, weird can be good. Anything else you need right now? Can I get you shoes to go with the dress? I've got a strappy heel that would be perfect."

"Yes, please, thank you," I say, pondering her words as I try on the sandals, agree that they're perfect, and dart into the dressing room to change back into my black skirt, vintage Smiths T-shirt, and Chucks.

She's right—weird can be good. Heck, that's practically my mission statement. If I hadn't embraced my weird at a young age, locking myself in my storage shed office behind our house and writing for hours while other junior high kids were playing video games, I never would have been published by seventeen or supporting myself and my sister on my royalties two years later. If I hadn't trusted the wild and weird stories that called to me, I might have blended in with the other make-you-jump novels and never connected with my rabid and wonderful readers.

And if I weren't open to weird, I wouldn't have become Colin's friend in the first place. Sure, he's a sexy, confident rock god now, but when we met, Colin was a home-schooled kid with a mop of hair, freaking out on his first day of normal-kid high school. As a musical prodigy who'd spent most of his early life in rehearsal rooms and stuffy concert halls, he was completely unprepared for the wilds of the public education system.

For weeks, he followed me around like one of the stray cats I seem to attract wherever I go, changing his course schedule so we'd have the same classes and lurking quietly at my lunch table until my other friends pulled me aside to ask what was wrong with him, and what they should do to make my strange new buddy more comfortable.

But Colin wasn't strange—he was a sheltered genius who had music unspooling in his head all the time. Incredible music that he'd play for me after school when we were hanging out at his place, eating nachos his not-insane-or-scary mother had made, and talking about everything under the sun.

We got so close that my boyfriend at the time—Gordan, a tragically serious graffiti artist who specialized in painting spoons on anything that would hold still—eventually emerged from his self-involved haze long enough to get jealous.

Just like Peter...

But neither of them had any reason to be.

Colin and I have always been just really good friends.

At first, I was too protective of my skittish stray to feel anything but platonic affection for him. Later, I needed him too much—needed his rock-solid support and knack for helping me loosen up and not freak out—to risk letting him know that there were times when he'd smile at me and I would secretly wish...

Murder meows, soft and low, as I emerge from the changing room and circle around to grip the handles of his stroller. "I know, I know. Your lack of enthusiasm has been noted. But no biting Colin this trip, okay? I expect you to be on your best behavior."

He grumble-purrs in response, a sound that could mean he's going to be good or that he's going to bite the hell out of Colin as soon as he's out of his carrier—

I'm fluent in feline, but cats like to keep people guessing.

I push him to the checkout, where Red already has my packages wrapped in tissue and tucked into classy silver-and-champagne-striped bags.

"Have so much fun," she says, waving as I head for the exit. "And tell Colin I love his music so much. 'Dear Abby Black' was basically my theme song in high school."

I force a smile and say, "Sure thing," but I'm a little thrown by the comment, a fact Colin notices as soon as I stop in front of the bench where he's furiously tapping something into his phone.

His fingers freeze, and his brow furrows. "What's wrong? Did you get the dress?"

"I got the dress."

"Then what's wrong?"

"Nothing." I nod to the right. "Ready to take the stroller back and get out of here?"

"Yes, but I'd like to know why your face is pinched, first."

"The sales girl recognized you," I say with a sigh, conveying her message in a rush before adding, "It still takes me by surprise, I guess. How often you get recognized these days."

His expression sobering, he falls in beside me as I push the stroller toward the exit. "Yeah. The past two years have been a game changer."

"But it sounded like that girl has been a fan for a while. It was nice of her to wait until we were leaving to say anything."

He clears his throat with a dubious sound. "Yeah, it

was. But she did ask me where I was staying half a dozen times while I was picking out a swimsuit for you."

My head jerks his way. "What?"

"I bought you a swimsuit. A red bikini. I know you prefer black like your soul, but you're going to look amazing in it. And I don't want to hear any bitching and moaning about putting it on or going out into the sun to frolic in the pool. Sun is good for you. You need a little color before you turn translucent."

"No, not that," I say, though I'm *not* on board with wearing an obnoxious bikini. I mean, hello? Do I look like a refugee from a 1980s hair band video? No, I do not. I look like Wednesday Adams if she decided to go blond and smile occasionally. And Wednesday Adams and a red bikini go together like salmon and dark chocolate.

But there's something more pressing that needs addressing at the moment. "She asked you where you were staying? And you...didn't tell her?"

He snorts. "Of course I didn't tell her. I didn't get a stalker vibe, but I didn't want to give her any encouragement to come find me, either."

"Of course not," I murmur, my stomach balling into a knot.

"And the hardcore fans have a network where they report sightings of band members. Last time I lingered too long in the Apple store in New York, I came out to a crowd at the bottom of the steps. Eventually, the police had to be called to keep the street clear."

I cringe. "That sounds awful. I'm sorry."

"Why are you sorry?" he says with a laugh. "Last time I checked, you didn't twist my arm and insist I become a rock star. If I remember correctly, you thought I should keep playing the violin."

"You're brilliant with a violin. Makes me cry almost every time."

He pauses in the shade a few feet from the valet stand and turns to me, brushing my bangs from my forehead. "I don't like making you cry."

"It's a good cry. A so-beautiful-it-makes-your-heart-fragile kind of cry."

"Is it just me or are you talking in poems today?" he asks, lips curving. "Everything you say, I want to write it down and turn it into a song."

I arch a dubious brow. "I think you're probably just sleep deprived."

"I think it was tasting you for the first time," he says, making my blood go thick and sticky in my veins as he leans closer and adds in a softer voice, "It was very...inspirational."

"Thanks," I say, my cheeks heating. "I hope you still find me inspirational when I confess that I told the salesgirl where we're staying."

He winces. "You didn't."

"I did, I'm sorry. I wasn't thinking. I thought she was just making small talk."

"Oh, well, it's not a big deal," he says with a shrug. "Maybe she'll keep it to herself. If not, there are worse things than having fans excited to meet you. Worst case, I have to spend some time signing autographs."

When we arrive at the hotel fifteen minutes later, Colin's words prove to be downright prophetic. There are, absolutely, worse things than a crowd of screaming fans. Much worse things, like a psycho ex-girlfriend wearing sky-high gold sandals, a gold lamé bikini, and a see-through fishnet cover-up lurking in the lobby.

Only the Dark Lord knows how she got to the Legacy so fast—and she must have made a deal with the devil to look this good while doing it. But whether it's cunning or coincidence, there she is, She-Who-Shall-Not-Be-Named, lounging in wait on a couch near the check-in desk, grinning like a vampire clown who found a juicy virgin taking a nap in her clown car.

CHAPTER FIVE

Colin

*S*hit. Fuck. Shittity-fuck-fuck-fuck.

There she is, the one person I was hoping I wouldn't run into while Kirby and I were in Vegas. Regina, looking like she's ready to claw Kirby apart with her bare hands and feed the pieces to the alligators over at the Wild Kingdom Casino. I'm sure most people looking at my leggy blond ex wouldn't notice the mad glitter in her eyes above her shiny white smile, but I see it, and there's no way I'm letting her anywhere near Larry.

I lift a finger to Regina and spin back to face Kirby.

"Get to the room," I whisper. "Hide. And don't come out until I tell you the coast is clear." I hand over the shopping bags as the valet rolls our luggage—and Murder's carrier—toward the front desk.

Kirby casts a concerned glance over my shoulder. "Are you sure you're going to be okay? She looks...blood-thirsty."

"It's you I'm worried about," I say. "Run. Save yourself. And if I don't make it out alive, burn everything in my blue file folder. That's where the bad poetry is."

"Are you sure you don't—"

"No, go. Relax. I'll be there soon." I force an encouraging smile and turn, crossing to where Regina is sprawled casually on a ruby-red couch as if she just happened to be hanging out in my hotel lobby. But, of course, we both know better. "Which message board was it?" I ask as I stop in front of her, crossing my arms over my chest.

"The Reddit one," she says, smiling as she stands, popping a thumb into her mouth and biting down in a way that used to make me hot, but now only makes me ponder how many germs she's introducing into her body by constantly sticking her hands in her mouth. "I was doing a product shoot for a new suntan oil, but I didn't figure you'd mind if I came over in my bikini." She arches a cool brow in Kirby's direction. "So you're here with your friend from high school? How sweet. She looks even more like a vampire in person."

"What do you want, Regina?" I ask, refusing to discuss Kirby with her.

"I want to talk." Her artificially plumped lips push into a pout.

"There's nothing to talk about. It's over."

"That's what you said last time," she says with a grin that's haunted by the ghosts of orgasms past. But that's what they are—the past—and this time I'm going to make sure Regina gets the message.

But first, to adjourn to a place with more privacy, where a nearly six-foot blonde in a tiny bikini won't attract so much attention—before one of the men walking by trips on his tongue and hurts himself or is knocked unconscious by an irate spouse.

"Let's go to the pool and talk," I say, holding up a hand when she starts to bounce in excitement. "We're just going to talk. For ten minutes. Then I have to go."

"That's what you say now," Regina says, shoulders swaying back and forth, making her ample breasts—also artificially plumped—bob from side to side. "But once we get to talking, you know how the time flies."

"After you." I motion toward the wide hall to the left, glancing over my shoulder toward the front desk as Regina stalks toward the pool in her sky-high heels. But it appears Kirby has already been whisked away to our room.

Good. She's safe. Now to get rid of Regina and get back to learning all the things that make Kirby's eyes light up when she's naked.

But sadly, operation Get-Rid-of-Regina gets off to a bumpy start. First, we end up at the spa instead of the outdoor pool deck and have to retrace our steps. Then the woman at the entrance to the lavish outdoor pool and gardens can't find my room number or reservation. By the time I run back to the front desk to fetch the information, return to Regina, and we find a seat in the shade near one of the fountains, it's been nearly twenty minutes.

I'm checking my phone, wondering if I should text Kirby and let her know this is going to take a little longer than I thought, when a flash of red by the check-in cabana catches my eye.

I turn to see a smoking hot blonde in a red bikini, matching red lipstick, a poppy-patterned cover-up that opens at the front, and reflective sunglasses strutting across the pool deck, her loose hair gleaming in the sun. She's so pale it's almost blinding, but the contrast between her porcelain skin and the vibrant suit only draws more attention to the places where the red fabric cradles her curves.

And curves, and more curves...

Holy shit, who knew Larry had a body like that? I mean, I've seen some of it up close and the rest in form-fitting clothes, but I never imagined her hips flared out so fetchingly at the sides, or that her legs would look so long in heels. She's only five foot three, but she's working every inch of her petite frame in a way I've never seen before. She looks confident, in control, and so fucking sexy that when she stops in front of the couch where Regina and I are sitting and runs a lazy hand through her hair, it's all I can do not to dissolve in a puddle of lust at her feet.

"Hey, I was getting lonely up in the room, so I figured I'd come down and check on you," she says, smiling as she holds up a hotel swim bag. "I brought your suit so you can change if you want."

"Thanks. A swim sounds good," I say, clearing my throat as I realize Regina and Kirby have never met, even though Kirby and I have deconstructed every aspect of this emotionally-unhealthy-and-just-plain-stupid relationship at least a dozen times. "Regina, this is Kirby. Kirby, Regina."

"So great to finally meet you, honey," Regina says, scanning Kirby from head to toe, a condescending sneer curving her lips. "You'd better get some sunscreen on you quick, sugar, before you burst into flames."

Kirby smiles. "So sweet of you to be concerned, but

I'm covered. Except my shoulders, I figured Colin could help me with those."

"Of course he will, he's a good friend," Regina says, laying a possessive hand on my knee. "This is so sweet of you, Colly, to bring your little friend, brush the spiderwebs out of her hair, show her a good time."

Regina makes it sound like Kirby's a tragically ugly old maid I've taken pity on out of the goodness of my heart. Before I can call her on her bullshit, Kirby laughs.

"Actually, I'm planning on showing *him* a good time," she says, sliding her sunglasses to the end of her nose, revealing wicked blue eyes that send a jolt of awareness straight to my undercarriage. She crooks a sexy finger. "Come on, Colin. It's way past time for me to get you out of those pants."

I make a sound somewhere between a laugh and a groan of anticipation and leap to my feet. "Yes, ma'am." I salute Regina and offer a quick, "See you later, Reggie. Or not. We've said all that needs to be said, and I'm here with Kirby so it would be best if you sent any further questions via email."

"But Colin, I—"

"Boundaries, Regina. Get some. And respect his," Kirby says firmly as she takes my hand, holding tight as she draws me away toward the dressing rooms on the other side of the pool, leaving Regina sputtering behind us.

I grin and ask in a delightfully scandalized whisper, "Are we really going to fuck in the changing cabana?"

"Do you really call her Reggie?" Kirby shoots me a narrow look over the tops of her glasses. "I thought I was the only girl in your life with a boy nickname."

"You are," I say, blinking. "Or you were. And you will

be again. If I never see Regina's face again, it will be too soon."

"Nope. Too late," Kirby says, lifting her nose higher in the air. "Now I really hate Larry. It doesn't feel special anymore."

"Oh come on, Larry. You're special." I exhale, taking her in again from head to toe as she pulls me into the cabana and draws the curtain behind us. "And you're fucking incredible in this suit. Like cherries and whipped cream. I could devour you in one bite."

She pulls her glasses off, tossing them onto the padded changing bench behind me. "I put it on for you, so I could come down here and save you from She-Who-Shall-Not-Be-Named. I thought maybe seeing that you're with someone else might help her get the message."

"You're brilliant, thank you. And maybe it will." I study her face, but her eyes are cool, giving nothing away. "So you're really mad? Because of the name thing?"

"No, not because of the name thing." She crosses her arms, causing her breasts to plump into a configuration even more delicious than before. My mouth is literally watering, but her energy is blaring "Do Not Approach" loud and clear.

"Then what's wrong?" I ask. "Tell me, and I'll make it right. I promise you, Kirby, there is nothing in the world I want more than to make it right. I'm dying to touch you." I pause before adding in a huskier voice, "To make you come for me again."

Something flickers behind her eyes, and she points an accusing finger at my mouth. "There! Like that. *That* bothers me. When did you get so comfortable with dirty talk? *I'm* the one who's had a series of intense, long-term, highly-sexual relationships. *I'm* the one who should be comfortable having a filthy mouth."

I blink. "Aren't you?"

"No, I'm not." Her arms flap at her sides. "I'm still faking it until I make it. But you act like it's your second language, and you didn't even lose your virginity until you were almost eighteen."

I grin as I bob a shoulder up and down. "I don't know. Guess I'm a fast study. Don't be jealous."

"I'm not jealous."

"You sound a little jealous," I say, carefully easing closer. "But you don't have to be. I can teach you my dirty-talking ways. And we can practice until you feel comfortable."

She rolls her eyes. "I don't need a sex tutor. I'm good at sex, thank you."

"I'm sure you are." I wrap an arm around her waist, pulling her against me, loving the way her breath rushes out in response. "But sex is like music, Ms. Lawrence. You should never stop learning." I kiss her temple. "Practicing." I kiss her jaw, right next to the seashell curve of her ear, where I whisper, "Pushing yourself to be the absolute best that you can be. So I want you to do something for me."

"What's that?" Her fingers tangle in the hem of my T-shirt as she shivers in a way that makes me certain she feels it, too—the rush, the electricity that vibrates between us every time we're close enough to touch. I don't know where it's been hiding the past fifteen years, but now that it's flowing, I'm not sure we'll ever get it back under control.

And why would we want to, when it feels this good?

"I want you to tell me what you want again," I say,

cupping her ass in my hands. "This time in as filthy a way as possible."

She presses closer, lashes fluttering as her hips rock against where I'm already hard. "Now? What if someone hears?"

"Now." I slip my fingers under her suit on the right side, tracing a slow path around the curve of her ass, pausing a few centimeters from where things start to get really interesting. "And no one's going to hear because we're going to be dirty and quiet."

Her hands smooth up to press against my chest. "I can't think of anything to say."

"Sure you can."

She shakes her head with a huff. "No, I'm going to be bad at it. And then you'll laugh, and the mood will be ruined."

"Nothing could ruin the mood, woman," I say. "Can't you feel how much I'm dying to bend you over that bench and fuck you until you scream?"

Kirby looks up, eyes flashing.

"See, you like it when I say naughty things. And I'm going to like it just as much when you return the favor."

"Speaking of returning the favor," she says, tongue slipping out to skim across her bottom lip, making me ache for a taste of her mouth. "Now would be a good time for..." She trails off, cheeks going even pinker than usual. "I can't."

"You can," I insist, sliding my fingers lower, skimming over the already damp curls between her legs and the slicker place between. "Come on, Kirby. Tell me what you want. You're already wet, so you must want something."

Her hands curl into fists against my chest as her breath rushes out. "I want your fingers inside of me."

"What else?" I encourage her, teasing my fingers lightly over her clit, making her breath catch.

"I want you to kiss me like you can't get enough of my mouth."

"I can't get enough of your mouth," I say, threading my free hand into her hair and fisting my fingers in the strands. "Or your pussy. I want you to ride my face the next time. I want to grip your thighs and feel you—"

"God, just kiss me already." She grips my face, pulling my mouth down to hers. Lightning strikes the same place twice, while a hurricane sweeps onshore, reshaping the world in its wild and windy image.

Hurricane Kirby kisses me like she's never going to get enough as we tumble to the floor of the cabana, lips tangled and hands roaming.

I've got my fingers down the front of her bikini bottoms, and she's tugging at the top button of my jeans when I hear the first girlish voice scream my name.

CHAPTER SIX

Kirby

"*H*e's here! He's here! Where is he?" The girl's voice pierces the sex haze, and I rip my mouth from Colin's.

"Shit," he mutters, pulling his hand from my bikini.

"He's still here, right?" another voice squeals. "We haven't missed him?"

"No, you haven't," Regina says from not-nearly-far-enough-away. "He's right over there, getting changed. Should be out any minute."

Colin and I exchange a panicked, wide-eyed glance and then we're on our feet, tugging our clothes into place, trying to look like we weren't seconds away from banging in the cabana, but it's not easy. My nipples are poking holes in the front of my swimsuit, and Colin's jeans are doing a poor job of concealing the direction his thoughts were headed a moment ago

I point at his fly and hiss, "You can't go out there like that. Those girls sound like they're twelve years old!"

"I know that," he hisses back, "but I'm having a little

trouble with self-control at the moment. Turns out I really want to bang you, Larry."

"I really want to fuck the hell out of you, too." My heart swoops as a smile blooms on his face, making him even more ridiculously handsome.

"See there? You're getting the hang of it. Now, tell me that you can't wait to ride my face."

"No." He reaches for me, but I bat his hand away with a scowl. "We have to get out of here. No more dirty talk."

"We barely even got started," he grumbles. "But agreed. We can continue our lesson when there aren't people around who shouldn't be exposed to my glorious hard-on."

My lips twitch. "Humble much?"

"You found it less than glorious?"

I laugh. "No. It seems pretty glorious. But a definitive conclusion is going to require further research."

"Yes, please." He darts in to steal a kiss. "We can play research scientist and test subject, and you can poke and prod me to your heart's content. Stay here. I'll lure them away to sign autographs, and you can slip out. I'll meet you in the room."

"Okay. Number fifteen ten," I say, glancing down again, uncertain whether to be impressed or disappointed that he's regained control. I like Colin out of control.

Probably like it way too much.

"Got it," he says with a wink. "See you soon. And if you're waiting for me naked on the dining table wearing nothing but sliced strawberries on your nipples and a smile, I wouldn't complain."

"Get out of here." I laugh, shooing him with both hands. "Go take care of your rock-god obligations."

He darts out from behind the curtain, inspiring a wince-inducing volume of girlish screaming. There are probably only five or six kids out there, but they make an impressive ruckus as Colin greets them, thanks them for loving the music, and suggests they move out of the sun to take pictures.

I wait until his voice drifts away before I grab my bag and my sunglasses and slip out from behind the curtain. With a quick glance over my shoulder to ensure no squealing fans have spotted me, I make a beeline for the lobby, only to run into a gigantic pair of boobs—face first.

"Sorry! I'm so sorry," I sputter, stumbling back to find myself face-to-chest with She-Who-Shall-Not-Be-Named.

Apparently, Regina decided *not* to take Colin's request to get lost to heart. She is still very much here and very much glaring down at me like a bug she would like to drown in her cleavage sweat.

"You. Me. Girl talk. Now." She loops her arm through mine in a way that makes it clear I'm not getting free without a fight, which is even more discomforting than it would usually be.

Maybe it's the fact that we're both semi-naked that's making it weird. Or maybe it's the fact that, even with my heels on, Regina's tall enough to make me feel like a kid getting into trouble at school. Whatever it is, by the time she whips me into the shadows behind the towel hut with a bump of her hip and a flick of her wrist, my heart is stuttering and anxiety is closing its iron fingers around my ribs, making it hard to breathe.

And then Regina leans down and says, "I'm only going to say this once, Short Stack. So listen up and listen good, or you're going to be sorry." And I'm suddenly certain that I'm about to be clawed to death by a jealous ex and my body will be discovered in a red bikini, and then my sister and all my closest friends will wonder if they ever really knew me at all, this stranger who thought prancing around in a barely-there red swimsuit wouldn't end in disaster for a spooky book nerd.

I've wandered way outside of my comfort zone, and now I will pay the price—with my life.

And yes, a part of me realizes that I'm being dramatic and that Regina probably won't kill me—at least not here, with so many witnesses nearby—but logic is no match for panic. Logic does nothing to stop the world from spinning or my vision from going black at the edges.

And then Regina shoves my shoulders, knocking me back against the hut wall as she says something that sounds like *"Wanh wanh woah wanh wa,"* to my anxiety-bedeviled ears, and then I'm going full fetal position, curling into a ball on the concrete by her shiny gold stilettos.

CHAPTER SEVEN
Colin

I get back to the room to find no sign of Kirby, and Murder's cat carrier sitting empty on the dining table. The suite is gorgeous, with two bedrooms, a sitting room-dining room-kitchenette combo space, and a large balcony with a Jacuzzi tub and lounge chairs overlooking a dramatic view of the strip.

From now on, Kirby and I can hang out in the sun in private, without any picture-hunting fans or crazy ex-girlfriends popping up to bother us. I'm imagining all the trouble we're going to get up to in that hot tub when pain flashes through my calf.

I curse, shaking off the hell beast latched onto my jeans with all four claws. He retreats in a blur, and I spin to point at the clearly unrepentant ebony feline crouched by the coffee table.

"No, Murder! Bad cat," I say—because that's what Kirby told me to say, not because I have any hope of getting through to Murder at this stage in our relationship.

By now, we have each other's numbers and have

settled into a pattern of quiet animosity interrupted by periods of sullenness and the occasional violent outburst. *His* violence, not mine, because I am a grown-up, dammit, and know how to control my homicidal urges.

So even when I grab the little monster by the scruff of the neck to escort him to the second bedroom for a time out, I do so with gentleness. Then I fetch him water and food from the supplies housekeeping left by the bar, push the litter pan inside so he can get to it when he decides to stop pouting and come out from under the bed, and return to the more pressing issues at hand.

Kirby. And where the hell she's gotten off to.

I do a full sweep of the space, but she's not in either of the bathrooms or hiding in the walk-in closet. I'm reaching for my phone to shoot her a text when it dings in my back pocket. I pull it out to reveal a message from Regina—*You need to come back to the pool and get your friend. She's having a meltdown by the towel hut. I'll stay to make sure she's okay until you get here.*

Cursing again, I jog for the door. It only takes a few minutes to get an elevator and another few to be carried back down to the ground floor and make my way through the lobby to the pool, but it feels like an eternity. An eternity during which something bad is happening to Larry, something bad that I would bet my strumming hand Regina is responsible for.

I stride out onto the pool deck, doing my best not to attract attention as I hustle over to the towel cabana and circle around behind it. My heart lurches into my throat as I see Kirby sitting on the ground, curled into herself with her arms wrapped tight around her knees. Regina stands over her like an evil Amazonian bikini queen about to hand down a death sentence.

She looks pissed, which is pretty strange considering Kirby is the distraught one.

I've only seen Larry like this a few times before—mostly in high school—but I remember each episode like it was yesterday. Seeing my calm, clever, rarely-loses-her-cool friend huddled in a trembling ball isn't something I'm ever going to forget.

"Finally." Regina heaves a sigh. "I don't know what her damage is, but you clearly shouldn't leave her alone, Colin."

"Step back, Regina." I glare at her as I hurry to Kirby's side and squat beside her, laying a gentle hand on her back. "Hey, Larry. It's me. You want to get out of here?"

"Yes." She pulls in a breath and lets it out with a shuddery sigh, but keeps her head tucked tight. "But can she go away first?"

Regina barks out a laugh. "Oh please, I didn't do anything to her, Colin. She's the one who started playing dirty. Have you read the book? Did you see what she did?"

"Any resemblance to people living or dead is coincidental," Kirby whispers, her voice muffled by her knees. "All characters are creations of the author's imagination."

"Right," Regina says, with an eye roll so hard her entire head gets involved. "You just happened to imagine a man-eating blond bombshell vampire clown with giant fake boobs. And then you just happened to make her devour one of your fan's favorite characters in the grossest way possible."

"Not the grossest." Kirby lifts her head. She's still alarmingly pale, but she seems to be rallying. "I could have thought of something grosser."

"Is that a threat?" Regina asks, propping a hand on her hip.

"Just statement of fact," Kirby replies. "I have a vivid imagination, especially when it comes to gross stuff. I'm sorry that you thought I was writing about you."

"Sure you are," Regina says, her voice tight. "And I bet you're sorry that I have horror nerds leaving shitty comments on all my social media posts. I'm an influencer, Miss Creepy. I have a happy, sexy, positive image to maintain, and you're screwing it up."

"I'm sorry." Kirby's shoulders hunch. "I'll make a public statement that you should be left alone. I didn't know my readers were bothering you."

Regina's expression morphs into a mask of false compassion. "Oh no? You didn't? Little Miss Innocent? Well, I think you're a liar. A mean liar who's had a crush on Colin for so long you were willing to do anything to get him in your bed, even resort to slander. Which I could sue you for, you know. My lawyer said so."

"Lawyers always say shit like that," I cut in, hoping to calm everyone down before this escalates any further. "They just want your money. And suing Kirby would be a waste of time and energy. You wouldn't win, and it would only draw attention to something you want forgotten. Leave it alone, and it'll all blow over in a week or two. People have short attention spans, you know that."

"Some people certainly do," Regina says, hurt flashing in her gray eyes before she shifts her gaze back to Kirby. "So be careful, Creepy. You might be hot stuff to him now, but in no time, you'll be yesterday's news."

Regina spins on her heel, stalking away with a grace any runway model would envy. She's a beautiful, self-possessed woman who can be a lot of fun when she isn't pissed off. But I still can't believe I ever got within ten feet of the Chapel of Love with her, let alone walked inside and said "I do." I must have been out of my damned mind.

Or just so lonely I wasn't thinking straight.

Turns out loneliness isn't something that goes away when you become rich and famous. In fact, sometimes it just gets worse.

"I'm so embarrassed." Kirby relaxes her hold on her knees, slumping back against the side of the hut.

"Why? You didn't do anything wrong. Regina gets under people's skin. It's her number one talent aside from taking really good selfies."

Kirby shakes her head tiredly, not so much as cracking a smile. "No, I overreacted. She pushed me, but not hard, and I just...crumpled."

I scowl in the direction Regina recently disappeared. "She shouldn't have laid a hand on you."

"No, she shouldn't have, but there was no reason to go into full meltdown mode." She drops her head back, looking up at the clear blue sky. "I haven't had an episode in over a year. I thought I was finally over this shit."

"But you don't ever get over PTSD, do you?" I ask, treading carefully. I know she hates to talk about this or anything else related to her shitty childhood. "At least not completely. It can always flare up again, right?"

Kirby's lips press together, but she continues to pointedly avoid looking my way. "Yeah. It can. Especially when you're already under stress."

"Which is why you need a vacation."

She slides her weary eyes my way. "No, that's why I need to go home. This plan has been a disaster from its inception, Colin. It's time for me to catch a flight and for both of us to forget the past twenty-four hours ever happened."

I sit down beside her, rocking my knee gently into hers. "It hasn't been a disaster. I can think of lots of nice things that have happened so far. I got to treat you to a belated birthday present, for one. And I got to see you in this swimsuit, which looks as banging as I thought it would, proving that I'm right about most things."

Her brows lift. "Most things?"

"Yes. Most. Not all, because I dated a crazy person for way too long. But nine out of ten ain't bad." I brush my fingers over the back of her hand. "I'm sorry my psycho ex went off on you."

Kirby's lips turn down. "She isn't psycho. She's hurt, and I feel terrible. When I was writing that character, it felt fun and harmless, but obviously, it wasn't. And now it's too late. I can't go back and rewrite it. The book's already going into a second print run, and my publisher would kill me." She sighs. "Or hang me up by my entrails for breaking the cardinal rule and basing a character on a real person."

"No one's getting hung up by their entrails. And you're not going to rewrite anything. The book is awesome the way it is, and there's no such thing as bad publicity. Regina's probably getting followers who never would have heard of her without you."

"I don't know, I have a lot of pervy dudes reading my books. The emails I get when they realize KB Lawrence isn't a guy are testimony to that."

I rest a hand on her thigh and give a light squeeze. "Is it all right that I want to cut the fingers off anyone who's written you a creepy or threatening email?"

She rests her head on my shoulder. "No, it's sweet. But you know what they say, a finger for a finger makes the whole world fingerless."

"No one says that."

"You know what I mean."

"I do." I rock her limp leg gently back and forth. "But I still want their fingers. I also want you to know that you can call me anytime you feel scared or need to talk. Okay? And I'll remind you that you don't have to be ashamed about it. Ever."

She sighs.

"Okay?" I insist.

"Okay," she whispers. "That might actually help. Knowing I can call. Hear your voice."

"Good," I say, feeling like shit that I didn't make the offer sooner, that I've always just assumed she would reach out if she needed me, even though I know that isn't Kirby's style. I need to do a better job of taking care of my number one. Starting now. "How about I carry you upstairs, run you a hot bath, and then tuck you into our sinfully cushy featherbed for a nap?"

"Nah. You know I'm a bad napper. A bad sleeper in general."

"Not today. Today, you're going to nap like a champ. And when you wake up, you're going to feel a thousand times better and be so glad we came."

"Well, *I've* come, you haven't yet," she says with a yawn. "But I'm too tired to deliver the goods right now. Shopping and girl-fighting are exhausting."

"And you didn't sleep well on the plane." I stand,

reaching a hand down to help her up. "You were mumbling nonsense pretty much nonstop."

"That's how I sleep when I finally get to sleep." She threads her fingers through mine, and I draw her up to her feet. "I'm chatty. Or moany. Yet another reason we should part ways now, before this friendship gets any more compromised by intimate details."

"This friendship isn't compromised," I scoff. "I love you even more than I did before we left. Put your arms around my neck."

Her eyes go wide. "No, Colin. You don't have to—"

I ignore her protest, swooping her into my arms and starting for the elevators.

"Put me down, psycho," she hisses as she loops an arm over my shoulder. "You're going to make a scene."

"It's Vegas. It will take more than a man carrying a woman through the lobby to make a scene. And this is good for me. Help keep me in shape." I curl her closer to my chest. "You're heavier than you look."

She narrows her eyes. "Thanks."

"You're welcome." I grin down at her. "I like my women solid."

"I'm not one of your women, I'm me," she says, clinging to my neck as I reach down to press the arrow by the elevator banks. "And don't forget it."

"Oh, I won't," I promise, holding her gaze. "That's why I want you to stay, Larry. I don't need romance or drama. I need a good friend with benefits, and I think you do, too." I step inside the elevator and hit fifteen while Kirby taps our key to the sensor to grant us access to the all-suite floor. "And your next benefit is a bubble bath, drawn to your specifications. Just tell me how hot and how many bubbles."

She hesitates but finally says, "Very hot. And lots of bubbles. I would like all the bubbles, please."

"All the bubbles, coming up," I promise, not nearly as sad about our change in plans as I'd have thought I'd be if someone had told me earlier that afternoon delight would turn into bath and nap time.

But I want Kirby happy and on board the Vacation train, and I'm willing to do whatever it takes to make her feel good about our impulsive decision.

Besides, we've waited fifteen years to have co-ed naked friend time. I can wait a little longer. Kirby is worth waiting for.

And she's going to look very sexy wearing nothing but bubbles.

"Do I get to watch the bath?" I ask as the elevator whisks us upward.

"No," she says with a laugh. "But maybe next bath. I'll forward your request to the help desk."

"The one in your brain?"

"Yes," she says, laying her head on my shoulder. "It's actually kind of nice to be carried. Thanks, dude."

"You're welcome, Larry." I kiss her head, a warm, happy-sad feeling spreading through me.

So beautiful it makes your heart feel fragile.

Yeah, that's Kirby. And that's exactly right.

CHAPTER EIGHT

Kirby

I refuse to think in the bath or as I dry off and don a fluffy robe in lieu of pajamas.

I still have my heels dug in on thinking as Colin tucks me into the sinfully delicious bed, kisses my forehead, and leaves me to drift off to sleep. With the last of my will power, I order my brain not to dream, and then I'm out like the proverbial light.

When I flicker back on again, feeling more rested than I have in months, the sky outside is rosy pink and I have to pee. Badly.

It's the peeing that does it. Sometimes when you really have to go, it feels so good to let loose it's almost orgasmic. Well, that's what it's like. Orgasmic, or close enough to it that my mind turns to the trouble at hand.

Mainly, the trouble outside on the couch, catching up on his reading, waiting for me to wake up and pounce on him like a tiger stalking a baby elephant through the jungle. It's against my moral code to hurt a baby elephant or any innocent creature—I haven't even eaten meat since I was eight—and I'm beginning to think getting sexually involved with my best friend should fall under the same protective umbrella.

Can you love someone *too* much to bang them?

I think maybe you can. And I think maybe I do.

Do I? Or am I just sabotaging myself? Pushing away pleasure because I'm afraid of losing control when I should be focusing on making hay while the sun shines?

I don't know, but I need to talk to someone other than Colin before I do something I can never take back.

Creeping back into the bedroom, I grab my cell from beside the bed and shoot a quick text to Bridget. I texted her earlier to let her know about the last-minute Vegas trip, but I spared her the scandalous details. I hate to drag my little sis into my drama, but she's the only person capable of understanding how serious this situation is. *Hey Bridge, you busy?*

Almost immediately bubbles fill the screen and then, *Not too busy to find out what the heck is going on with you. How on earth did Colin talk you into going to Vegas? You hate Vegas.*

I sigh and tap, *To be fair, I've never been to Vegas, but you're right. Last night was pretty crazy. Crazy enough that I think if I don't catch a cab to the airport in the next ten to fifteen minutes... Well, I think Colin and I are going to sleep together.*

A wide-eyed emoji pops onto the screen followed by, *What?! But you're friends! Best friends. You've known each other since you were fourteen! I've always thought of Colin as our brother.*

Ew, I reply, nose wrinkling. *He's not like my brother. Yes, we've always been friends, but I've had other feelings around him sometimes. Those kinds of feelings.*

Another wide-eyed emoji and *SEX FEELINGS?!* is Bridget's clearly not-on-board response.

I never should have texted her. I should have known better. Bridget is as much my friend as she is my sister, and she's known Colin as long as I have, but she's not the most sexually experienced person. She's only had one serious boyfriend, and she clearly hasn't reached the point in her banging journey where she can understand why a person might want to mix pleasure with friendship.

We're both in between relationships, I shoot back, doing my best to explain. *Colin's looking for some low-key fun before he goes on a sex fast to write songs twenty-four/seven, and I need someone to help me get over the post-breakup hump. I haven't been with anyone since Peter, and the celibacy is starting to drive me crazy.*

A skeptical looking emoji rears its yellow head. *So you're going to let Colin hump you over your hump? And probably ruin fifteen years of friendship in the process? Is it worth it, Kirby? Really?*

I hesitate, nibbling my lip as I watch the lights glitter on across the skyline. It's the same question that's been pinging around in my head since I woke up on the plane. Sort of. Bridget is missing one key part of the puzzle, however—one she needs in order to give comprehensive advice.

Heart racing, I take a deep breath and type out the truth for the first time, *If secretly having a thing for him for the past few years hasn't ruined it, maybe sleeping with him won't, either?*

Bubbles fill the screen, then stop. Bubbles, then stop. Bubbles, stop, bubbles, stop, until I've nearly chewed a hole in my lip by the time Bridget replies, *Oh, Kirby. I'm sorry. I had no idea.*

Eyes squeezing shut, I flop back on the bed with a muffled groan. I hate pity. I always have, even back when I was the kind of kid people couldn't help but feel sorry for. But no matter how many times my mom screamed at me or locked me in the pantry for daring to back talk on a day when mental illness had taken her beyond the bounds of decent behavior, I didn't want pity. Help, support—yes, but never pity.

My phone buzzes again, and I look down to see, *Have you told him how you feel?*

Throat locking down at the thought, I type, *No!*

Maybe you should. Maybe he feels the same way.

I sigh. *No. He doesn't. He loves me—he even says it—but not like that. If I tell him, things will be weird. Maybe for a long time. Maybe forever. And the benefits will definitely be off the table, and I think I would like more of the benefits. The ones I've sampled so far have been bleeping incredible.*

Bridget sends a blushing emoji. *Well, then... I guess you just have to decide—are the benefits worth the potential fallout. And how are you going to feel when the vacation is over, and Colin starts seeing other people again?*

I press my lips together, willing myself to stop stress chewing before I do myself damage, and search my heart. It's always hurt a little to see Colin with other women, but I've lived through it and managed to find happiness with other men.

I loved Peter. For a while, I even thought we might end up together for the long haul. Yes, my feelings for Colin were always there, lurking in the background, but they were like white noise, something I could ignore most of the time. My heart is a stubborn fool who wants things it will never have, but it's also a realist who doesn't want to be alone forever.

Or even for very long.

For all my prickliness and hermit tendencies, I don't like to be alone. I like to emerge from my writing attic at the end of a long day and know there's someone there to wrap me up in his arms for a long hug. Someone who will insist I'm fed and watered and walked around town until I float down from my dream world and slip back into my body again.

Growing up, I took care of my sister, shielding her from my mother's violence as often as I could, and making sure she had clean clothes and something in her lunch box every day before she left for school. I took care of my mother, too, when she'd let me, putting her medicine on her nightstand, calling her in sick on days when she couldn't get out of bed to go to work, and making sure the bills were paid before the electricity was shut off.

But I didn't take the same care with myself. I learned to push myself, challenge myself, to use up every bit of energy until there was nothing left. I've been on the verge of burning out too many times to count. I don't know when to stop or how to be gentle and nurturing with myself. I never learned that particular life skill.

That's part of why I fell for Colin in the first place. He was the first person to bring me food when I forgot to eat, to insist I take a mental health day when I'd pushed so hard the words wouldn't come anymore. He would take my hand and drag me out of my writer's lair and into a world where things like sunsets and rain on your face and sand between your toes help put all the creative drama in perspective.

He was the first person to show me the most basic, care-taking, need-meeting kind of love, and he will always have a piece of my heart because of it.

I guess that's why I'm so torn about what to do next. If I sleep with Colin, I don't think I can keep it a friendly, uncomplicated romp between the sheets. If I sleep with Colin, I might end up confessing my secrets through a kiss or a touch.

And then he'll know. He isn't stupid. Oblivious at times, yes, but he knows me too well. If I go soft on him, he's going to see it, feel it, and no number of orgasms is worth death by embarrassment.

Heart sinking, I shoot off a final text, *Thanks for the chat, Bridge. You helped put things in perspective. I'm going to skip the madness and grab a cab to the airport. I'll text you when I have my flight information.*

Bridget sends a thumbs-up, accompanied by a hug emoji. *I'm sorry, Kirbs. I know that probably isn't a happy-making decision, but I think it's the right one.*

Clicking my phone off, I set it on the bedside table and pull on one of the lace bras I bought at the mall, panties from home, a black T-shirt with an angry Chihuahua playing a keyboard on the front, and my new jeans—an outfit that says "I'm going to the airport," not "I'm coming to ride your cock like a roller coaster." Then I open the door to the bedroom to find it almost eerily quiet in the suite.

I scan the spacious main area, but there's no sign of Colin.

I pad deeper into the room in my bare feet, gazing past the kitchenette area to the second bathroom in the hallway by the door, but the light is off and the door ajar. He's not at the dining table or out on the balcony, either.

I'm about to head back into the master bedroom to grab my phone when I catch a soft snuffle from the couch. A few more steps and a peek over the edge of the posh leather reveal a sleeping Colin, sacked out with a book open on his chest.

He's reading a space opera series I turned him onto last year, the kind of science fiction men who secretly like a little romance with their action gravitate toward, though most of them would never admit they like the kissing parts.

Or the feeling parts.

But Colin would. He's a romantic, the kind of person who falls in love at least once a year, only to end up with his heart broken when Princess Charming turns out to be someone different than the idealized portrait he's painted in his mind.

And that's why he'll never fall for me. He knows me too well. I will never be Princess Charming. I'm Larry, his buddy, the kind of woman he feels comfortable jumping right into the dirty talk with, no need for hearts or flowers.

So maybe it would be okay.

I've never spit out my feelings for him before; the tone of our conversations never made it feel reasonable or appropriate. So why would sex be any different? If Colin's banging me like his best friend, I'm not suddenly going to start kissing him like my true love.

My resolve is already melting when Colin's eyes crack open and a smile curves his lips. "There you are. I was dreaming about you."

"Yeah?" I ask, heart beating faster. "Good dream I hope."

"The best," he says, reaching up and grabbing me

under the armpits. And then he's dragging me over the edge of the couch and on top of him, his fingers fisting in my hair as he kisses me hard and deep.

And my resistance is going...

Going...

CHAPTER NINE
Colin

*I*n my dream Kirby was wearing that red swimsuit and dripping cool pool water onto my chest as I tugged the fabric down, baring her breasts to my mouth. In real life, she's wearing a rabid Chihuahua shirt and a modest black lace bra, but real life is still a thousand times better than any dream.

By the time I have Kirby naked from the waist up and straddling me in the pink light streaming in from the picture windows, I'm so hard it hurts.

Almost as much as it hurts to look at her.

She's doing it again, making my heart turn to glass.

"You're so beautiful." I cup her breasts, dragging my thumbs lightly over her nipples, things low in my body twisting as her lips part and her breath shudders out. "I like you like this, all flushed and hungry looking."

"Starving." Her fingers wrap around my wrists, squeezing as she rocks against my cock through my jeans. "And sensitive. So be gentle."

"Sensitive here?" I roll one nipple between my fingers

and thumb, summoning a moan from low in her throat that is hot as hell.

"Yes, there," she breathes as I attend to her other nipple, making it harder, pinker. She's all creamy skin painted with shades of peach and dusty pink, and I can't wait to unwrap the rest of my lovely friend.

Fingers around her neck, I drag her down for another deep kiss as I reach between us, flicking open the button on her jeans and dragging at the zipper. I push the denim and the panties beneath down far enough to bare her ass, an expanse of sinfully soft skin I can't resist giving a spank.

She exhales sharply into my mouth. "What was that for?"

"For being so damned sexy." I squeeze the flesh I just swatted as I confess against her lips, "Just a warning, I'm probably going to last all of five minutes the first time. It's been about six weeks since I've been with anyone."

"Try nine months, asshole," she says, her hands diving under my T-shirt and shoving it up. "It feels like I'm dying, I want you so much."

"So much," I echo, helping her dispose of my shirt. "All I can think about is being inside you."

"Yes. Please. Inside me." She shifts her legs between mine, helping me wiggle her jeans down her thighs before reaching for my fly.

Somehow, we end up tumbling to the floor, Kirby rolling under me as we land by the coffee table. I shove it to the side, giving us more room on the carpet by the couch as I dispose of my jeans and boxer briefs.

Kirby watches, her eyes mirroring the urgency that clutches at my chest and pulses through my balls, making them drag heavy between my legs. I can't remember the last time things got this hot, this fast, but thankfully I'm not too far gone to remember protection.

"Condom. Stay here, just like this." I skim my hands up Kirby's thighs, spreading her legs wider, revealing my favorite pink part of her. I look down, brow twisting in sweet agony as I get my first clear view of her, all swollen and wet, leaving no doubt she's as desperate for relief as I am. "Yes, just like this."

"Or this?" Her knees tip out a bit more, nearly giving me a heart attack.

I don't remember getting up or running to the bathroom to grab a condom, but I must have sprinted because by the time I return to her, my heart is pounding in my ears. I kneel between her legs, holding her gaze as I unwrap the condom, my pulse racing faster as she reaches for me, "Hurry, please," she whispers. "Please."

I roll it on with shaking hands and tumble eagerly back into her arms, lengthening myself over her as her legs wrap around my waist. I reach down, but her hands are there, fitting me against where she's so ready for me that all I have to do is glide, melt into her tight heat. I groan against her lips as she shifts beneath me, taking me deeper until I'm buried completely inside her. And fuck, it's good. So good I force myself to hold still for a moment, committing every spark and sizzle to memory.

She cups my face in her hands, pressing a softer kiss to my lips, hers trembling lightly against mine. "God, it's so good. You feel so good, Colin."

"Perfect." I pull out and sink slowly back in, head spinning. "I can't believe how perfect you feel. We should have been doing this for years."

"Years," she agrees, arching into me, her breasts

rubbing against my chest, all soft and swollen sweetness. "All the time. Every day."

"Every day." I grip her ass, pulling her closer at the end of my next thrust. It takes a few adjustments, but eventually, I find the money spot, the perfect point of entry that makes her cry out.

"Yes, there," she says, lifting into me. "Right there. Oh, God, Colin, don't stop. Don't stop."

"Never," I promise, cupping her breast as I ride her harder, deeper, loving how responsive she is. The way she gasps and moans and writhes beneath me, the way I can feel her pleasure building, burning higher, hotter, until she comes crying out my name, her fingernails digging into my ass, pulling me so deep I can feel her inner walls clenching around my cock.

"From behind now," she pants. "Behind."

"Any way you want it," I promise. "Just tell me how you want me to fuck you."

"Like this." She comes onto all fours in front of me and reaches back, but I'm already there, sliding into her again with a relieved groan. Even five seconds apart was too much. She arches her hips, welcoming me in, and I can't resist threading my fingers into her hair.

I make a fist, tugging her head back as I drive forward again, nearly losing it as she cries out and her body goes molten hot around me. Thank God she likes it when I pull her hair because I am instantly obsessed with watching the delicate muscles in her neck strain as we drive faster, harder, headed for the edge where we spin out with matching sounds of primal bliss.

"Damn, Kirby." I come so hard I fall forward, bracing one hand on the carpet beside her as I hold her close with the other until the waves of bliss finally taper off.

As soon as they do, I breathe into her hair, "Let's do that again."

"And again and again," she says with an unconcealed enthusiasm that makes me grin as I pull out, carrying her with me as I sit back and draw her onto my lap. She's smiling so wide that I start laughing. I can't help it.

"What?" she asks, still beaming

"Nothing," I say, cuddling her closer with another chuckle. "You're looking at me like I'm a roller coaster. I like it."

"Better than a roller—" She breaks off, her smile falling away as she points at the window. "What the heck is that?"

I look up to see a drone hovering over the hot tub on our supposed-to-be-private balcony. A drone with a red light glaring at us from above the lens affixed to its center, leaving little doubt that we're being recorded.

Or that every private thing we just did is about to become fodder for public consumption.

CHAPTER TEN

Colin

*R*age dumping into my bloodstream, I grab a throw pillow from the couch and press it to Kirby's chest to offer her cover before leaping to my feet and jogging for the door to the balcony buck naked.

"Colin, be careful!"

But I'm not going to be careful. I'm going to get my hands on that drone and obliterate it. And then I'm going to track down the shit stain with the remote control who violated our privacy to get some smut to sell to the highest bidder and make him sorry he has opposable thumbs.

What just happened between Kirby and me wasn't smut, and it sure as hell isn't anything anyone else ever deserves to see.

I hurl myself through the door just as the drone reverses course, cruising away from the window—fast. But I'm faster. I lunge forward, grabbing it by the base before it can clear the railing, and then I spin, slamming it into the wall beside the Jacuzzi—once, twice—until the spinning blades shatter and I'm left with a gargling black box in my hand.

It won't be flying anywhere, ever again, which the person operating it must realize. A moment later the engine shuts off, and the red light goes dark.

"Fuck," I curse, wishing it had stayed on so I could have delivered a few choice threats to whoever's watching. If they dare to leak so much as a hot second of what they recorded online, I'll kill them.

Dead.

With a guitar pick, so it will hurt more.

"Please tell me that isn't what I think it is." Kirby appears in the balcony's doorway, wearing her T-shirt and underwear and cradling a spooked, crazy-eyed Murder in her arms. "Tell me someone didn't record us having sex. Tell me that this is all a horrible dream, and I'm going to wake up in a few minutes and regret the bad fish we must have had for lunch."

I drag a hand through my hair, feeling like the lowest form of shit. It's my fault this happened. Me and my stupid celebrity. "I wish I could tell you that, Larry, I really do..."

"Oh God." She steps out onto the balcony only to sit down hard on one of the cushioned deck chairs. "What are we going to do, Colin?"

I turn the drone over in my hands. It's not your average toy from a box store. This is pro-level equipment, with a solid but lightweight design and a high definition camera. Whoever bought this invested serious bucks to get quality footage.

And it looks like he's local. There's a sticker on what's left of one of the blades, a thin blue and white tag with the store name—Vegas Photo City—written along the top in red.

"We're going to Vegas Photo City," I say. "And we're going to find out who bought this thing. And then we're going to track them down, and I'm going to shove my guitar so far down his throat he won't be able to breathe without coughing up a lullaby."

Kirby hugs Murder to her chest, stroking the cat's thick fur with anxious fingers. But he doesn't seem to mind the nervous handling from his main squeeze. Kirby could probably put the cat in a pillowcase and swing it around over her head, and he would stumble out purring and climb right back onto her lap.

He loves her to distraction.

So do I. I want to gather her up in my arms, promise her everything's going to be fine, and kiss away the sick look on her face, but I can't.

"You can't do that," she says, eerily echoing my thoughts. "But maybe we can offer to buy the footage or something? Or get the police involved? Revenge porn is illegal in most states now, so shouldn't stealing porn be illegal, too?"

"I don't know," I say, crossing to crouch beside her chair. "But that wasn't porn. That was you and me having an amazing time together, and I'm just..." I sigh. "I'm so sorry, Kirby. I'm sorry some asshole ruined it by invading our privacy."

Murder grumble-growls low in his throat, but Kirby silences him with a soft, "Hush, now," and sets him down to prowl the balcony before meeting my gaze with an almost shy smile. "It wasn't ruined. It was still very good."

I curl my fingers around the back of her knees. "Only

very good? Because I can't remember the last time I had that much fun. And we haven't even gotten to the kinky stuff yet."

Her lips purse as her eyes cut to the right. "The hair pulling was a little kinky for me. But I liked it."

"Yeah?" I grin.

She nods, her hair sliding forward to frame her face as she adds in a more serious voice, "Yes. But if our amateur sex tape ends up on the internet where everyone and my sister can see it, I'm going to have to crawl into a hole and die. You know that, right?"

"You're not going to crawl into a hole. We're going to hunt this guy down and get to him before he has a chance to hit publish."

"Good." She casts a pointed glance down at the rest of me before refocusing on my face. "But you should probably put some clothes on first. Preferably *before* Murder decides your balls are cat toys."

I whip my head over my shoulder to see the wretched cat crouched low and wiggling his haunches, clearly intending to pounce and destroy my tender bits. I stand up fast—too fast, bringing my cock bobbing into Kirby's face. "Sorry," I say, taking a step back with a laugh.

"Don't worry about it." She rolls her eyes, flapping a hand in my direction as she stands. "Are you always this comfortable waltzing around naked?"

I prop my hands on my hips. "I don't waltz, Larry. I stride manfully to my destination." I stalk toward the door, exaggerating the length of my stride and the bend in my knees to deliberately look ridiculous. A husky Kirby laugh rewards my efforts.

"You're such a clown," she says, shaking her head.

This is what we should be doing—enjoying more coed naked friend time. Laughing, clowning, ordering room service, and fucking in every room in the suite until we finally get to the bed and I show Kirby what I can do to her body with the assistance of a few well-placed pillows and maybe a belt or two if we're feeling adventurous.

Instead, we're dressed and out the door in ten minutes, with Murder accompanying us on his leash because Kirby is afraid he'll decide to shred the curtains as revenge for being abandoned and cause damage our one-hundred-and-fifty dollar per night pet deposit wouldn't begin to cover.

"Sorry," she says, snuggling the purring cat on the way down in the elevator. "I know Murder isn't your favorite, but things are going to turn around for you two. I can feel it."

"He tried to eat my balls. Ten minutes ago."

She rolls her eyes. "He did not. He was just going to rip 'em off and play with them a little. He's not a monster, for God's sake." She grins. "And he's open to a truce. He told me so while you were getting me socks."

"Yeah? Fetching your socks? That's all it took to soften him up?"

"Actually, he liked your funny naked walk. But he also knows that my toes get cold, even when it's hot outside."

"You've got cute toes." I put an arm around her waist, and to my surprise Murder refrains from sinking a claw in my pectoral muscle. "Almost as cute as your boobs."

Kirby sighs. "I just hope that's a secret you, me, and the handful of guys I've banged can keep to ourselves. I do not want my boobs made famous in a rock-star sex tape."

"We're going to figure this out. Don't worry."

But I'm worried, too. I don't want to share Kirby's boobs with anyone else, either. I don't even like the thought of sharing them with that handful of guys she mentioned, even though they're in her past. But I met almost all of them, and none of them were worthy of her.

And you are?

The thought zips through my head, and almost instantly a voice from deep in my bones shoots back, *Hell yes, I am.*

Because I care about her more than all of those other losers combined.

And I'm going to fix this. Or die trying.

CHAPTER ELEVEN

Kirby

*B*y the time the car drops us off at Vegas Photo City, it's almost nine o'clock—I slept longer than I realized and thought it was earlier, thanks to the late-setting Nevada sun—but thankfully the store is still open.

The strip mall is hopping, filled with couples pushing strollers from the fountain on one side to the ice cream shop and playground on the other, people standing in line for movie tickets, and a group of performers in tight black pants and T-shirts practicing fake-punching each other in the grass outside Sin City Acting Studios.

As we pass by, I can't help but stare.

Some of them are awful, reacting seconds after the fake-punch fake-lands, but some of the performers are impressive. "They look like they're really fighting," I whisper to Colin as we cross the grass to the entrance to the photo shop, wincing when a tiny brunette sucker-punches a large bald man, sending him to his knees with a convincing groan of agony. "Ow. That was a good one. I wish I could fight like that."

"Fake fight like that, you mean?" Colin asks, arching a brow.

I consider the question. "No, really fight like that. In the event of an emergency or a zombie apocalypse, I'd like to be able to kick ass and take names. Or at least take out a larger opponent. I think it might help me... freak out less."

He pulls out his phone, typing something into the notes feature.

I grin, "Song lyrics attacking again?"

He finishes and tucks it back into his jeans' pocket. "No, making a note to hire you a fight coach. Bet we can find one who will make house calls, so you won't even have to leave your lair to learn how to kick ass."

"Thanks," I say, touched. "That's sweet."

"No, it's selfish. Ever since you told me about that letter, I've been worried. This will put my mind at ease a little. Knowing you've got a leg up on the creeps."

My nose wrinkles. "Speaking of creeps, I've been thinking about Regina."

Colin pauses beside the glass doors leading into the store. "What about her?"

"Do you think she might have had something to do with this?" I motion toward the demolished drone in his hands. "I mean, it seems like an awfully big coincidence, doesn't it? The encounter by the pool and then a video drone outside our room later that same day?"

"Excuse me, sorry." Colin steps out of the way as an older woman with an armful of camera equipment hurries out the shop.

He touches my waist as he moves, guiding me farther from the door with a confidence that sets off shock-waves of awareness inside me. My brain instantly starts replaying highlights from Sexy Times with Colin, no video recording required, and within seconds, I'm so flustered I've managed to get myself tangled in Murder's leash and almost fall on my ass trying to step back into the grass.

Colin catches me, his hands firm on my hips. "Gotcha," he says, helping me unwind myself, while I bubble and fizz and things low in my body unzip, unspool, unravel.

I did my best to avoid touching him on the way over here for just this reason. Touching him makes me feral. Our first time—a first time that was so comfortable and intimate and perfect—did nothing to take the edge off my hunger for him.

If anything, I've gotten even more ravenous. I want to be naked with Colin again as soon as humanly possible. I want to memorize his taste, his smell, and the feel of his skin warm beneath my lips. I want to tattoo the way he kisses me into my memory banks, right along with the feel of his teeth on my shoulder, his hand down the front of my panties, his fingers tangled in my hair.

Just looking at our legs so close together in the car—his thigh thick and muscled beneath his jeans: mine shorter and curvier—made my panties wet all over again. I want to straddle his thigh and squeeze mine tight, making it clear he isn't going anywhere until I've had my way with him.

Who cares that our benefits will expire in a week? A week of the best sex of my life is worth it.

I'll just have to save up my memories and thumb through them later when I'm alone and wishing I wasn't.

"I don't know," Colin says, once I'm free of the leash and Murder is lounging in the grass, alternating between aggressively licking his crotch and watching the stage fighters roll around with a bemused expression that conveys exactly what he thinks of humans and their ridiculous hobbies. "The timing *is* odd, but Regina's the jealous type. I can't see her being okay with watching me bang another woman. We used to go to this sex club together, but she never wanted to actually do anything while we were there. She was too possessive to let me take my clothes off."

My brows lift, but I try to play it cool as I ask, "Did you...want to take your clothes off?"

He shrugs. "Not in front of other people, no. But I could have been into trying one of the private rooms. She wouldn't even do that. She was afraid they had cameras hidden in there somewhere."

"See!" I poke a finger at his too-trusting chest. "She's paranoid about cameras. Probably because she's a secret drone enthusiast who films people without their knowledge!"

Not only is Regina a logical suspect, she'd be easy to find. She lives in Vegas. All we'd have to do is cruise by her condo, demand all copies of the incriminating files be purged from her hard drive upon penalty of Serious Lawyering Up, and we'd be back at the hotel with our hands all over each other in no time.

"Eh, I just don't see it," Colin says, doubling down on defending his evil ex. "She's not the most tech savvy person. She has an assistant who helps her manage her social media. If she can't figure out how to post a story with a universal link, I seriously doubt she's going to know how to fly a complex piece of machinery."

I prop a hand on my hip. "But Regina heard me tell you what room we were in."

"So could have anyone hanging around the lobby while you were checking in. Or one of the staff could have leaked the information. The Legacy is known for their discretion, but if the price was high enough..."

I purse my lips. "Okay, so who do we suspect, then? A sleazy celebrity gossip site?"

He shakes his head. "No. At least, I don't think so. We were inside our hotel room, not in a public place or even out on the balcony. From what I understand, not even Star Blanker traffics in content that's such an obvious violation of privacy. I'm thinking it has to be a paparazzo working on his own, branching out into Peeping Tom videos to boost his bottom line."

"Gross." I shudder. "I know I should be more worried about the world watching us doing it, but right now I'm just as skeeved that some sicko has already seen both of us naked and vulnerable."

"I know. Me, too." Colin gathers me to his chest, his forearm settling in the hollow of my spine as he cradles the back of my head, making my body light up despite the reason we're hugging in front of this store. "I didn't want to share that with anyone but you."

I rest my cheek on his chest, coziness and dismay warring for supremacy inside me—joy and grief, dancing their endless, circling dance. I close my eyes, focusing on the cozy feeling. I refuse to start mourning the end of this when we've barely gotten started.

I pull away with a sniff of determination and find Colin shooting Murder a suspicious look. I glance down at my cat, who is still happily cleaning his junk, and then back at Colin. "What's up?"

"I hugged you again, and he didn't try to carve out any of my internal organs."

I smile. "See. I told you. You guys have turned a corner."

Murder rumbles softly from the grass, almost as if he understands Human as well as I understand Cat, making Colin and I both laugh. "Come on, baby. Time to purse up to go inside." I gather Murder in my arms and tuck him into my bag, supporting his weight from beneath. He pokes his head out from between the straps and immediately starts to purr.

Colin shakes his head as he reaches for the shop door, holding it open. "I can't believe he actually likes being in there."

"I used to keep catnip in there when he was a kitten," I say, passing into the icily air-conditioned store with a shiver. "Now he associates my purse with feeling high and happy."

"I get it," Colin says, his hand lingering at the small of my back as we start toward the Help Counter on the right side of the store. "I could easily come to associate being inside your purse with feelings of happiness and well-being."

I arch a wry brow his way. "Oh yeah? Are you sure we're still talking about my purse?"

"Or something else that starts with P," Colin says, pinching my waist. "Now stop talking about your pussy before you get me hard in public again, Larry. You're shameless with that shit."

I huff with laughter, but we're at the customer service desk before I have time for a comeback. A squat man with a tiny red goatee, incongruously dark black hair hanging in greasy clumps to his chin, and a nametag that reads BENDER, steps away from the open camera case on the table behind him to face us across the carpeted counter. "Hey, can I help you?"

"Yeah, I'm Colin and this is Kirby. We were hoping you might know who purchased this drone," Colin says, setting the battered piece of machinery between us. "It looks like a pretty high dollar item. Probably don't sell a ton of these, right?"

"What happened to it?" Bender says, reaching for the drone.

"Retribution," Colin says vaguely. "So what do you think? Is it ringing any bells?"

The other man shakes his head as he turns the machine over. "Nope, I don't work the sales floor. But this isn't a model we sell. It's a rental. See?" He points to what's left of the Vegas Photo sticker on the blade. "Cute cat, by the way. I have three."

"Thanks so much," I say as Colin and I exchange hopeful glances and Murder purrs louder inside my bag.

"So if it's a rental there will definitely be a record of who checked it out," Colin says.

Bender nods. "Yep. And the credit card on file will be charged the full amount for a replacement. This thing is too wrecked to repair."

Colin smiles, taking pleasure in the damage he's inflicted. But I'm not so sure this is a good thing. I doubt having a credit card charged to replace an expensive drone is going to make this douchebag happy or eager to play nice once we finally track him down.

And I'm betting getting his info won't be easy, either. But I have to try. "So, do you think you might be able to tell us the name on the rental?" I lean in, batting my lashes, earning myself a snort of amusement from Colin, who I kick beneath the counter as I continue to flirt in Bender's general direction. "I know that's probably not protocol, but we'd really appreciate it."

"It's not," Bender confirms. "Sorry, but records are private."

I wrinkle my nose. "I totally get that, but we really need to find this guy."

"Yeah, he had the balls to— Ow!" Colin's words cut off with a yelp of pain as I kick him again.

"He had the balls to film a music video and run off before he got paid or even gave us his real name. Everyone on set just called him Boss 'cause he was so good," I say, lashes batting faster as I will Bender to believe me.

If there's one thing I've learned from interviewing cops to add real-life flavor to my tales of supernatural mayhem, it's that you get more information when people think you're one of the shiny, happy people. Drama and conflict clam people up; goodwill and appreciation keep tongues flapping.

"And he did a stunning job," I say, my eyes going wide. "I can't believe some of the aerial shots he got. They're devastatingly good. We're definitely going to use them in the final cut of the video, aren't we Mr. Donovan?"

I drop the famous last name, and Bender's lips go twitchy. And then his ears. And then his gaze cuts back and forth to Colin and me as he debates what to do next and apparently decides to play it cool.

"Well, I usually wouldn't share private information on a customer," Bender says. "But since the equipment was damaged and he's going to be charged, it only seems right to make sure he gets paid."

I dazzle in his direction. "Oh, thank you so much. That's so sweet of you, you're the absolute best."

Bender's cheeks flush as he bobs a little bow in our direction before jabbing his thumb over his shoulder. "I'll go grab the paperwork from the back. This was checked out earlier today, so it won't be in the computer system yet."

"Earlier today," I hiss to Colin as soon as Bender is out of earshot. "So it could have been Regina!"

"Or anyone else who read the message board and found out we were staying at the Legacy," he says, smirking down at me. "Nice feminine wiles, by the way. You kind of looked like you were having a seizure there for a little bit, but clearly, that does it for Bender."

I sniff. "Hey, it worked. I don't see you getting any information out of reluctant informants."

"True, you're the master," he says, drumming his fingers impatiently on the counter. "I wonder who it is? The suspense is killing me."

"If it's Regina you owe me five bucks."

"How about five orgasms instead," he says, making my nerve endings hum.

"Five bucks and five orgasms," I whisper as Bender swings back into view at the end of the row of shelves.

"Done," Colin murmurs behind his hand. "And if it's not Regina you're going to sing karaoke with me at my favorite Vegas dive bar later this week."

My lips part to make it clear I will be doing no such thing—I do not sing in public, ever—but Bender is already slapping a sheet of thin yellow duplicate paper down on the counter. "P. Eater Incorporated."

I blink. "Excuse me?"

He shrugs and taps the bottom of the page. "P. Eater,

Inc. That's all I've got. And the credit card number, but I can't give you that."

"Of course not," I murmur, spirits sinking.

"No address?" Colin asks. "Somewhere we could mail the check? We'd really appreciate it."

"We just want to make things right," I add with an earnest nod.

Bender exhales, rubbing a hand across the back of his neck as he glances toward the front of the store. "I'll write it down for you, but don't tell my boss, okay? Or anyone else."

I lift three fingers in a salute. "Scouts honor. Thank you so much."

Bender writes the address on a sticky note and discreetly passes it to Colin, who hides it in one palm as he lifts his other hand to bid our accomplice goodbye. I thank Bender again, cuddle Murder closer, and follow Colin to the door. He waits until we're outside in the warmer air, crossing the now empty grass outside the acting studio before he glances down at the note and grunts.

"What is it?" I ask, pausing to let Murder out of my bag. He gives a full body shake, stretches, and proceeds to sniff the grass with an intensity that makes me think there must have been food in the vicinity not long ago.

"A post office box," Colin says, pulling his cell from his pocket. "In Texas."

I frown. "So someone from out of town, but not Los Angeles. I thought all the stars and star parasites lived in California."

"Not necessarily," Colin says, tapping something into the search field on his browser. "Austin has a pretty serious music scene. But this guy could have just based his corporation in Texas and not necessarily be living there full-time. You owe me karaoke, by the way. And I will be collecting."

"No, you won't. I don't sing in public. You know this."

"But you should. You've got a great voice." His attention is fixed on his cell, so he misses the gagging face I make. I add a sound effect to make sure he gets the message, and he smiles but continues to tap away at the screen. "You do. And you already have a flying phobia."

"So?" I prop a hand on my hip.

"So you only get one phobia. You can either be irrationally afraid of flying or irrationally afraid of singing in public, not both. Those are the rules. Okay, I think I found something." His brows lift only to swoop back together again a second later. "Never mind. This is P. Eater *Events* Incorporated. And they're based in Montana, not Texas."

I shift to stand beside him, looking over his arm at the screen. "Well, they could have moved right? Or given a fake address?"

"Doubtful," he says. "Looks like they manage competitive eating events."

I skim the welcome message on the site with a shake of my head. "I'm constantly amazed by how many strange jobs there are in the world. I wish I'd known competitive eating management was a career option in high school. I think I missed my calling."

"You absolutely missed dinner," Colin says, swiping the search window closed and tucking his phone back in his pocket. "And so did I. The furball is the only one who's eaten since lunch. Want to grab food here before we head back to the hotel and ponder next steps?"

"Sounds good." I nod toward the opposite side of the strip mall, where a cluster of outdoor tables gleam red and white beneath the bright lights illuminating the theater entrance. "We can eat outside so Murder doesn't have to hide in my bag the entire time. He's usually good in there, but more than ten minutes or so in captivity might strain his patience. The only thing he and my other little monsters have any real patience for is stalking baby mice. They're shamelessly cruel about it, but I guess death demands attention."

Colin smiles down at me. "You're doing it again. Talking in song lyrics. The first time I'm away from my guitar in months and songs are popping up all over."

"Then let's get you a guitar." I lean into him as he wraps an arm around my waist. "Vegas has music stores. And I owe you a belated birthday present, too."

"I'll buy my own guitar. The only present I want from you is your pussy coming on my mouth again as soon as humanly possible."

I bite my lip, and I'm positive I'm blushing, but I don't look away as I say, "I think that can be arranged. But first I'm going to suck your cock like it's my job."

His eyes darken as his hand slips down to cup my ass through my jeans. "Like it's your job, huh? Hmmm... And I know how devoted you are to your work."

I press closer, my breasts flattening against his chest. "Very devoted. As well as committed to excellence."

"Maybe we don't need food, after all," he says, his fingertips digging into my hip. "I can survive on sex alone."

"Orgasms are probably rich in vitamins and nutri-ents," I murmur, moving in for a kiss only for my stomach to growl—loudly—right before my lips meet Colin's.

He laughs. "Food it is."

"No, I don't need food. Ignore my stomach. It's not calling the shots around here."

Colin takes my hand, threading his fingers through mine. "Food, woman. We've gotta keep your strength up. You have some very important work ahead of you."

I grin. "Not sure about important, but I'm definitely looking forward to it."

"Me, too," he says with a smile that could break my heart if I let it. But I won't. At least not yet.

CHAPTER TWELVE

Colin

*W*e get chicken pita sandwiches and lemonades from the Greek restaurant a few shops down from the theater and take them to the outdoor tables. Kirby ties Murder's leash to one of the chairs and gives the cat water in a bowl she pulls from her purse and a few pieces of her chicken.

And then Satan's spawn curls up beside my foot to eat without even attempting to devour a chunk of my flesh as an appetizer.

I'm cautiously optimistic—maybe a vacation was all we needed to turn our relationship around—but also committed to never taking my pants off in front of him again.

Almost bite off my balls once, shame on you.

Almost bite off my balls a second time…

"So what do you think?" Kirby casts me a tortured look over the top of her pita. "Should I text him? Or call maybe?"

"Call who?" I claim my own sandwich. "Sorry, I was

lost in thought. Who are we calling?" I take a bite and chew, pretty sure I've never had a pita this good.

"Peter," she says, pulling a face. "I mean, he *is* a private detective. He might be able to help. And we wouldn't have to tell him what the drone recorded while it was filming us."

"Then how would we justify how badly we need to get our hands on the footage? Or explain why we're sharing a hotel room in the first place?" I ask as she takes her first bite, moaning her appreciation around a mouthful of Mediterranean goodness. "Good, right?"

"So good," she agrees, plucking a napkin from the center of the table as I continue to chow down. "We wouldn't have to tell him we're sharing a room. The suite has two bedrooms. And he knows we're just friends. I made that abundantly clear to him when we were dating." She rolls her eyes. "He used to get so jealous."

I cock my head. "Really? Why?"

Kirby shrugs. "He thought we had a strange vibe."

"Strange vibe?" I scoff. "We don't have a strange vibe. If anyone's strange, it's him. What kind of weirdo quits his job as a high-paid attorney to become a private investigator? That's like...a job for guys who live under bridges and lurk in pervy movie theaters."

She laughs around a bite of pita, swallowing before she says, "It is not. It's a perfectly respectable job that gave him flexibility he didn't have as a lawyer." Her smile fades as she takes a deep breath. "And he did it partly for me. So we could travel more. But we know how that worked out."

"Actually, we don't. I mean, I know you broke up while you were in Ireland, but you never shared the gory details."

"Oh, well..." Kirby suddenly becomes very interested in the straw in her lemonade, twirling it in a slow circle. "He, um... He asked me to marry him."

I freeze mid-bite. "Seriously?"

She nods. "Seriously."

As long as I've known her, Kirby has been vehemently anti-marriage. I can't believe after two years of dating, Peter didn't get the message. "So you said no, and that was it? He was done?" I ask, setting my sandwich back on the paper.

"I told him I thought marriage was an outdated institution. And fairly insincere, really, considering we live in modern times and divorce is always an option. So why act like a forever promise is *really* going to last forever when there's a good chance it won't?" She gives the straw another spin. "He said that was all a bunch of bullshit. An excuse to hold people at arm's length because I don't trust anyone enough to let them in." She presses her lips together, hesitating before her gaze lifts to mine. "Anyone but you."

My chest tightens, and the last of my appetite fades away. "Me?"

"Peter thought you were the only person who got all of me." Her shoulders lift as she looks away, watching the people streaming out of the theater. "He said it felt like..."

I study her tense features, feeling like shit for upsetting her, but sensing that I need to know whatever she's holding back. I reach across the table, running my fingers lightly across the back of her hand. "He said it felt like what?"

She glances down to where our hands touch. "Like I was having an emotional affair with you. By that point, he finally believed that we'd never had sex, but it didn't matter. He said emotional cheating was just as bad, and that if he and I were going to stay together without getting married, then I had to promise to stop talking to you so much. That I could see you when you came into town for a show or whatever, but that was it."

"Fuck him," I say, temper flaring hot. "What a controlling, manipulative piece of shit."

Kirby's lips quirk. "Yeah. I said something similar. I told him there was no way I was turning my back on fifteen years of friendship because of his insecurities. He said I was deluded, we argued some more, and then...he left. Flew home before he'd seen a single castle." She sighs. "And he was really excited about seeing the castles."

I sit back, pulling my hand away from hers. "So that's why I didn't get the gory details, huh? Because your break up was my fault?"

"It wasn't your fault." She pulls a piece of chicken from the remaining half of her sandwich. "It was my fault. I guess I did a shitty job of making him feel loved." She extends her arm under the table and a purring Murder hurries over to pluck the treat from her fingers. "He also hated that I fed Murder from the table. Said it was bad cat parenting."

"I didn't realize he was an expert on cat parenting," I say, laying on the sarcasm. "In addition to being a licensed psychoanalyst qualified to judge whether or not you were having an emotional affair." I exhale through my nose. "And what about you and Bridget? You talk every day. Was he jealous of her, too?"

Kirby blinks and reaches for her purse. "Shit, that reminds me, I should text her. Tell her that I decided not to come home tonight, after all, before she starts to worry."

I cock my head. "You told her you were coming home tonight? When?"

"Um, right before I found you on the couch," she says, avoiding my gaze again as she digs for her phone. "I thought maybe it would be better to leave before things got any more physical between us."

I start to ask her why, but she stands, phone in hand. "I'll just call her. I'm pretty sure she'll still be awake since her routine has been disrupted." She motions toward the base of the table. "Keep an eye on Murder for me?"

"Sure thing." I glance down at the cat as Kirby moves away, seeking privacy for her call. "So you think your mom regrets sleeping with me?" I ask, earning a murderous look from Murder and my first hiss of the night. "You're right," I say. "That was an inappropriate question to ask a fur kid about his mom. I apologize."

I shift my attention back to Kirby, watching a warm smile bloom on her face as Bridget answers the phone. She's only three years older than her sister, but their relationship is more mother-daughter than the typical sibling bond.

Kirby has always protected Bridget. First from their mother, then from bullies at school who sensed that shy Bridget was easy prey, and eventually from the rest of the big, bad world. Kirby paid for Bridget's degree in hotel management and then as a graduation present, bought her a bed and breakfast to run.

That's probably why Mr. Possessive wasn't jealous of Kirby's relationship with Bridget. Kirby's honest and open with her sister, but she doesn't tell her everything.

She protects her from the hard truths of the past, glossing over all the times she stood between Bridget and trauma at the hands of their mother, not wanting Bridget to feel guilty or upset.

I'm not even sure that she knows that Kirby has PTSD, or that there are times when it brings her calm, controlled sister literally to her knees. She certainly doesn't know that Kirby was hooked on sleeping pills for a while, had a nasty time getting off of them, or that she's still suffering from insomnia years later.

That's when we talk on the phone, late at night, after I've finished a show and am too ramped up on adrenaline to turn in at a decent hour, and Kirby's awake because she's always awake. But there are times, at least a couple of nights a week, when I'm able to talk her off to sleep. She jokes that I'm just *that* boring, but that's not the real reason my voice sends her off to dreamland.

It's because I make her feel safe. Kirby lives a quiet life these days, but when you grow up constantly on edge, waiting for the other shoe to drop, you tend to stay on edge. On edge becomes a pattern, a ghost that lives inside you, keeping the anxiety going long after the original source of stress has gone.

Kirby hasn't spoken to her mother in years, not since Georgia moved to Florida with her biker boyfriend the summer after our junior year of high school. But Georgia is still with her in spirit, in the dark quiet, when the worries that hide in the shadowed corners of our mind come out to play.

But my voice can sometimes send the worries away.

It makes me wonder what my arms could do if they were wrapped around Kirby every night, holding her close.

I blink, shocked by the thought. It's not a "just friends" thought, or even a fuck-buddy one. But before I can examine it too closely, my phone buzzes in my pocket, once, twice, a gazillion times, leaving little doubt who's texting me. Regina apparently has a motto in life —why send one text when you could send seven?

Sure enough, when I pull up my messages there are a cluster of new ones from my ex that read—

We need to finish our conversation. Alone.

I deserve the chance to talk to you in private, without your new girlfriend around.

I still can't believe you're dating her, by the way.

She's so short. And pale. Ugh...

I seriously don't get what you see in her.

Is she super kinky in bed or something? If that's it, you don't have to go slumming with Creepy to get what you need, baby. I've got a kinky side a mile wide, you know that. We can even play in public if you want, have some make-up sex neither of us will ever forget.

But meet me at the Spot tonight, and I'll pull out all the stops for you, Daddy.

Nose wrinkling with distaste—why on Earth would she think I want her to call me "Daddy;" that's nowhere on my kink radar and never has been—I text back a firm, *There's nothing left to talk about, Regina. It's over. Good luck with whatever and whoever comes next for you.*

Almost instantly, she shoots back—*Are you sure about that?*—followed by a picture of a pregnancy test with a plus sign in the little pink window.

Fuck. Me.

CHAPTER THIRTEEN
Kirby

*A*nother car and another ride across Vegas—this time to that top-secret sex club Colin is apparently a member of—and we're no closer to finding out who filmed us or whether they can be convinced to hand over the recording.

And now yet another steaming pile has hit the fan.

"It can't be mine." Colin's voice is muffled by the hand lingering over his mouth as he stares out at the lights streaking by, but I have no trouble understanding him.

It helps that he's said the same thing about a dozen times since Regina sent her live grenade sailing into his text messages.

"It can't," he repeats. "We haven't been together for four months, and we used protection. And wouldn't she be showing if she were that pregnant? You saw her today. She looked ready to model for Sports Illustrated. Like she hadn't eaten a sandwich in days, let alone gotten knocked up over four months ago."

"I don't know," I say with a sigh. "I'm no expert, but

I've heard a lot of women don't show much with their first pregnancies, at least, not until they're farther along."

Colin curses beneath his breath, and I rest a hand on his arm. "Let's talk more when we get there," I say, casting a pointed look toward our driver, a middle-aged Indian man who appears not to be paying attention, but recent events have made me paranoid.

Jaw clenched, Colin nods and turns back to the window as we pull off the busy four-lane road onto a narrower residential street.

I shift my purse on my lap and stroke Murder's head, wishing I'd left him in the room, after all. Shopping and dinner accompanied by a feline friend is fairly easy, but confronting an ex at a sex club sounds like something best done without a capricious animal in tow. Murder doesn't usually bite people—except for Colin—but he comes by his name honestly.

In the first week after his adoption from the pound, when he was still a barely-weaned kitten, he killed four baby birds, ate all my beta fish, and wholly disemboweled a squirrel he dragged in from the backyard.

That's how Baby Whiskers became Murder, and I realized I had to step it up to protect the native bird population from my adorable black menace. I started keeping Murder on a leash when we went outside and stopped letting him roam the garden without supervision, but he still manages to slaughter something weekly, even if it's just a cockroach from the basement or a mouse unfortunate enough to wander into our attic.

Hopefully, they won't have a fish tank at this sex club, or I'm not going to be able to take my eyes off of Murder for a second.

Maybe I should stay outside with him while Colin goes in alone.

Honestly, the more I imagine what it might be like to wander through a home where strangers are naked and doing kinky things to each other right in front of me, the more staying outside starts to sound like a lovely idea. I'm no prude—far from it. I love sex as much, if not more, than the next girl. But I like my sex private and observed only by the other person involved in the sexing.

And occasionally a random cat. I try to make sure all the felines are out of the bedroom before making out commences, but sometimes I forget, and it's not like they'll be traumatized by anything they witness. Sex is a natural, no-big-deal type of thing for animals.

People are the only species that make it weird.

No sooner has the thought drifted through my head than our driver pulls to a stop in front of a perfectly normal looking adobe ranch house set back from the street. Colin opens the door and swings out of the car with a tight "thank you" to our driver as I scoot out behind him.

"Have a nice night. Be safe," the man says, lifting a hand. I return the wave and shut the door before turning to inspect the sex lair with a sharper eye.

But it still looks benign. Tasteful black solar lamps light the cobblestone path to the front door, the porch boasts a cozy wooden swing and two rocking chairs, and the curtained windows glow with welcoming orange light. It's not even that loud. I strain my ears, but all I catch is faint music emanating from somewhere within.

I glance up at Colin, who's staring at the ranch with a curiously blank expression on his face.

"Hey, you okay?" I shift my purse full of cat to one arm so I can reach out and take his hand with the other.

"I want to be a father someday," he says softly, "but not like this. I've always been so careful, using condoms even when my partner was on the pill or had the shot or whatever. Because I didn't want to be that guy, the one who was never around. Like my dad." He glances down at me. "Or your dad."

I squeeze his fingers. "And you won't be. If this baby is yours, you'll step up and be a part of his or her life. You might not be able to be around as much as other fathers, but you'll still be there. Your kid will know you and know that you care, and that goes a long way."

He pulls in a deep breath, holding it for a moment before letting it out with an uncertain nod.

I want to say something else, something wise and insightful that will make him truly feel better, but my dad finally disappeared for good when I was five years old, and my mother is a sick person who never should have had children. What I know about parenting can fit inside a thimble and still have enough room left over to get a spider drunk.

So I just squeeze his hand again and say, "I'll be right here when you come out, okay? You've got this."

He shakes his head. "No, you're coming in. If you don't, you'll never forgive yourself."

"What? Why?" I ask, digging my heels in when he tries to pull me toward the path leading to the front door.

"Because it's a sex club, Larry," he says, widening his eyes at me like he's beginning to wonder if I have any sense at all. "Don't tell me your curious little storyteller mind isn't dying to see what's in there."

I waver, but resist being tugged onto the paving stones while I hitch a sleepy-looking Murder higher on my hip. "I have no desire to watch strangers having sex."

"Then don't go down to the basement," he says, nodding his head toward the house. "The first floor is chilling out space, the second floor is private rooms, and the third floor is where the food and entertainment is."

I narrow my eyes. "Private rooms. You said that before, but why go to a sex club to have sex in a private room?" I ask, my resolve weakening as my curiosity increases. "Why not just have sex at home in a private room?"

"Because these private rooms have fun things inside them, my sweet sex-club virgin," he says, mischief dancing in his eyes. "If you play your cards right, maybe I'll give you a tour before we leave."

I roll my eyes. "I'm sure Regina would love that."

"Then Regina can leave," he says, his jaw going tight again. "She's the one who insisted we meet here. She can deal with the fallout."

"She also insisted you come alone," I remind him.

"Which proves she knows nothing about me. If she did, she'd realize how little I enjoy being told what to do."

"This is not going to end well," I say with a sigh, "I can feel it already." But when Colin tugs on my arm again, I allow him to lead me down the path and up the stairs to the front door. There, Colin gives a strange syncopated knock, and a moment later a woman in a cute straw cowboy hat and overalls opens the door.

"Hey, C, good to see you," she says, grinning as she motions us inside.

"You, too, L," Colin says warmly, making it obvious

he feels comfortable here, or at least with this woman. "Been a minute since I've been in this neck of the woods."

"It has, but we're always thrilled to have you in town." She hands Colin an iPad from atop a small desk set against one wall of the snug foyer. The space is partitioned into its own cozy nook by a thick blue curtain hanging in a semi-circle around the door, with nothing but the desk and a water cooler visible from this side of the veil.

"If you'll just sign in here," Cowgirl L says, "and check the box for one guest in attendance, I'll get your lady set up with the nondisclosure agreement." My brows shoot up, but our host rushes to reassure me, "It's just a standard NDA, stating that you won't share anything you see here and vice versa. It's to protect everyone's privacy and make sure this remains a safe space for all of us."

I nod. "Of course. I just didn't expect paperwork at a, um... At a place like this."

Cowgirl grins. "Half of us are lawyers, hon, so we're all about red tape with our whips and chains." She laughs as she takes the iPad from Colin and swipes until a signature page pops up on the screen. "But we're a chill group, don't worry. The biggest rule is no names, just initials, and no entering a private play space if there's a red scarf on the door handle. Anything else, I'm sure C will help you figure out." Cowgirl turns Colin's way as I skim the form and sign it. "You won't need an attendant tonight, I'm assuming, since you're not a dungeon player?"

Dungeon player? Good grief, what am I doing here?

The only thing I like to do in dungeons is set fictional torture scenes in them.

I start to turn around, but Colin discreetly grabs my arm.

"Actually, I'd love to hire someone for an hour or two. Not for us, for him," Colin nods toward my purse.

Cowgirl turns to look, staring for a long moment before she gasps and presses a hand to her chest. "Oh my God, you've got a cat in your purse. That's a first." She laughs. "I've seen a lot of things smuggled in here, but never a pussy in a purse." She reaches for the bag. "Aw, and he's a cute one. Hand that sweet baby over. I'll cat-sit for you guys; no need to pay anyone to do it."

I hesitate. "Are you sure? He can be a handful, and if there are any fish or mice around, he will kill them. Violently."

She laughs again as she gathers purse and cat into her arms. "No fish or mice around here, and I'm sure. I've got this. I'm a cat lady from way back." She leans down, peering into Murder's face as she scratches his neck. Almost immediately he begins to purr.

"Thank you so much," I say, some of the tension easing from my chest. "If you need to leave your desk, you can tie his leash to the chair. He can be trusted alone for a few minutes at a time."

"Nah, if I have to hit the ladies, I'll bring him with me," she says. "Now you two go, have fun. Don't worry about us. We'll be fine."

We're about to step through the curtain when Cowgirl adds in a "just remembered" voice, "Oh, and C, just FYI, the coast is all clear now, but R just ran out the back door before you came in, and she was piiiiissed."

Cowgirl draws out the word into three or four syllables while Colin curses softly beside me.

"Oh no, should I have kept that to myself?" Cowgirl asks. "I just thought you might want to know. In case she decides to come back."

"No, it's fine, I—" Colin breaks off as his phone chimes three times. He pulls it out, staring at the screen for a beat before he turns it my way with a sigh.

I read—*You didn't come alone. I hate you. You're never going to see this baby ever!*—and sigh, too, with frustration.

And relief.

At least now we have a good excuse to get out of here.

But Colin doesn't show any signs of leaving. In fact, he seems to be reaching for the curtain...

CHAPTER FOURTEEN

Colin

*K*irby looks stricken by the Regina news, but I can't bring myself to be too upset.

Yes, I want to get to the bottom of this latest madness and find out if she's really carrying my baby. But I also really want to show Kirby around the club without stressing about my ex, and watch Larry's seen-it-all eyes go saucer-wide.

And maybe find out what flavor of kinky makes her go pink in all the places I love to watch her turn pink.

"Thanks, L." I tuck my phone away. "We'll just be an hour or so." I push the curtain aside, drawing Kirby through.

"Shouldn't we leave?" she whispers.

"No, we're not going to leave. We're here now. Might as well stay a while." I guide her around the edge of the living room, where a few couples are chatting around a fire that's irresponsible, considering the air conditioning is running, but it casts a pretty glow on Kirby's skin as she frowns at me. "Don't frown. It will be fun."

She grunts, arms folding at her chest as we step into

the elevator next to the kitchen, and I hit the button for the third floor.

"It will be," I insist in the velvet silence inside. "Just wait and see." The doors open, and I step out in the bar and pool room, followed by a still glowering Kirby. "And stop scowling. You look constipated."

"Maybe I am," she grumps.

"Pita regret so soon? Do you need me to massage your gassy tummy later?" I ask in an overly solicitous voice that earns me the hint of a smile.

"No, jerk," she says. "I'm fine. But don't you think you should at least text her back?"

I lift a hand to the waiter with the champagne tray on the other side of the room.

"No, I'm not going to text her," I say. "She's playing games, and I don't like games. And she won't be able to stay home on a Saturday night, or off social media for more than an hour or so. As soon as she posts, I'll know where she is. We'll follow and catch her off guard." I take two glasses from the tray and thank the waiter before handing one to Kirby.

She accepts the bubbly with a dubious look. "So shouldn't we head back to the hotel and drop Murder off so we're ready when the post drops?"

"Eventually, yes. But first, we're going to enjoy our vacation. I think we deserve a little R and R mixed in with hunting down the creep who filmed us and dealing with my difficult ex, don't you?"

She lifts a finger into the air. "Oh, speaking of the guy who filmed us. I forgot to tell you in all the Regina-could-be-pregnant uproar—Shep was at Bridget's place when I talked to her. And apparently, he knows a guy who is all up in the dark web's butt."

"All up in its butt, huh?" I sip the champagne, enjoying the way the crisp bubbles burn on the way down.

"Yeah. Who knew Shep had it in him?" she says, her eyebrows rippling. "It's always the quiet ones you have to watch out for, though."

"Like your sister," I tease. "What was Shep doing at her place, anyway? It was nearly midnight their time, wasn't it?"

Kirby rolls her eyes. "Oh, stop. Shep's staying in her spare room while he's helping his mom renovate her cottage. It's too much of a hot mess for anyone to live there. His mom is in Montreal staying with her sister while he's knocking down walls or whatever."

"I remember him saying something about that. I asked him why he didn't get one of his eleventy-hundred siblings to do the heavy lifting. Or hire someone to renovate it and protect his hands, but he acted like *I* was the crazy one. Said he could play drums without hands if he had to—just duct tape his sticks to whatever's left."

She laugh-winces. "Ouch. But I'm sure he'll be fine. He's always been good at handyman stuff. Remember back in high school? He practically built a skate park in his backyard. And he fixed the steps to the old tree house in Gordan's back yard so we could make out in it. Never fell once."

I glower at her until she grins.

"What?" She sips her champagne, looking awfully pleased with herself.

"Some of us spent high school being scrawny and awkward and getting zero action. No need to rub it in, teenage dirtbag."

She laughs again, harder this time, a throaty sound

that's sexy as hell and attracts the attention of one of the silver fox assholes drinking scotch at the card table.

Time to take this to a more private location, before one of them decides to come sniffing around to see if Kirby's into playing games with strangers and I have to bite his hand off.

"It's not my fault I used to be great at nailing down make-out partners," she says as I guide her toward the stairs. "And you weren't awkward. You were in the middle of an intense learning curve. I love your mom to bits and pieces, you know I do, but she kept you ridiculously sheltered."

"And then threw me to the public-school wolves when she had to go to work. Yes, I remember." I smooth my hand up her back to curl my fingers around the warm skin at her neck. "Thank you for saving me, by the way. I don't know that I've ever properly thanked you for that."

She glances up at me but turns back to the banister too quickly for me to read what's going on behind her eyes. "You don't have to thank me, silly. You were a kindred spirit, I could tell. And you don't let kindred spirits drown in their teenage angst and loneliness." She takes the stairs slowly, elegantly, and I wonder how I've failed to notice how graceful she is.

I guess it's something I've always taken for granted, another lovely part of my lovely friend who I can't imagine my life without. She's right—without her, my early teen years would have been pretty damned lonely. I didn't hook up with Shep and the rest of the band until the summer before junior year or really find my feet socially until the start of senior year. Kirby kept me from drowning.

And now, even though I'm all grown up and lucky

enough to spend my work life making music with my best friends and my free time with beautiful, talented, entertaining women, I still count on her to keep my head above water. She's still the first person in my thoughts when I have good news. Or bad news.

Whatever it is, I want to share it first with her.

As we emerge onto the second-floor landing and move through a smaller sitting room toward the hallway on the other side, I can't help but think that maybe her annoying ex-boyfriend might have had a point about that emotional affair.

And now we're having a physical affair. Or just sex, I guess, since neither one of us is in a relationship at the moment.

Except it feels like more than sex.

More intense, more intimate, more...everything.

I catch her elbow before she steps into the hall. She stops, lifting her gaze to mine. "What's up?"

I look into her eyes, but she's got her game face on, giving nothing away. "You okay with checking a few things out? We don't have to if you think this is weird."

Kirby's lips purse and shift to one side. "I don't think it's weird, I just... I guess I can't stop thinking of you here with her."

"Jealous?" I ask, the word sounding strangely hopeful, even to my own ears.

"Maybe. A little," she says. "What if I am?"

I draw her closer, letting her feel what it does to me.

"Oh yeah?" Her lashes flutter as she rocks her hips lightly against my hard-on. "So you like me possessive?"

"I do," I murmur. "I really do." Something primal inside me loves the idea of Kirby all snarly, scaring other women away from her man.

Her man.

I've always been hers, in one way or another. And now...

Now I want her again. I want her all over me—her smell, her kiss, her wetness on my fingers, my cock.

"You should see the look in your eyes," she murmurs. "You look like you're going to—"

I silence her with a deep, hungry kiss that goes from zero to sixty in seconds flat. I pull back long enough to set both of our champagne glasses on a hall table, and then we're all over each other again. My hands are everywhere, and hers are, too, skimming over my ass, rubbing my hard-on through my jeans, while she makes mewling, fuck-me-now sounds that are going to get me in trouble if I'm not careful.

I've been a member of this club for too long to get kicked out for out-of-bounds banging in the hallway.

"A room," I breathe against her lips as I back down the hall. "Let's find a room."

"Yes."

I glance to my right to see a red scarf on a door handle, then to my left to find the way clear. I have no idea what's in this particular space, but it will have to do.

I need to be alone with her. Now.

We tumble into soft blue light and dreamy mood music and close the door behind us, turning to find ourselves surrounded by people.

No, not people...reflections.

"Oh my." Kirby glances around, taking it all in—the mirrors on every side, the plush king bed covered with a tight black-fitted sheet and nothing else—before turning to me with glittering eyes. "Guess we get to watch, after all."

"Do you like to watch?" My belly flips as she reaches for the bottom of her T-shirt.

"I don't know. But I'm game to find out." She slowly draws her shirt off, and the other Kirbys follow suit, each stripping down to her lacy bra while I soak her in from every angle—the front, the back, the left and right, where her irresistible side boob is taunting me again. I strip off my own tee, tossing it over my shoulder. Kirby hesitates a beat before dropping hers to the floor with a shaky exhalation.

I search her face, but she's wearing an expression I don't recognize. I step behind her, circling her waist gently with my hands. "Nervous?"

She shakes her head, meeting my eyes in the mirror. "No, just...surprised."

"By what?"

"By how pretty we look together half naked," she says, her fingers trailing up my thigh, making me shiver and my cock pulse behind my zipper.

I skim my palms up her torso to cup her lace-clad breasts, taking my time with her, cupping each perfect curve in one hand, lifting them higher on her chest, watching as her cleavage goes from sexy to flat-out deadly.

"You know what I think will be even prettier?" I ask, slowly drawing one lace cup to the side, revealing a tight pink nipple lovelier than anything hanging in any of the world's museums.

"What?" Her breath rushes out as I circle her tight tip with my thumb, teasing around the edge where the satin-soft skin begins to pucker.

"When we're all naked," I whisper, pressing a kiss to

her neck as I pinch her nipple tight enough to make her gasp.

Gasp and claw her fingers into the ass of my jeans, pulling me closer, arching into my hand as she says, "Yes. I want to see all of you. Every single inch."

Before I can promise to oblige, she's tearing at the close of my jeans, and I'm popping the clasp on her bra, and we're rolling onto the bed where I discover an unexpected treat. There are mirrors on the ceiling, too, granting me a heart-stopping view as Kirby straddles my hips, her bare ass a perfect peach shape without a hint of a tan line.

"I've changed my mind," I say as she nibbles her way up my neck and I smooth my hands over her sweet ass like it's a crystal ball that will answer all of my most burning questions. "I like you pale, glowing in the dark. Just for me."

"For you," she promises in a husky whisper, and then she bites my ear and presses her slick center against where I ache, and I lose the ability to think about anything but how good she feels in my arms.

CHAPTER FIFTEEN

Kirby

I'm not a visual person.

Yes, I like pretty things, but not in *that* way. I've never watched porn or collected naughty gifs or stashed magazines beneath my bed. If I want to get in the mood, I track down a sex scene from one of my favorite novels and skip straight to the good parts. And then all I need is closed eyes and my own hand, no elaborate toys or tricks required.

But now, as Colin flips me over on his chest and says, "Look up," a rush of heat jolts through me as I take in the sight of us together in bed.

He's right. We're even prettier completely naked. And watching his hands roam over my body as I spread my legs and reach down, stroking the hot velvety length of him that juts out between my thighs, is the sexiest thing that's ever happened to me.

"It's like I'm feeling it twice," I murmur to Colin as he plays with my nipples, making me squirm and my breath come faster. "Once from seeing you touch me and once from feeling it. We are so, so pretty. So sexy."

"Except that you sort of look like you have a cock coming out of one thigh," Colin says, laughing as I adjust my grip on him and shift my hand to make it look even more like I'm touching my own raging erection. "You're a sick cookie."

"No, I'm not," I say, teasing my thumb around the leaking tip of him, dying to fit him to where I ache and feel him inside me. "I'm just comfortable imagining myself as a hot hermaphrodite. The ancient Romans thought they were erotically irresistible. Some of their most talented sculptors devoted years of their lives to carving beautiful, curvy women with a little of this and a little of that." On "that" I stroke him harder, making him moan and his hands tighten on my breasts until it sends a pleasant zing of pleasure-pain zipping along my nerve endings.

"Only you," Colin says, hands moving to grip the inside of my thighs, spreading them farther apart, destroying the illusion. "You're the only one who could make me hot talking about your hypothetical extra penis. God, Kirby, you make me crazy. I want you so much."

"Then take me," I say, guiding him to my entrance, a fresh wave of arousal zapping through me as he starts to push inside only to stop at the last second.

"Condom," he grits out through clenched teeth. "Let me get one from my wallet."

"I'm clean and on the pill," I say, circling my hips, teasing the tip of him while my inner walls clutch and squeeze, dying for him to be inside me again. "As long as you're clean, we're safe. I promise. You can trust me."

"And you can trust me." He holds my gaze in the reflection, his expression pained. "I'm clean. I was tested a couple of weeks ago, and I've never been with a woman without something in between."

"Never?" I ask, surprised.

He shakes his head, the pain rippling to tense the rest of his face as I tilt my hips and an inch of him pushes inside. "Fuck, Kirby, we have to stop. If I'm getting a condom, I have to get it now. Or I'm going to —" His words end in a groan as I take him in the rest of the way.

I cry out, and the shameless girl in the reflection's lips fall open as she begins to move, riding the beautiful man beneath her as his hands write music on her skin, each note echoing in her bones, taking her higher.

Higher...

And then his fingers close around her throat—gently but firmly. He pins her to his chest as he squeezes her hip tight with his other hand and pumps deeper, harder, and she's on her way into orbit.

Breaking the sound barrier in three, two—

I come, fighting to keep my eyes open so I can watch as Colin drives into me, fast and wild, the sight of him losing control while his fingers still circle my neck with perfect, insistent pressure turning me molten on the inside.

Within seconds of coming down, I'm on my way back up again, swiftly losing my mind and any remaining sense of propriety. I claw at him with my nails, begging for what I need, and he gives it to me, flipping me over onto my back and ramming into me with enough force to scoot me across the tightly fitted sheet.

I cling to his shoulders, watching in fascination as the thick muscles in his backside flex and release. He fucks me like he's never going to stop, never get enough, never be as deep as he needs to be.

The sight of it is enough to make another orgasm snatch me up in its merciless jaws, shaking me back and forth until the pleasure is so intense my head swarms with drunk bees singing a hallelujah chorus.

I come back to my body just as Colin is reaching a fever pitch that gets me buzzing all over again.

"Oh God, Kirby, baby," he breathes into my ear as he brushes my bangs from my forehead with a shaking hand. "You feel so good. I'm going to come. I can't help it, I'm going to—"

"Come, yes. Yes," I encourage as he stiffens against me with an animal sound that becomes a stream of worshipful cussing as he rides out his release with slower, gentler strokes and I hum and sigh.

And giggle.

Though, I don't realize I'm giggling until Colin pulls back to gaze down into my face with a bemused grin. "Want to share the joke with the class, Larry?"

I realize I'm the source of the giggling and giggle harder before I pull myself together enough to apologize. "Sorry. I don't know why I'm laughing. I just...feel so fucking good. And happy." I beam up into his face. "And great. So great. You're way better than a roller coaster."

He laughs, too, because he loves to see me happy and has way too big an ego to ever imagine I might be laughing at his sexual performance. "You, too. And you're really pretty when you're coming on my cock. Your body just..." He shudders, and I grin even wider.

"Your body does that to me, too," I say, tracing the hollow of his spine. "But I do feel a little sad, too."

He tilts his head. "Why's that?"

"I never got to suck your cock." I push my lips into a pout, which isn't easy with all the smiling I'm doing, but I manage. "And I'd really like to, so very much."

A shaky breath from Colin rewards me, along with the feel of him getting hard again inside me, and I grin.

"You're a bad girl," Colin says, smiling back at me.

"But good at it. You just wait and see." And then I roll him onto his back, kiss my way down his tight, trembling stomach, and show him that he's not the only one who knows a thing or two about being wicked.

Or wonderful.

CHAPTER SIXTEEN

Colin

*T*here are moments in life that stick with a person forever, scrawled on the pages of their memory in permanent ink.

I have a few from childhood—my dad's sad, stony face the last time he came to visit, when I somehow knew in my gut I was never going to see him again. The smell of fresh tar the first time Mom took me to Six Flags and we rode the kiddie roller coaster together at least a dozen times. A standing ovation in Vienna at an overseas show when I was eight, the air roaring with applause and something in my head clicking as I realized it didn't matter where I was in the world—music was my universal language, and it was never going to let me down.

But I confess that, since the age of seventeen or so, most of my forever memories have something to do with sex. Because let's face it—sex is a whole lot of fucking fun. It's the high without the hangover, the chocolate cake without the calories, a thrill ride to the top of the world that doesn't cost a dime.

It's another universal language.

Whether you speak English, French, or Korean, "Oh please, right there, that's it, don't stop," is exactly the same. When a woman's breath hitches and her muscles pull tight and the rock of her hips takes on that urgent edge, I know what to do, no words required.

But of all the racy material glued into my mental scrapbook, I somehow know Kirby in the blue light, holding my gaze in the mirror as I slid into her from behind is always going to be my number one. It's moved to the front of the binder, where it will stay. Forever.

Even now, in a none-too-fresh-smelling taxi at almost midnight, with a cranky cat meowing in the seat between us—Murder was sleeping in L's lap when we came down and wasn't thrilled about being disturbed—all I can think about is the feel of Kirby's skin, the bliss of her body tight and hot around me, the look in her eyes as I took her over the edge and she started to laugh.

I never imagined a woman laughing in bed would make me so fucking happy, but I am. I'm giddy, floating, so ridiculously pleased with us that I can't quit smiling. Every time I catch Kirby's gaze, I smile a little harder, until my jaw starts to ache and I'm halfway to being hard again.

My phone buzzes, and I pull it out to see a text from the other side of the car—*I've almost started giggling at least three times. I think I'm drunk on sex.*

Casting a quick glance her way, I type back—*You're cute when you're drunk on sex. Is it okay that I can't stop thinking about watching you suck my cock in the mirror? Or your pussy? Or how good our pussy and cock are at being best friends?*

She makes a soft, snorting sound, and one hand flies

up to cover her mouth as she types her response with one thumb. *Stop! I'm going to lose it, and Murder will freak. He doesn't like it when I get the giggles. It scares him. He's used to my dark and broody side.*

I like your dark and broody side, I reply. *But I love you like this. I love seeing you this happy and knowing I had something to do with it.*

She arches a brow my way and whispers, "Everything to do with it."

I shake my head. "Nah. It takes two to make a thing go right, Larry."

"Rob Base and D.J. E-Z Rock?" she asks, her dimples popping.

"I only quote from the masters. Eighties rappers and Shakespeare."

She laughs. "If music be the food of love, play on? How many times have you used that one on some unsuspecting girl?"

"A few," I confess, "but for you, I think..." It comes to me, the words I want to say, the simple line I've always thought was the most romantic thing the Bard ever wrote.

Maybe the most romantic thing anyone has ever written.

But now that it's here, on the tip of my tongue, I hesitate. Not because it isn't true, but because it is. It's true, and it's Kirby, and the two things are starting to feel more and more like one and the same, and what the hell am I supposed to do with that?

With her?

With the growing suspicion that what I've been searching for has been right in front of me all along?

Her brows lift. "Don't tell me your famous memory is failing you."

"No." I shake my head, the words wanting out too much for me to hold them back. "For you, *The Tempest*, Act Three, Scene One. I would not wish any companion in the world but you."

Her face softens, opens, giving me a glimpse of something hiding beneath the surface before she looks back down at her phone. A beat later, she types, *Me, too. Thanks for being my very best friend.*

Throat tight, I whisper, "My honor and pleasure." And it is. Even helping her wrangle her ridiculous cat as we tumble out of the cab and head for the elevators—Murder yowling like he's being tortured by lesser demons the entire time—I wouldn't want to be anywhere in the world but with this woman.

I've got a tempest of my own swirling inside, reshaping the Colin landscape. It's so distracting that I walk right past the new developments by the suite door without noticing them until Kirby coos, "When did you order flowers? They're gorgeous, and coral peonies are my very favorite!"

I turn, frowning at the simple but elegant bouquet of six plump flowers on the entry table. "I didn't," I confess, gaze sliding to the black case behind the door. "But it looks like someone ordered a guitar, too?"

She shoots a confused smile my way as she lets Murder out of the bag and he slinks away to the spare bedroom with a wounded look that makes it clear what he thinks of being kept out this far past his bedtime. "I had Bridget order it. I can't believe it got here this fast, though. It's nothing special, just a middle-of-the-road instrument to write songs on, but it should get the job done."

"It's completely special, thank you," I say, feeling like a rat for being out-romanced this early in the game. But then, I didn't realize Kirby and I were romancing until maybe a few minutes ago.

We are romancing, aren't we? Or is the guitar just a kind and generous gesture from a good friend?

Fuck. I'm so fucking confused.

A state of being which only gets worse when Kirby opens the card beside the flowers and reads, "How do you live with yourself? With all the lies you've told? You owe me an apology, and I will be collecting it, one way or another."

Kirby's gaze jerks to mine. "Well, this clearly isn't from Bridget."

"Clearly," I agree, crossing back to her and taking the small card from between her fingers. But it's a typed note, no handwriting or anything else to clue me in as to who might have sent it. Still, I can make an educated guess. "I guess Regina is more pissed at me than I thought."

"But these are *my* favorite flowers," Kirby says, frowning at the blooms.

"Coincidence?"

She purses her lips. "Maybe, but they aren't in season and they aren't cheap. I doubt that Regina called up a florist, said give me a quickie bouquet to use as cover for a threatening note I want to send my ex, and the florist offered up six gorgeous coral peonies. They're like eight dollars per stem out of season. I know because I asked Bridget to paint some watercolors of them for me a few years ago. She likes to paint from real life, so I ordered a dozen for her to work with. It ended up costing a small fortune."

"But the pictures came out great," I say. "The ones in your bathroom, right?"

She blinks up at me. "Yeah. I'm surprised you noticed."

"I notice things," I say, silently adding *especially things about you*. This mental shift is too new for me to know exactly what to think, let alone how to clue Kirby in on it. Especially with all the other drama swirling in the dry Vegas air. "Well, I know one way to get to the bottom of this." I pull out my phone. "We find Regina, and we get some answers."

"And why not just text you?" Kirby adds, fingers playing lightly along the base of one bloom in a way I find inexplicably erotic.

"Maybe she didn't want evidence that the message came from her," I say, scrolling through my InstaChat feed until I find what I'm looking for. When I do, I grunt and my eyes narrow. "And look at this." I tip the screen Kirby's way, and her eyebrows shoot up.

"Um, I'm not expert," she says, "but that doesn't look like expectant mother behavior."

"No, it doesn't." I screenshot the image of Regina in a skin-tight gold mini skirt and an artfully ripped black tee, standing on top of a bar with her head thrown back in laughter and a martini in hand. My jaw clenches tight. "She'd better be lying about being pregnant. If she's not..."

Kirby rests a hand on my shoulder. "She has to be lying. She's a little out there, but she's not crazy or stupid. She would know better than to drink while she's pregnant and put her baby at risk."

"Maybe, maybe not," I say, running a hand through my hair. "Regina likes to party, and there comes a point in the night when she stops caring about the consequences. That, and way too much scotch on the rocks, is how we ended up at the Little White Chapel at four in the morning."

"Well, to be fair, you were part of that decision, too." She peers up at me. "When did you know you'd made a mistake?"

"She was saying her vows," I admit. "All of a sudden, I sobered up and had the most intense 'oh shit, what the hell have I done' moment of my life. But it felt like it was too late to turn back at that point. So I said my part, went back to the hotel, and passed out, praying that I'd wake up and it would all be a dream. When I woke and it wasn't, I called my lawyer and started the paperwork for the annulment." I lean back against the wall beside the entry table. "And then I kept sleeping with Regina on and off for another year and a half, even though I knew I shouldn't. Because I'm a fucking idiot."

"You're not a fucking idiot. Relationships are messy. They don't always end nice and clean, tied up with a bow, the way they do in the movies." She crosses her arms, glaring at the bouquet. "But I think it's past time to wrap this one up. I say we go to the club, find Regina, and get to the bottom of a few things. Specifically, whether or not she's really pregnant, and if she sent these flowers. Hopefully, if we catch her unaware, red-handed with a baby-unfriendly drunk on, she'll fess up without a fuss."

I nod. "Maybe. Especially if I go in solo."

Kirby's forehead wrinkles. "You want me to stay here? It's fine if you do."

"Hell no, woman." I hook my fingers in the loops of her jeans, loving the way her eyes darken as I pull her close. "I want you to come with me and show me your dirty disco moves."

Her hands smooth up my chest as a naughty smile teases the corners of her mouth. "I'm not sure you can handle my dirty disco moves. They're pretty scandalous."

I lean closer, brushing my nose against hers, pulse beating faster as her breath rushes over my lips.

"You know I'm an animal on the dance floor," she adds, all rough and sexy.

"I do know this about you," I say, one hand sliding down to grip her ass as I add, "I spent most of the prom fighting a hard-on, and my date had very little to do with it. It was all you dirty dancing in that puffy yellow dress."

She pulls back, brows popping up. "Really? I gave you a hard-on in high school?"

"You gave me multiple hard-ons in high school. Teenage boy penises are pretty unruly, Larry. They don't care if a girl is a friend. If she also happens to be sexy and trouble on the dance floor, a hard-on is pretty much a done deal."

Kirby grins, and her hips give a satisfied wiggle. "Is it weird that I find that flattering?"

"Not weird at all." I wince, fingers digging deeper into her ass as her hips continue to twitch from side to side. "Though, I'm starting to think you might have been a cat in your last life. And that maybe I was, too, because this little tail wag thing is really doing it for me."

"Speaking of cats, I should put out some fresh food for Murder before we go." She leans in, arms going around my neck as she rocks harder against where I'm already plenty happy to see her. "And I want to put on my sparkly dress for you." She kisses me, taking my breath away before she adds in a wicked whisper, "and torment you with glimpses of my side boob for the rest of the night."

I groan. "Fuck, yes. Torment away, baby. I can't wait."

"Masochist," she says, her swift inhalation becoming a giggle as I smack her ass. "What was that one for?"

"Because you're bad, and I love it and—" I cut off mid-sentence, biting my lip with a groan as I pick her up, guiding her legs around my hips as I carry her toward the bedroom. "And I need a quickie," I add, pretending it was what I planned to say all along, even though "I love you" almost slipped out of my mouth, and if it had, it wouldn't have been a lie. "Just real fast, in and out, promise you won't feel a thing."

She laughs and murmurs in between kisses, "Oh yes, I will. I'm already feeling lots of things." She sighs, her fingers threading into my hair. "I can't wait to have you inside me again. I want you inside me all the time."

"Every second of every day," I agree, and then we're on the bed, tearing at each other's clothes and coming together with a perfection that shreds the last of my preconceived notions.

Either friends with benefits is what I've always wanted in a relationship, and I've just been too stupid to realize it, or this is what love is like—simpler and sweeter than I ever imagined.

And right and good and hot, God, so fucking hot I can barely believe I'm lucky enough to be in this body, in this bed, inside this woman who is my perfect fucking match.

CHAPTER SEVENTEEN

Kirby

*T*he crash is going to be awful. Going back to being just friends when all this is over is going to hurt like nothing I've ever felt before, but at the moment I'm too high on sex to care.

I float through my brief shower on a cloud of bliss and hum along to Colin's strumming from the bedroom as I put on my makeup, not even minding for once that girl readiness takes so much longer than boy readiness or that eyeliner is my nemesis and getting it straight always takes at least five tries.

When you've come as many times as I have in the past twenty-four hours, no troubling thing is very troubling.

"I've lost track of how many orgasms I've had," I murmur to Colin as we step into the elevator, my nerve endings humming as he teases fingers under the hem of my dress, tracing the line where my panties give way to butt cheek.

We're alone in here, but even if we weren't, I'm not sure I would care. I am past caring, surfing the Happy

Sexy Fun Orgasm wave like the good times are never going to end.

"Seven if I was reading the signals correctly," he says, nuzzling his face against my neck. "You go pink all over when you come. It's my new favorite color."

Nipples tightening, I turn his way with a smile. "I'll buy you a pink shirt tomorrow."

"Please do. I'll wear it to dinner," he says, fingers sliding beneath the elastic on my panties. "I made a reservation at Sinatra, by the way. Figured we'd need something special to celebrate the successful completion of our missions."

"Or to drown our sorrows," I remind him. "Shep might not be able to track down the P. Eater, our sex tape could be online by morning, and Regina could actually be pregnant."

Colin scoffs as he takes the finger-teasing to its inevitable conclusion, gliding a finger into where I'm already wet, making my eyes flutter closed and my words emerge as a breathy whisper, "Stop. They probably have cameras in here."

"That's why I'm keeping my hand hidden beneath this naughty little skirt," he murmurs into my ear. "This is a very bad dress, Larry. Lift your arms too high, and everyone on the dance floor is going to see these pretty panties."

"That's why I wore the sparkly ones," I say, grinning as he pulls back to pin me with a disapproving glare.

"You're a shameless hussy."

"Says the guy who's fingering me in the elevator."

He smiles, wickedly, perfectly, and my heart break-dances in my chest, doing that head spin move that always seemed impossible before, but is now as easy as falling wildly in lust with my best friend.

Though, of course, it isn't just lust. It's other things, too, things that make me cup his cheek and whisper, "Sinful bastard," in a tone that says, "You are everything I want, don't ever leave me."

Trouble. I'm asking for it, giving heartbreak a handwritten invitation, but I can't seem to help myself.

Colin is gravity, a law of nature I can't escape and wouldn't want to.

He leans in, his lips moving closer to mine as his fingers take me closer, closer to the edge, only for the elevator to purr to a stop seconds before my knees go weak. Colin pulls his hand discreetly from under my clothes as two older ladies wearing black dresses and elaborate red hats hustle in, laughing loudly at some shared joke.

I suck in a breath and fan my face with one hand, fighting to pull myself together and look like I wasn't just on the verge of orgasm.

The taller one does a double take before wiggling her fingers our way and asking, "Y'all having a good night?" in a thick Southern accent.

Before we can reply the shorter, stouter one hoots, "Of course they are, look at them. They're young, beautiful, and in love." Her gray eyes sparkle between us. "And headed somewhere fabulous, I bet. Dinner? Dancing?"

"Dancing," Colin says, sliding his arm around my waist. "I'm going to try like hell to keep up with her."

The taller woman laughs. "You do that, honey. And bring a stick to beat back all the other men." She winks at me. "You look gorgeous, sweetheart. And I love your books. Scare me so bad I'm afraid to go to pee in the night without turning the light on and checking the shower and the toilet bowl for monsters first."

I sputter out a laugh. "Well, thank you. I try." I feel my cheeks going hot and can't help but add, "This is only the second time I've ever been recognized."

Both women make sounds of disbelief before the one who pegged me says, "I can't believe that. The first time I saw your picture on a dust jacket, I thought to myself —that's why you don't judge a book by its cover. Who would have thought that sweet little angel face had such a twisted mind sitting behind it?"

Colin laughs as the elevator door opens, and we move out into the lobby, our new friends waving goodbye as they join a group of other red-hatted, black-dress-wearing women and a man holding a "Haunted Vegas Night Tour" sign that's intriguing. I can't help peering at the group as we move toward the exit.

"Angel face. Twisted mind," Colin says. "I should get that printed up on a T-shirt for you, Larry."

I narrow my eyes at him. "Oh, stop. I don't have an angel face. She was just being nice. Angels don't have noses and chins so sharp you could cut yourself on them if you're not careful."

Colin stops just outside the sliding glass doors, turning to me with a serious expression as the cool air rushes out behind us, ruffling my skirt. "Are you serious?"

"Of course. I do own a mirror you know." I shrug. "But I don't care."

"Well, I do." A frown bunches between his brows. "You're beautiful. And anyone who's ever told you different is a fucking idiot."

"Okay. Thank you." I shift in my heels, glancing over my shoulder, hoping we're in someone's way. But we're not. The lobby is nearly empty, and the valet station in front of us is calm for the first time since our arrival, with just two attentive but tired-looking men standing at attention beside the desk.

"Why did that make you uncomfortable?" Colin asks, sticking his nose in, the way he always does when he catches wind of something I don't want to talk about.

"Why are you so comfortable asking uncomfortable questions?" I counter.

"Born that way," he says. "And probably poor boundaries, but boundaries are overrated. Especially with people you care about. Why should I ignore your weirdness and let you keep believing dumb things about yourself?"

"Maybe because the fucking idiot is me, Colin," I say, voice shakier than I expect it to be. I take a breath and add in a lighter tone, "No one ever told me I was a troll person except me, okay? I did it to myself. Since I was a kid."

He threads his fingers through mine and shakes his head. "Not true, Larry. Kids don't come out thinking they're troll people. Someone teaches them that, maybe not with what they say, but with what they don't."

With my ribs in an emotional vice, I look up at the giant chandelier hanging from the ceiling of the covered drive, pretending to be interested in the artistry as I nod. "You could have something there, I guess."

"You think?" he asks dryly.

"But it's not a big deal," I say, willing myself not to tear up. I refuse to mess up my eyeliner because Colin makes me feel my stupid feelings the way no one else ever does. "Seriously. I don't care about looks that much, anyway."

"Fine." He shrugs and tightens his grip on my hand. "Then I'll care about it for you. I'm going to tell you you're beautiful every day, Kirbs. Every day until I know that you believe me. So just fucking prepare yourself."

I shift my stinging gaze to him with a sigh. "Well, that's going to be obnoxious. But I guess you gotta do what you gotta do."

He grins and says, "I love you, too," and it's all I can do not to start bawling my eyes out right there.

But thankfully, the car Colin ordered upstairs pulls up to the curb before the waterworks can get started. Before I can throw my arms around Colin's neck and confess that I love him, too, but that I've gone and messed up our easy, breezy thing by getting too much of myself involved.

He's more than my kindred-spirit friend. He's my brain's favorite sparring buddy, my vagina's most treasured companion, and such a big chunk of my heart that if he were ever cut out of it, I'm not sure I'd survive the separation.

"Ready to take this bad dress out for a good time?" he asks, nodding toward the car.

"Ready." I sniff away my tears and force fear and worry into the shower and pull the curtain. They'll be there, waiting to jump out and hack me to bits when this is all over, but tonight is not that night.

"But seriously, I think you should stay at the bar while I talk to Regina," he says, lifting a hand to the driver before opening the back door for me. "This dress is going to need a bodyguard on the dance floor. I'm not comfortable leaving it or you alone in a crowd."

I roll my eyes as I slide into the cool car, but say, "Yes, sir."

Colin makes a happy growling sound as he dips in behind me. "And we'll do that later. You can be the naughty school girl who disobeyed the dress code, and I'll be the stern headmaster who's going to teach her a lesson about wearing short skirts."

I giggle as he pulls me closer and press a finger to his lips as the driver pulls out of the drive. "Okay, but hush. The first rule of kinky playtime is we don't talk about kinky playtime in public."

"Yes, ma'am," he says, nipping at my finger, the feel of his teeth dragging across my skin making butterflies swarm low in my body. "I really hope tonight has a happy ending. I'd much rather head home with you knowing I'm not going to have to figure out some way to keep Regina from drinking during her pregnancy and fucking up our kid."

I brush his hair from his forehead. "Me, too. But if it comes to that, we'll figure something out. Together."

"Together," he echoes, looking happy about it.

If only he meant it the way I do. But he doesn't. I keep reminding myself of that as he snuggles me close, kissing my forehead as we zip down the strip, the lights a blur and his heartbeat strong and steady beneath my cheek.

CHAPTER EIGHTEEN

Colin

I'm in love with Larry.

I'm in love with Larry, and I told her I was in love with her, and she blew it off because she thought I meant friend love.

But I didn't. I meant that I want to tell her she's beautiful every night before we go to bed and first thing when we wake up in the morning. I meant that I want to patch up all the places in her heart that her mother scratched up so she can see herself the way I see her—as one-in-a-million.

My one-in-a-million, because no man is ever going to appreciate every spooky, quirky, kind, creative, thoughtful, sexy, brave part of her the way I will.

I'm going to have to clear up the misunderstanding, take a gulp and a breath, and hurl myself off the ledge into the great unknown hoping she'll catch me.

But first, to find out if I'm going to have a baby with another woman...

I wouldn't blame Kirby for not being on board for a situation like that. I'm not sure Kirby even wants kids.

It's not something we've ever talked about, but I wouldn't be surprised to learn children aren't on her wish list. She spent her childhood cleaning up her mother's messes while being a surrogate parent to Bridget. She might very well want to spend her adulthood just taking care of herself and a shitload of cats.

I turn to her, about to ask what she thinks about kids, but swallow the words at the last second.

"What's up?" she asks, reaching for the car door handle.

"Nothing." I lift a hand to the driver. "Thanks for the ride."

"No worries," the young guy says with a yawn. "You guys should check out the exhibit if you get the chance. Super cool old stuff. I think this is the last night for it."

"Will do," I say as I step out behind Kirby.

"What exhibit?" She takes the hand I hold out, making my heart do goofy, not-just-friends things in my chest as she threads her fingers through mine.

"No idea. I was just trying to get rid of him. I'm a little distracted."

She nods, shaking my arm gently as she exhales. "Understandable, but you've got this. And I can come with you if you want."

I shake my head as we start up the wide, curving staircase leading to the second floor of the Cairo hotel, an Egyptian themed behemoth that recently got a swanky facelift and opened one of the hottest clubs on the strip. "No, you should wait at the bar. I'd love to have you there, but Regina clearly sees you as a threat."

"I am pretty threatening," Kirby says dryly before adding in a monotone, "Growl. Snarl. Snap. Grr."

"Terrifying," I agree with a smile.

"Speaking of terrifying, I'm not going to drink any more tonight. After last night's debauchery under the porch, I want to keep things respectable."

"Good idea. I'll follow your example." Staying sober is also an excellent way to keep from spitting out premature romantic confessions. I point to the coffee shop tucked into a corner behind a bank of slot machines at the top of the stairs. "You want to grab a coffee, then? And I can come back for you when I'm finished?"

"No way," she scoffs. "I want to be up in da club, fam, getting turnt."

I hold out a hand, covering her face. "Stop. You're embarrassing yourself."

"What?" She giggles. "That slang was on point, bae."

"Awful," I insist, as she pulls my arm down. Even though I would happily be her Before Anyone Else. "You sound like an alien. Or my mother."

Her brows snap together. "Wow. Can we get a RIP in the chat for poor Katherine. Your mom is the most Gucci lady I know, dude. Not cool."

"Speaking of cool, are you going to be warm enough?" I cast a pointed glance at her arms, where the little blond hairs are standing on end. "The air conditioning is working overtime in here."

"I'll be fine. Especially once we start dancing." She curls her fingers around my bicep, staying close as we weave through the last of the poker tables and step into the glass elevator that will whisk us up to Elevation, the strip's current "cool kid" club. "And I bet they have tea or coffee at the bar. If I get too chilly, I grab one and warm up while I wait for you."

"Hopefully I won't be long." I cover her hand with mine, keeping her fingers on my arm as I cut right out of the elevator instead of left, where a line of people snakes away from the club entrance all the way down the hall toward the shops and restaurants on this floor. "This way. No time for the line tonight."

"So you're going to be the obnoxious rock star who uses his famous face to bypass the queue?"

"I am. Can you forgive me?"

"Yes, I can," she says. "The only thing worse than a long line is a long line in heels. And there ought to be some perks to your crazy life, to go along with the stalking fans, crazy touring schedule, and pervasive lack of privacy."

I make a sound of agreement and lift an arm to high five Jorge, one of the bouncers I've met before. We exchange a few pleasantries as he opens the rope, angling his large body to shield Kirby and me from the curious stares of the people at the front of the line, who are already starting to murmur my name. But I'm too busy wondering if my fans, touring schedule, and lack of privacy are going to be a deal breaker to pay much attention to the talk.

Kirby likes her privacy. A lot. She's a happy little hermit 90 percent of the time, and she's always done her best to fade into the woodwork when we're out after a show and someone comes over to ask me for a selfie.

Unlike Regina, who squeezed into every shot, as in love with the way I boosted her social media reach as anything else I had to offer. But her love of attention has given me a good idea where to find her, proving almost every trying thing in life has a silver lining.

I lean close to Kirby's ear, raising my voice to be heard over the music pulsing from the dance floor. "I'm betting Regina is in the champagne suite upstairs. As far as she's concerned, the more exclusive, the better. So I'm going to try there first. Where do you want to wait?" I motion to the massive twin bars to our left and then to the balcony bar on the second floor that overlooks the writhing, jumping, twisting bodies below. "Big bars or balcony bar?"

Kirby points to her left. "I'll wait at the big one closest to the wall. More likely to have coffee and tea, I think." She glances down at her phone, which she's pulled from her tiny handbag. "And I'm getting good Wi-Fi, so I can check email and do some research on haunted Pennsylvania while I'm at it. I'm thinking of setting a series there."

"Perfect. I'll be back soon." I kiss her forehead. "Don't work too hard."

"Good luck," she says, lifting her crossed fingers as I head in one direction and she in another.

I duck my head, concealing my face as I thread my way through the crowd at the edge of the dance floor, heading for the not-so-secret secret entrance hidden in one of the cigarette machines on the other side of the club. The vintage dispensers are part of Elevation's theme. Everything here is "elevated" to serve a function finer than the one for which it was originally intended.

The couches in the champagne suite are made out of antique bathtubs, the glittering dance floor is composed of thousands of bottles of various colors, crushed and covered in lightly bouncy plastic, and the old soda and cigarette machines along the wall deal out art from local artists for five bucks a pop.

Except the one in the corner, the one with another massive bouncer stationed in front of it to keep non-VIPs from tugging handles they shouldn't. *That* machine leads to the champagne suite, a glass-walled room with a view of the entire club and a third, catwalk-style dance floor that's a popular selfie attraction.

As I approach the bouncer, I lift my head and make meaningful eye contact, but the guy doesn't blink. His brown eyes remain flat, and his meaty arms stay crossed at his chest.

Looks like the famous face isn't going to get me far with this dude.

Luckily, I know the password.

"I'm here for the old-fashioned," I say, but when I reach for the golden handle in the center of the machine, the bouncer holds out a hand.

"Sorry, we're full up." He points a finger overhead, where the glass wall of the champagne suite juts out into the room just enough to catch a glimpse of the bartenders' shoes as they rush from one side of the bar to the other. "You'll have to wait for someone to leave."

I nod, even though I fully intend on getting up there —now. But nodding always makes people feel better about letting you break the rules. "I'll only be a second, man. I just need to talk to someone who's up there. I'll be in and out in five minutes."

"Fire code." He shifts to the left, blocking access to the handle that serves as the open sesame button for the door to the hidden staircase behind it. "We could get shut down if we're caught with more than fifty people in the suite."

"But you won't get caught," I say with a reassuring smile. "Because I'm going to be so fast no one will even know I was there. Seriously, what are the chances the fire marshal is going to show up at this time of night? And even if he does, he'll need more than five minutes to get through the club, and by then I'll be gone."

"I'll comp you a drink," he says, not budging. "That's the best I can do."

"I don't need a drink." I pause, deciding to bring out the big guns. "I need to talk to my ex. She just posted a picture of herself getting wasted on her InstaChat page not two hours after telling me she was pregnant with our baby."

A spark of interest flickers behind the mountainous man's dark eyes. "Dude, that's fucked up."

"Right? Hopefully she's lying about being pregnant. But if she's not, my baby's brain could be getting pickled as we speak. And that cuts deep. If my kid ends up damaged for life because the club was too full the night I came to stage an intervention with his mom..." I sigh, giving that a moment to sink in. "I don't know how I'm going to live with myself."

The bouncer's chin puckers, and his mouth scrunches up like he's taken a bite of something he's not sure he wants to chew, but I can tell he's wavering.

"I swear I will crawl under the bar and hide if the fire marshal shows up. He or she will never know I'm in there." I lift a fist, hoping he won't leave me hanging for the bump. "Do a guy a solid just this once?"

His gaze darts toward the front of the club and then over to the DJ booth before returning to me. "I'll let you up, but you'll have to be quick. There's a guy keeping count up there, too. Once he realizes we're over capacity, the last person to sign in up top will be out." He reaches for the handle, tugging it and sending the hidden door sliding open, revealing a gas-lamp lit staircase.

"Thank you, man." I slip inside, throwing my next

words over my shoulder as I climb, "I'll be quick and stealthy, I promise."

I jog up the circular stairs, arriving at the top slightly out of breath, but the girl in an old-school flapper dress at the sign-in desk is too dazzled to notice. "Oh my God, hi," she says, laughing as she waves a hand in front of her face. "I'm sorry. I just love your music. I couldn't live without Better Day."

"Thanks so much, catch you on the way out," I say, signing my name in the ledger and ducking through the curtain behind her before she can ask for a selfie.

I'm sure she's not supposed to ask patrons for pics, but most people today don't give a shit about the rules. They will totally put their job on the line for a juicy, status-elevating social media update. It drives me crazy, honestly. And makes me wish I'd been born fifty years earlier, back when modern medicine was still doing decent work, but before technology got so fucking annoying.

There are days when contributing to Lips on Fire's online presence is like selling my soul for the kind of love that gets lonelier with every click.

I pull my phone out, making a quick note of the thought as I prowl the edge of the intimate room, searching for Regina's fluffy blond locks, notes and rhythm already humming to life in my head and itching to find their way out of my fingertips.

The past day has been magic, inspiration-wise, making it clear I didn't need a sex break to connect with my muse. What I needed was to get my ass on the right path with the right person.

"Can I get you a drink, sir?" The cocktail waitress sporting two long black braids looks familiar. Hopefully, she's worked here long enough to know the regulars.

"No drink, thanks, but I'm looking for Regina Williams." I hold up a hand beneath my nose. "About this tall in heels, blond, tan, smile so white it's blinding?"

The girl bites her lip and shakes her head. "That's a lot of women around here."

"She only drinks clear alcohol so her teeth don't get stained? Gets upset if her dirty martini is too dirty, even though olive juice doesn't have a color, and will send it back at least twice, no matter what?"

The server's eyes light up. "Oh yeah. I remember her. She was in tonight."

"Was," I repeat, spirits sinking. "So I missed her?"

"You did," the woman says, "but not by much. She just left. Maybe ten minutes ago? I remember because she made Joan let her use the back elevator, even though it's supposed to only be for handicapped guests." Her brows lift as she adds in a more pointed voice, "She said she needed to avoid someone coming in the front. A guy with a history of abuse, she said."

My head rears back as I blink like someone threw acid in my face. "What the hell? I..." My mouth opens and closes, but no words come out. "I don't even know what to say to that. Except that it's bullshit, and I'm sorry she involved your staff in her drama. She texted me a positive pregnancy test earlier tonight and then decided to go clubbing instead of talking things over like reasonable adults. That's why I'm trying to find her."

The girl nods and some of the wariness fades from her eyes. "Yeah, I remember you from before. You never acted like a douchebag when you were with her. And I've seen some stuff go down here that you wouldn't believe.

People can be awful when they're drunk and feeling fancy for getting to play in the secret room."

"I bet," I say, brow furrowing in commiseration. "So I don't suppose you have any idea where she went?"

"Sorry, no." The server jabs a thumb over her shoulder. "But I can let you go down the elevator. Maybe someone downstairs will have seen her. The projector games are there, so sometimes people stick around for a while."

"Thank you so much." I press my palms together in gratitude and follow her around the back of the raised dance floor, where several women in skirts even shorter than Kirby's are flashing sparkly panties not nearly as cute as hers. Then we go down a hall with bathroom doors on one side and soundproof chat rooms with phone charging stations on the other, finally reaching a door marked "Staff Only."

I follow her through, glancing around at the gray and light brown color scheme that takes effect the instant we're out of the public eye.

"I know, right?" The girl grins as she punches the down button near the oversize gray elevator doors. "If they really wanted to 'elevate' the club, they'd give us something to look at back here aside from beige lockers and instructions on how to give the Heimlich maneuver. You should buy this place and take it up another notch. I have ideas, and the owner's looking for a buyer before the cool factor wears off."

I cock my head. "Own a club. I've never thought about anything like that."

"You should," she says, jabbing the button again. "Entertainers with pull are making insane money in Vegas. You guys could play here a couple of months a year and then pop in for unannounced guest appearances whenever. People would be lining up even harder than they are now."

The doors trundle open with a thunking sound, and I step inside, holding an arm in front of the sensor as I extend the other to my guide, a twenty between two fingers. "Colin Donovan."

"Yeah, no duh." The girl rolls her eyes good-naturedly and takes the bill. "Theresa Chin. I've been here longer than anyone but Bill, the marketing guy, including the general manager. If you want to chat more, give a call and leave your number. I work most nights."

"Maybe I will. Thanks, Theresa Chin." I pull my arm away from the sensor.

Theresa waves as the doors slide closed. "Good luck."

I pace the elevator, pondering Theresa's suggestion. A club of my own would be a great place for the band to try out new music, give us a feel for what's resonating with our fans before we head into the studio. And if I am going to be a father, being close to Regina, who's lived in Vegas all her life, for at least part of the year would probably be a good idea.

The thought sours my excitement, but only a little. No, I don't want to have a baby with Regina. But if there's already one on the way, I'm going to do everything I can to be a positive force in his or her life, and that includes being physically present as often as possible.

I exit the elevator and do a quick scan of the people waiting their turn to play a space-themed virtual reality game projected on the wall to my right. The current players are wearing headgear that completely covers their eyes and ears, so they won't be any help, but maybe one of the people near the front of the line...

I approach two curly-haired kids who look way too young to be in a twenty-one and older club, and I tap the boy gently on the shoulder. "Excuse me," I say when he turns. "Have you seen a tall, blond woman with big hair wearing a very short gold skirt walk by? And if so, could you tell me where she went?"

"I saw her," the girl says, pointing up and over the dance floor. "She was walking really fast that way. Toward the exit, I think."

Cursing inwardly, I thank the girl and jog off in the direction she pointed, taking a hard look at every blond I pass, but none of them are Regina. I reach the exit and hesitate, torn between telling Kirby I'm heading out to search the casino and not wanting to give Regina any more time to get away from me. Finally, I split the difference, calling Kirby on my cell as I hurry past the bouncers and over to the balcony to scan the casino floor below.

The phone rings several times before sending me to voicemail, but I don't worry. It's loud as hell in there, and there's an excellent chance Larry can't hear her phone.

I make a mental note to try again in a few minutes and jog down the hallway, searching the various shops and bars, ignoring the nagging feeling in my gut that something's not right. Not right at all.

CHAPTER NINETEEN

Kirby

I'm halfway through the unanswered messages in my inbox—and a quarter finished with a cup of the worst coffee I've ever tasted—when the bartender sets a fizzy red drink garnished with a plump strawberry on the bar in front of me.

"Your friend bought you a drink," he says, his eyes crinkling as he flashes a mouthful of even teeth. "Thank goodness. I was about to buy you one myself. To apologize for the coffee. I think that bag of French Roast is older than you are."

I set my phone down on the bar beside me with a smile. "It's fine." I glance around the bartender, but there's no sign of Colin. Maybe he called the drink in from the champagne suite?

"No, it's not fine." He braces his hands on the bar, the better to display his flexed forearms. "I feel terrible. I didn't know it was shit brew until my coworker poured himself a cup and spit it out in the sink. I'm a tea guy. Love a good Lapsang souchong or anything rich and smoky." He pushes the bubbly red concoction closer to my hand with a flirty wink. "But this is almost as good. House-made strawberry lemonade, squeezed fresh every morning."

"That sounds great. Thank you." I grip the glass lightly in one hand while I push the coffee his way with the other. "There's no alcohol in this, right?"

He lifts a hand, his flirty vibe vanishing. "Yeah, there is, actually. A shot of lemon vodka, and a touch of peach liqueur. But if you're sober, I can make it virgin. It's no problem."

"Oh, no, I'm not sober." I shake my head with a wince. "I mean, I am presently sober, but I'm not in a program." I shrug. "I was just trying to take it easy tonight. But a shot of vodka isn't a big deal. You don't have to remake it."

"Are you sure?" he asks as he dumps the coffee in the sink behind the bar. "It's no trouble. Things are slow. After two o'clock or so, the team on the dance floor side gets all the action."

My eyes widen as I take my first sip of lemonade, tongue tingling as the tart liquid prickles down my throat. "Wow, I didn't realize it was that late. I don't feel two-in-the-morning tired."

He points toward the ceiling. "That's because the casino is pumping pure oxygen into the joint to keep people awake and gambling."

"Is that right?" I take another sip, catching a sliver of sickly sweetness this time, a not-quite-right flavor that makes me think this guy was hired more for his impressive forearms than for his skill with slinging a drink.

"It is. At least, they say it's just oxygen." He leans closer, adding in a confidential tone, "But I wouldn't be surprised to find out they've slipped something else in the mix, something to keep people amped up and reckless. My roommate thinks it's just the desert air that makes people crazy around here, but I'm not sure. There are more things in heaven and earth, right?"

"Shakespeare," I say, smiling. "You're the second man to quote Shakespeare to me tonight."

His eyes narrow as his lips curve. "Bummer. I like to be first. Hopefully, I'm better looking, at least."

I bare my teeth and turn my palms to the ceiling in a "Sorry Charlie" way that makes Forearms laugh. But then, if Colin ordered this drink for me, Forearms should have seen with his own eyes that he's up against some pretty intense competition. Colin must have called it in from somewhere else, which makes me wonder how much longer he's going to be.

If he anticipated a quick return, surely he wouldn't have ordered me a drink.

"Oh, well, can't win 'em all," the bartender says with another wink. "Enjoy your drink, and let me know if I can get you anything else."

"Thanks, will do." I'm about to reach for my phone when I hesitate and call after him, "Did my friend give you a message for me? Maybe a hint as to how much longer I'll be waiting?"

He crosses his arms over his chest with a shake of his head. "No, sorry."

I wave a hand. "It's fine. No worries. I'm not in any big rush." I point to the ceiling. "And I'm not sleepy, so…"

Forearms grins. "The casino's evil plan is working."

"No, it's not," I say, taking another drink. It's a little odd-tasting, for sure, but still way better than the coffee.

"I don't gamble. So I'm getting oxygenated for free. I win this round, casino."

He laughs. "Good for you. I don't gamble anymore, either. Every time I lost forty bucks in the slots, I kept thinking that was a month's gym membership, with a couple of protein smoothies thrown in."

I hum in agreement, even though I've never set foot in a gym. I get my sweat for free, pounding the pavement from my place to the marina and back again. And I figure lifting my fattest cat, Hitchcock, off my mattress before I head to bed every night is all the weight lifting any reasonable woman needs.

"But if you're looking to kill time while you're waiting," the bartender adds, "you should check out the carny exhibit." He points toward the entrance. "It's just down the hall to the right, before you get to the arcade. They've got some cool stuff. A bunch of those old fortune-telling machines that spit out cards and a display from an old Mummy's Curse ride."

I sit up a little straighter at "Mummy's Curse," intrigued. "So it's close?"

"Real close. And you can take your drink with you if you want. Just get your hand stamped so you can come back through the exit without waiting in line again."

"Thanks, I will." I slide off my stool, tucking my phone into my little purse and collecting my drink.

"Cool. Enjoy it." Forearms lifts an arm, looking sad to see me go. But then, he's right—it's dead on this side of the bar. It's strange to think that people would rather wait in line closer to the dance floor than walk twenty feet to reach more readily-accessible alcohol, but people are often a mystery to me.

It started in elementary school, when other girls my

age were crushing on boy-band members I found repulsive and continues to this day as the people in my inner circle drag me to sporting events. They insist I'm going to love Sport X once I see it live, but I always find the snacks the most riveting part of any competitive performance. And honestly, I'd rather eat my popcorn in the dark, staring at a movie screen, the way God intended.

But old carnival equipment? There's a temptation I can't resist.

I collect my hand stamp at the exit and drift down the hall. I consider calling Colin to let him know where I'm going, but it seems like he's going to be a while. And if he arrives at the bar to find me gone, he'll call me, and I can answer. Better that than I risk pestering him in the middle of a tricky conversation with his ex.

I reach the entrance to the exhibit—a giant, bug-eyed clown's face with a six-foot hole cut in his mouth—and grin. Oh yeah, this is in my wheelhouse all right. Sipping at my increasingly tolerable drink—my taste buds are going pleasantly numb from the combo of alcohol and citrus—I wander into the first display room.

There, I find a few fortune-telling machines, arranged haphazardly in the space, almost as if someone has already started breaking down this part of the exhibit. But still, there are a few things left, including an ancient-looking wheel-of-fortune type apparatus and a couple of the more modern gypsy-mannequin-behind-glass variety. Picking my favorite mannequin, an old man in a turban with a leathery-looking face, I slip a quarter into the slot, punch the "Tell my Future" button, and watch as his glass eyes light up from the inside.

The red glow and the spooky accordion music pumping from the speakers above his head are creepy enough to make me take a bracing drink. His arms lift and his head rolls before he touches a jerky hand to the green jewel in his turban and announces in an ominous voice, "Your fate is sealed, no turning back now. Give Soloman more coins to learn more about your future."

The machine spits out a crisp eggshell-colored card that I collect from the slot beneath Soloman's glass window. Turning it over, I read, "There is nothing to fear, but fear itself," and harrumph. "Thanks for the platitude, Soloman."

I consider trying the other machine to see if I can score a better fortune but decide I should keep moving. I have no idea how large this exhibit is, and I'd like to at least skim through all of it before heading back to the club to get my groove on with Colin. Though, I have to confess, dancing is starting to sound like more effort than I'm up for tonight. The casino must have cut the oxygen supply in here.

I can feel my lids getting heavier as I cruise through mostly empty rooms—they've definitely started breaking this down, and I'm beginning to wonder if I should even be in here—and into a long hallway lined with mirrors.

I wander across the carpeted space, head spinning as I watch my body morph from a squat goblin with an impossibly long neck to a ten-foot-tall girl with a body like stretched taffy. The images are disconcerting, making me think back to my conversation with Colin before we left the hotel tonight.

So much of the world is a funhouse mirror, reflecting false images that it can take an entire lifetime to realize are lies. Without good friends and people who love us to help undo the damage, where would we all be?

"Lost. All lost," I murmur, draining the last of my

drink and smacking my tingling lips, wishing Colin was here so I could thank him for caring enough to challenge me when I need challenging. He's a good one, my friend. My sweet, sweet friend that I love so much it hurts.

I fumble for my phone to send him a sappy text, but the drawstring on my purse is being impossible and my fingers are stupid, so I give up.

Hmmm...stupid fingers. Fuzzy head. Heavy eyes.

I suspect Forearms must have done a heavy pour on the vodka, a suspicion that is all but confirmed as I totter deeper into the exhibit, getting progressively freaked out by things that usually wouldn't bother me. I love stuff like half-rotten clown costumes and portraits of people who worked the Freak Show circuit.

But not tonight. Tonight, I can feel hidden eyes watching me, and spirits lingering too close. By the time I reach the velvety near-darkness of the Mummy's Cursed Tomb, the one room that still looks pretty complete, my heart is racing, my palms are sweating, and my knees are so wobbly, I really wish there was a place to sit down.

But there's nothing horizontal except the coffins scattered throughout the room, and those are filled with mummies in various stages of decomposition. There are freshly wrapped mummies sitting stock straight, their arms extended like sleepwalkers, and mummies with blackened bandages and skeletal faces crawling out of their coffins, as furtive as naughty children sneaking out to steal cookies after they've been tucked into their beds.

And then there are the rest of them...

Whoever put the finishing touches on the near-naked mummies has horror-movie magic flowing through his or her veins. The monsters are utterly terrifying, rotted corpses with wild eyes that would be at home in a zombie film—one of the really scary ones that keeps you up the rest of the night making your Zombie Apocalypse plan even though you know that the end times aren't going to go down that way.

"The end times are going to be stupid," I tell one of the scary mummies, leaning in to get a closer look at his utterly gross face. "We're going to get killed by weather, Mr. Gloppy. Or pollen. And sneeze and snot ourselves to death."

"God, you really are weird as hell, aren't you?" a familiar feminine voice behind me asks.

I spin, and the world spins with me. I stagger to the left, dropping my empty glass as I trip over my own feet and nearly take a tumble to the floor.

"Easy there, Creepy," Regina says, righting me with firm hands on my shoulders. "Here, let me take that for you." She grabs my purse, snatching it from my tingling hands with ease before she asks, "Facial recognition on your phone lock screen?"

I frown. "Wha za wha…"

I smack my lips, struggling to make actual words come out, but the room is spinning again, whirling, colors swirling into a mix of muddy green, brown, and the candy apple of Regina's red lips.

"Sleep it off, sweetie, and you'll be fine," she says with a mean laugh. "And I know just the place where a tragic thing like you will feel right at home."

I lunge for the mirrored hallway, still sick and confused, but knowing that I have to get out of here, away from Regina. I barely make it one wobbly step in my heels before her arm locks around my chest and drags me backward.

And then the ceiling is on the floor, and the floor is on the ceiling, and I'm floating, falling, tumbling into something soft, but dusty.

Really dusty.

I sneeze, hard, and it clears my head just long enough to realize Regina has put me to bed in one of the mummy's coffins before the black circle at the edges of my vision closes in.

CHAPTER TWENTY

Colin

*F*ifteen minutes later, I reach the end of the long colonnade of shops and a staircase leading to the lobby of the Cairo's connected sister casino, the Valhalla, without any sign of Regina. I do, however, see hammered frat boys spilling French Fries all over the marble floor, a wasted man with urine dripping out from his pants' leg screaming at his wife about his pension on the phone, and several twenty-something girls retching in potted plants, all of which make me grateful that I'm not a casino custodian.

With all the free booze flowing, I'm sure repulsive messes are par for the course.

I'm bracing myself for the return trip when the first notes of 'Spooky Little Girl Like You' emanate from my back pocket. It's the Hidden Kill Bay Bed and Breakfast ring, a realization that's immediately alarming. Bridget wouldn't call me in the middle of the night unless it was an emergency.

"Hey Bridge, what's up? You okay?" I ask before she can get a word in.

"I'm fine, but I'm worried about Kirby," she whispers, "I've tried to call her four times, but she isn't picking up her phone."

"She's in a dance club," I say, starting back down the hall at a brisk clip. "She probably can't hear the ring over the music, but I'm headed back to check on her now. I'll report back as soon as I find her."

"Thank you so much," Bridget says. "And once you find her, stay with her okay? Until we figure out what's going on with Peter?"

My brows snap together. "Peter? Her ex?"

"Yeah, Shep came down to the kitchen while I was starting the scones for breakfast," she says softly.

I frown harder. "What time is it over there?"

"Five forty-five. I always get up early to get the baked goods ready on Sundays, and Shep had his email set to ding so he'd know when the Dark Web guy got back to him. Anyway, the guy found out who's behind P. Eater, Inc. It's Peter, Kirby's Peter. He's the CEO."

"What?" The fingers of my free hand curl into a fist.

"Like Peter Peter Pumpkin Eater, the nursery rhyme. It's his company."

"So he's the one..." I trail off, uncertain how much Kirby has shared with her sister.

"Who filmed you guys kissing in your room," Bridget pops in, making me grateful I didn't spill the beans. "Yeah, probably. Or he at the very least hired the person who rented the drone."

"Sick fuck."

"Looks like it," Bridget says sadly. "I'm hoping there's an innocent explanation—I liked Peter, even though he and Kirby were wrong for each other. It's hard to believe he'd violate her privacy like that. It's blowing my mind almost as much as knowing you and Kirby are make-out buddies."

"I'm sure that is a little weird. Sorry." I take a breath, holding it as I hurry past the potted plants by the elevator, where a guy with sweaty red curls has taken over plant-puking duty. Shuddering, I make a note never to stay out past two in the morning in Vegas again. Clearly, this is the time of night when the debauchery takes a turn for the repulsive.

"I meant blowing my mind in a good way," Bridget says. "The more I think about it, the more it feels like a no-brainer. I mean...of course, right? Of course you two are perfect for each other."

"I, uh, um... Yeah, I think so, anyway," I say, the words ending in a cough as I pass the entrance to the buffet, where the sickly-sweet smell of waffle batter mixes with the scent of steamed fish from the dinner shift.

Definitely heading home early next time.

"But don't tell her I said that," I say once I stop hacking, shocked to find my cheeks warmer than they were before. I can't remember the last time I blushed— have I ever blushed? "I'm still trying to figure out how to break the news that I've got a thing for her that's more than a friend thing."

"Aw, it makes me so happy to hear that." Bridget sighs happily. "And I promise I won't tell Kirby. But please have her text me when you find her, okay? So I know she's all right?"

"Absolutely. I won't let her out of my sight until this situation is resolved. And hopefully, now that we have evidence to connect him to the drone, we'll be able to get Peter to hand over the footage without a fight."

"My fingers are crossed for you guys."

"Thanks. And thank Shep for me, okay? Tell him I'll call later?"

"Of course," Bridget says, a hint of something strange in her voice that I can't quite pin down. "As soon as he wakes up. He went back to bed after he delivered the news. He isn't used to going without sleep. Or being up at the crack of dawn."

I snort. "Yeah, the last time Shep was up before noon was—" I cut off at the hum on the line, signaling an incoming call. Pulling the phone away from my ear, I see Kirby's name and breathe a sigh of relief. "Hey, Bridget, it's your sister. Let me take her call, and we'll text you in a few."

"Okay, tell her I love her and I'm sorry Peter's being awful!"

I promise I will and click over to the other line with a smile. I hate that I have to be the bearer of bad news about her ex, but I'm still ridiculously excited to hear Kirby's voice again. Twenty minutes apart is too much, "Hey, Larry, sorry to keep you waiting. I'm afraid it's been another shit show. Regina saw me coming and ran off again, and I just got a call from your sister with some pretty fucked-up news."

"I'm so sorry to hear that," purrs a voice that is *not* Kirby's, making my smile drop so fast it shatters on the marble floor. "I hope her sister is okay, because your fuck buddy sure isn't."

I stop dead in the middle of the hall, my blood freezing. "What did you do to her? I swear, Regina, if you hurt her, I'll—"

"Uh, uh, uh, watch it there, big boy. Don't want to say anything you can't take back," she says, before adding in a coy voice, "And I didn't do anything to your little precious. She got wasted, wandered into a restricted area, and got carted away by casino security. I hate to break it to you, but I think she's got a drinking problem, Col. Like...a serious one."

"Said the woman who's out at the club swilling martinis while she's four months pregnant," I snap back. "And what the hell are you doing with Kirby's phone?"

"Jesus, relax, asshole. They were virgin martinis. And she dropped it when she passed out before the cops dragged her drunk ass outside. I picked it up so I could call you and get it back to her." Regina sniffs. "Last time I do a good deed."

"A second ago you said casino security," I say, dread worming through my gut. Regina's lying, I can feel it. But why? And where the hell is Kirby? "Now it's the cops who took her out? Which is it, Regina?"

"I don't know, guys in uniforms all look alike to me. But she's fine. They'll take her somewhere to sober up. And in the meantime, you and I can finally talk without a third wheel in the way."

"I'm not talking to you, Regina. Not until I know Kirby's okay and find out where she is. She wasn't even drinking tonight. She could have passed out for some other reason and be headed to the hospital. I need to find her so I can—"

"Oh, please. Relax. She's not headed to the hospital. She's fine." She sniffs before adding with a dramatic sigh, "I can't, however, say the same for our relationship. If you don't meet up with me and make this right, I can't promise to play nice with you, Colin. I mean, I'm sure you'll *say* you want to see your baby, but how can I trust a man who's so busy worrying about his fuck buddy he has no time for the mother of his child?"

"Tell me what really happened," I growl. "Now."

"I told you! She passed out. But it's no big deal. She'll wake up in a few hours with a fuzzy head and a dry mouth and no damage done. Probably won't even have a headache."

The blood drains from my face. "You did something to her, didn't you?"

"What? No, of course not," she screeches, sounding guiltier by the second.

"What was it?" I demand. "Chloroform? An injection or—"

"Jesus, psycho, no. I'm not a criminal mastermind." She huffs. "I just put a pill in her drink while the bartender was looking at my boobs." I curse, and Regina hurries on in a slightly slurred voice that makes me positive she's been drinking more than virgin martinis. "A tiny little one. Baby pill. Small. And I tucked her in safe and sound." She giggles. "Creepy's probably feeling right at home right about now."

"Where is she?" I demand. "Tell me now, or I'm calling the police."

"No! Colin, please, I just want to talk. She's fine, I—"

"Goodbye, Regina. I have to call 911."

"No, no, no!" she whimpers. "Okay, I'll tell. I'll show and tell. Meet me downstairs by the ice cream shop. I'll take you right to her, I swear."

"You'd better. I'm not playing any more fucking games with you, Regina." I hang up and storm the rest of the way down the hall to the elevator. I make it through the mezzanine level of the casino, down the curved staircase, and through the lobby to the ice cream shop and kids' indoor play structure in no more than five minutes. I give Regina another ten minutes to get her ass in gear before I call Kirby's phone.

But there's no answer, just a series of rings and then Kirby saying, "Can't come to the phone right now. Leave me a message. Or, better yet, send me a text and I'll get back to you as soon as I'm out of the word cave. Later."

The sound of her voice makes the worry gripping my gut squeeze tighter. She's out there somewhere, drugged and unconscious. Anything could be happening to her. I have to find her and keep her safe. If I don't, I'm going to lose my fucking mind with worry. I'm about to call again—and call and call until Regina picks up—when fluffy blond hair bounces around the lobby desk.

But when Regina's face comes into view, her expression is anything but bouncy. Her mascara is smudged beneath her eyes, and her face is almost as pale as Kirby's.

"What's wrong. Tell me," I demand, crossing to meet her near the empty shoeshine station.

"I didn't mean for this to happen," she whimpers. "I promise, Colin."

"Tell me," I say, panic tightening my voice. "Please, Regina. As quickly and efficiently as you can."

"I took Kirby's phone so I could look through her texts and see if you were cheating on me with her while we were together," she says, focusing on my face as she does her best to oblige. "But I read through a ton of messages and didn't find anything. So then I decided to check her email since she'd left it open in her browser."

"Fuck, Regina," I grumble, unable to help myself. "You can't just invade people's privacy like that. And no, I was never cheating with Kirby."

"I know, I'm sorry," she says, holding out Kirby's purse, which I take with as little violence as possible. "I didn't find anything in her email either, or her chats with friends or photos. But even looking through all that, it didn't take me that long, you know? I mean, no more than thirty or forty-five minutes could have passed before I called you." She blinks tear-filled eyes. "But when I went back to make sure she was okay before I came down to get ice cream with you, it was gone."

"What was gone?" I demand.

"The coffin where I left her to sleep it off," she says sheepishly, as my brain explodes. "It was gone. All of it was gone, the entire carnival exhibit. It's like it just vanished into thin air. So maybe ghosts are real, after all? Maybe it was all haunted and just...disappeared?"

I pull out my phone, hitting 911. I could keep trying to understand what the hell Regina is talking about, but I don't know how much time Kirby has. She could be in serious trouble. "I need to be connected to the police," I tell the woman who answers. "My friend has been drugged and potentially kidnapped. She's been missing for at least an hour, maybe longer. I have the woman who drugged her here with me."

Regina's eyes go wide as she whispers urgently, "No, I can't, Colin! I can't get arrested. I took way too much shit tonight. I'll fail a drug test." She bites her lip with a wince. "But don't worry, I'm not pregnant. Sorry. I only lied because I needed to talk to you so much."

I glare at her as I answer the operator's questions, "No, I'm not in any danger. I just need the police. Yes, I'll hold."

I cover the receiver as I hiss at a retreating Regina,

"You stay right there. I want you to tell them exactly what you gave Kirby and where you—"

"I can't, gotta go, sorry!" And then she turns and sprints away. Actually sprints—in heels, her muscled, former-track-star legs carrying her across the lobby and up the stairs to the street so fast catching her wouldn't be easy.

And if I chase after her, I won't be here when the police arrive. So even though a part of me wants to take off after my ex and insist she stay to face the consequences of her actions, I hold tight where I am and have a talk with the Vegas Police Department.

Officers Davidson and Goodnight arrive just a few minutes later, and together, with the help of casino security, we get to the bottom of what happened. We watch most of it on tape, in fact—Kirby walking into the carnival exhibit, not noticing the "Closed" sign that had been tipped over beside the clown entrance. Kirby collecting her fortune from one of the remaining machines while the guys packing up the exhibit were on a break on the loading dock. Kirby emerging from a hall of mirrors, and then Regina confronting her in the mummy display and finally hoisting her into a coffin.

I watch Regina struggle with Kirby's limp body, hold up Kirby's phone to her face to get access, and then slam the lid of the coffin closed like she's just finished taking out the trash. And then the movers return and load up the last of the carnival display without realizing that there's a girl inside one of the coffins.

The last footage we have is of the moving truck leaving the underground parking garage half an hour ago.

"She won't suffocate in there, will she?" I ask in a tight voice.

"She shouldn't," Officer Goodnight says. He's by far the nicer cop so far. Davidson, a broad woman with a no-nonsense chin, has barely spoken at all and keeps shooting suspicious glances my way. "It didn't look airtight, but we should find her as soon as possible. We'll put out an APB on that truck. And your ex-girlfriend."

"In the meantime, can you come back to the station with us, answer a few more questions?" Davidson asks.

I nod, even as a sour taste fills my mouth. I'm not surprised—the boyfriend is always the lead suspect—but it still makes me sick to know this woman thinks I had something to do with Kirby's disappearance.

But I guess I did. If I had handled Regina better, Kirby wouldn't be missing right now. I blame myself. And if she isn't okay...

No, I can't go there. Not yet, hopefully not ever.

After a quick call to Bridget to explain what's happening, and comfort her as best as I'm able, I climb into the back of the police cruiser and let the officers take me downtown, praying that they will find Kirby soon.

But they don't, and eventually the police send me back to the hotel, where I watch my first sunrise in Vegas alone, feeling more scared and helpless than I have in my entire life.

CHAPTER TWENTY-ONE

Kirby

I wake up to pitch blackness, and for a second, I'm certain I'm dead.

But for some reason, I'm not scared.

I mean, it's disconcerting—to wake up dead, in the dark—but I'm also warm and cozy, and there's a gentle rocking motion that jostles me lightly from side to side, reminding me of last summer when Peter was away on a PI Job and the boys in the band were in town for the Fourth of July weekend.

They rented a boat to take Bridget and me out on the water, and we spent the entire day basking in the sun and waiting for tugs on our fishing lines, while the boat rocked pleasantly and Cutter told every horrific shark story he could remember from his long, sick, and twisted obsession with shark attacks.

And then Colin got out his guitar, and he and Zack whipped up a ridiculous song they titled "Losing My Teeth For Love"—because sharks keep losing teeth and making more for as long as they're alive—and Bridget laughed so hard she had to jump into the water to pee because Cutter was already in the tiny boat bathroom. And then Shep jumped in after her because she couldn't stop laughing, even while she was peeing, and he was afraid she was going to drown, and then Bridget almost died of embarrassment because Shep jumped into her pee.

It's one of my best memories, filled with laughter and sun and the people I love.

Love…

That's my only regret about being dead. I've always had a keen sense of my own mortality—multiple near-death experiences when I was too little to run damage control on my mother's poor life choices left a lasting mark on my psyche—but I'm weirdly grateful for that. Too many people take tomorrow for granted, thinking they have all the time in the world to get over their fears and hang-ups and start really living, where I've always known that tomorrow isn't a given. For the most part, I've lived my life so that if for some reason a particular day turns out to be my last, I'd be at peace with checking out.

But I wish I'd told Colin that I'm in love with him. Even if he doesn't love me back the same way, I wish I'd let him know that he's that kind of special to me, my very favorite person in the whole world.

He knows a voice in my head assures me *Now close your eyes and get some rest. It's going to be a while before we get there.*

On some level I realize my inner voice is talking out of its ass—it has no idea where we're going or when we'll get there—but I'm so tired and warm. So snugly on the soft mattress beneath me. It makes it hard to…

Keep…

My eyes…

. . .

WHEN I BLINK ON AGAIN, the world is still dark, but with slivers of light streaming in through cracks in a rectangular shape above me.

I am also hot as hell, not simply warm, and my mouth is so dry it feels like I placed first in a sawdust-eating contest. The heat evaporates the fog in my brain, and in a rush, I remember everything that went down last night.

Specifically that—

1. I was drugged.
2. I was pushed into a coffin, where I passed out.
3. The coffin was moved while I was still pretty out of it.
4. I do not remember crawling out of the coffin, which means...

A soft keening sound like an orphaned puppy fills the hot, cloying air, and it's coming from my own bone-dry throat.

I clap a hand over my mouth, silencing the hysterical sound. I have to keep my head on straight. If anyone is equipped to survive being buried alive, it's me. I wrote the book on being buried alive—literally.

In the third installment of the Funhouse series, a serial killer kidnaps Amy and buries her alive, and Beau has to become a wolf shifter to get a nose sensitive enough to track her to the place where she was interred before it's too late. I did enough research that I'm able to make a very educated guess about how much air is left in this crate and how long I have to get out before I suffocate.

I'm thumbing through my mental files, pulling anything that might help me stay alive long enough for Colin to find me, when I push on the lid and it pops off without a bit of resistance.

My adrenaline levels plummet and a disappointed, "Oh," escapes me, because apparently, some not-right part of me was looking forward to the challenge of outwitting the person who buried me alive.

"Sicko," I mutter as I sit up, squinting in the bright desert sun.

It takes my eyes a few moments to adjust, but when they do, I see that, other than the coffin, everything around me has changed. Now, instead of the cool darkness of the casino's Mummy Curse room, I'm surrounded by a junkyard full of random shit, which is surrounded by a high, barbed wire fence, which is surrounded by lots of middle-of-nowhere beige desert and some faint blue mountains in the distance.

I twist to look behind me, hoping for a more encouraging view, but I can't see anything past the giant clown face grinning back at me. The entire carny exhibit has been dumped out here to bake in the sun. It's equally enraging—these are irreplaceable antiques—and troubling.

If the owner of these treasures abandoned them, it doesn't bode well for me finding help before I die of thirst. I'm already so parched that my tongue feels three sizes too big for my mouth.

Still, I can't resist the instinct to call "Help," in a scratchy voice. And then "Help me, please," a little louder.

But the only response is a gust of wind that scatters gravel across the ground beside my coffin and the soft cry of a crow far away.

Shivering despite the sweat dripping down the hollow of my spine to soak into my sparkly panties, I stand up, wobbling on my bare feet on the lumpy mattress. I glance down, searching the bottom of the coffin for my shoes, but they seem to have vanished, along with my purse and—

"Shit. My phone." I press my fist to my chest, willing my once-again racing heart not to punch a hole through my ribs. My phone, and getting in touch with Colin, should have been my first thought. It wasn't, which proves my head isn't completely clear yet. I have no idea what Regina slipped into my drink—or if Forearms the bartender was in on the plot—but it was some serious stuff. By the angle of the sun, I'm guessing I've been out for at least seven hours.

Still, it could have been worse, I realize as I step out of the coffin and pad gingerly across the gravel lot, looking for signs of life. I'm thirsty and my head is fuzzy, but I'm not sick to my stomach or unsteady on my feet.

Or dead.

"Not dead is always good," I mutter, the sound of my own voice comforting in the ringing silence. I can't remember nature ever being so quiet. In my neck of the woods, there are always waves crashing and birds chirping and tree leaves whispering in the breeze.

Here there's just quiet, a rush of desert wind, then more quiet.

I circle a wooden cut-out of a strongman and find several rows of slot machines covered in a fine coat of sand and the top half of a life-size Tyrannosaurus Rex, his mouth open in a roar. But Rexxy is clearly a home-grown job. His proportions are all off—teeth too big, snout too small, and eyes disturbingly close together—and the spots where his protective coating have eroded reveal tufts of papier-mâché material beneath. Still, he's pretty fabulous kitsch, and some TLC could return him to his former glory.

"People throwing away perfectly lovely things," I tut as I continue my hunt for a way out.

And now I'm one of them.

Regina pushed me into a coffin and threw me away. And if I can't manage contact with the outside world—or at least get out of this barbed-wire-surrounded island of misfit toys—I could die here.

It's a worst-case scenario, and the rational part of me knows that if someone brought me here, someone will likely show up sooner or later, but my pulse isn't listening to reason as panic sets in.

I rest a hand on Rexxy's warm flank, forcing my shoulders to relax as I inhale to a count of four and exhale the same way. Freaking out is a waste of energy. I have to remain calm and make choices that will increase my odds of survival—starting with getting out of the sun and protecting my ghostly-pale flesh from a burn.

Clinging to the pockets of shade, I make a circle of the storage lot, passing more orphaned slot machines, a collection of lightly dented go-carts, a plastic statue of a bearded man in a yellow chicken suit, and enough pink plaster pillars to create a Pepto-Bismol colored Grecian temple, but nothing that looks like a guard house or anyplace that might have a phone.

And when I reach the gate, it's wrapped in heavy chain and secured with a padlock.

"Shit," I whisper again, tangling my fingers in the chain link as I stare at the road outside my prison.

It's not much more than a set of ruts in the sand, stretching so far into the distance that it disappears into the horizon. Even if I figure out a way to bust out of here, I'm going to have a long walk ahead of me, and the longer I wait, the weaker and more dehydrated I'm going to become.

"Think, Kirby, think," I chant as I finish my exploration and come up with nothing of use except a knock-off Mary Poppins statue, complete with a faded gray umbrella that I appropriate for sun protection.

Back at my coffin, I search the lumpy padding at the bottom again for signs of my shoes or purse—still no dice—before turning to survey the yard again. There's a weak place in the barbed wire not far away, where the wind has twisted it into a knot small enough to step over, but the chain link is too small to get a decent toehold. I could try, but chain link messes up your feet pretty quickly.

I learned that the hard way, sneaking over the fence to swim in the pool at the apartment building down the street from my childhood home. I usually made it, but the fence was shorter, I was lighter, and there were still times when I'd tear the skin between my toes on the way over, making the chlorinated water sting the entire time I swam.

If I hurt myself on the way over this fence, I'm going to have at least a two-mile walk through the hot sand in my bare, bloodied feet after.

"Something to cover them," I say, congratulating myself on my creative problem solving as I rip the satin lining out of the coffin and tear the aging fabric into strips I can tie into makeshift shoes before I start my walk.

But first to get over the damned fence...

If I just had a ladder, so I'd only have to deal with the chain link on the way down. Or a rope, maybe, or...

"A giant T-Rex head." I shoot a narrow glance Rexxy's way, already knowing he's not as heavy as he looks. When I put my hand on him earlier, there was an echo. I'd bet money that he's hollow inside and that I can probably push him up against the fence, where his head will be level with the weak spot in the barbed wire.

Tucking my strips of coffin lining through one side of my halter top and resting my umbrella on the ground by Rexxy's torso, I lay my hands on his sun-warmed side and push, sending him scraping across the sand only an inch or two. He's heavier than I thought, but that's a good thing. That means he'll be less likely to collapse under me as I'm climbing onto his head.

Rolling my shoulders back and bending my knees, I push from my center of gravity and am rewarded with a nearly foot-long scratch in the sand. I keep it up— pushing and resting, pushing and resting—slowly giving birth to hope as Rexxy and I inch our way over to the fence.

By the time his nose butts up against the barbed wire, I'm covered in a sheen of sweat and my mouth is stuffed full of cotton balls, but I'm not nearly as frightened as I was before. I have a plan, and I'm getting out.

Pinning my umbrella under one arm, I scramble up onto Rexxy's shoulder.

The climb from his shoulder to the top of his rounded skull is harder. I slide off several times, impeded by my umbrella until I realize I can toss the umbrella up first and then claw my way up after. Still, the last few inches—straining every muscle in my body while wedging my bare toes into the corner of Rexxy's open mouth—take it out of me.

I collapse onto the top of the dino's head, breathing hard, silently promising the universe that I will start lifting weights and rock climbing and doing other womanly muscle-building activities aside from jogging if it will just loan me enough strength to get to civilization. A breeze picks up a moment later, cooling my flushed skin and carrying a hint of something that smells like... diesel exhaust.

And where there is diesel exhaust, there are trucks and people driving trucks who will take pity on a girl abandoned in the desert and loan me their phone so I can call Colin to come to pick me up!

Then we'll grab Murder from the hotel and head straight to the airport, where we will jump on the first flight home. "Because it's been real, Vegas, and it's been fun," I say, rising onto my knees on Rexxy's head. "But it hasn't been real fun."

Swiping my forearm across my sweaty lip, I grab the umbrella and toss it over the fence first, ignoring the way my stomach flips as it takes a good second and a half to hit the sand on the other side. It's a long way down, but I can make it. Half of this climb is equal to one over-the-pool-fence climb, and I can jump the last few feet if I have to. I really only have to spider monkey down ten or twelve feet until I'm in the clear.

"Easy peasy," I say, my scratchy voice barely audible over the pounding of my pulse in my ears. But still, I add in a firmer tone, "You've got this, Larry. The bad guys don't get to win. You're going to win, and then you're going to kill off Regina's character in the most horrible, bloodthirsty, torturous way you can imagine."

Soothed, and pleasantly distracted by thoughts of all the ways I can make the fictional Regina suffer—after I inform the police of the real Regina's actions and get the psycho charged with a few crimes—I grip the fence and swing a trembling leg up and over the top.

CHAPTER TWENTY-TWO

Colin

*M*urder looks like he wants to murder me, and for once I can't blame him. I've lost Kirby. I've fucking lost Kirby, and for all we know she could be hurt, or sick from the drug Regina slipped into her drink.

Or worse.

"Please ring. Fucking ring already," I beg my phone, driving my fingers into my hair and digging the heels of my hands into my eyes. The police sent me home four hours ago—promising to call as soon as they contacted the moving company who'd taken the exhibit job—but I've watched the temperature heat up to a brutal ninety-eight degrees without any word from the authorities.

"They probably still think I had something to do with it," I say, earning myself a "no shit, Sherlock" meow from the cat in front of me on the coffee table. I lift my head, expecting an incoming claw aimed at my face, but Murder's still curled up in a ball, apparently willing to let me live—for now.

But his glare makes it clear what he thinks of me. He

thinks I'm an idiot who's sitting around with my thumb up my ass, waiting for a phone call that's not coming because the cops think I was working with my ex-girlfriend to get rid of my current girlfriend. Even though I told them that Kirby isn't my girlfriend, just a friend who I would *like* to be my girlfriend, but I didn't have a chance to tell her that or how much I cared about her before she was pushed into a coffin and moved to God knows where.

The casino rented the exhibit from an entertainment company, who in turn hired the moving company. Both the entertainment company and the moving company were closed until eight this morning, but my millionth check of the time says it's nearly ten. Surely the police must have something by now.

I grab my cell, intending to ring the station and demand an update, when it vibrates in my hand and Bridget's name pops up on the screen.

Fuck. When she hears there's no news, she's probably going to want to kill me, too. She and Murder can join forces to claw me to pieces and cook me into a stew to serve to the guests at the B&B.

But hopefully they'll let me live long enough to know that Kirby's safe first.

Please let her be safe, I beg the powers that be as I answer the call. *Please.*

"Hey, Bridge." I sound as strained and worried as I feel. "Nothing yet. I'm sorry. But I promise I'll call you as soon as—"

"It's okay, we've got something," she cuts in. "Shep and I have been working our Google-Fu to try to get to the bottom of this, and it looks like there's been a mix-up with the delivery."

I sit up straighter. "What kind of mix-up?"

"The exhibit was supposed to be delivered to a movie set in the desert, but the movers took it somewhere else instead. It never showed up on set last night."

"How did you figure this out?" I ask, feeling like shit for sitting around on my ass waiting for the police while Bridget and Shep were solving the mystery.

"Shep's friend with the dark web connections did some—" She cuts off as a deep voice murmurs urgently in the background. "Shep says I'm not supposed to talk about that part. Forget I said that." She clears her throat uncomfortably. "Do you think people are listening to our conversations, Colin? Or is Shep being paranoid?"

"I have no idea," I say. "But better safe than sorry. There's already one Lawrence sister missing—no need for the other to end up in jail for cybercrimes."

"Right," Bridget says with a rush of breath. "So, knowledge was acquired by means we won't talk about. But that's where the trail ends. The shipment never made it to the set, but we have no idea where it did end up. The men who did the delivery were subcontracted through a local company. They haven't turned in their paperwork to the main company yet, and none of the workers have been reachable by phone. Considering they work the night shift, however, that's not super alarming. Yet. They could have their phones off so they can get some rest. Now, if it gets to be four or five o'clock and they still aren't answering or returning messages from concerned family members and the police, then we have to start considering whether foul play might be involved."

I surge to my feet, pacing toward the windows.

"What kind of foul play? You think these guys were in on it with Regina?"

"Maybe," Bridget says, adding in a tighter voice, "Or maybe they just discovered a beautiful unconscious girl in a coffin and decided to do something awful."

Rage claws at my throat and something snaps in my head. "If they hurt her, I'm going to kill them. Hunt them down and rip them to pieces with my bare hands."

"I'll help you," Bridget says. "But we shouldn't go there yet. This could all be a big mix-up and we'll get a call from Kirby any minute, saying she's stranded at a storage locker or something."

I perk up again. "Storage facilities. We could check those, right? I could start calling them now, see if they had any deliveries come in after three in the morning last night."

"You could. But Shep had a better idea. I'll let him fill you in." Bridget whispers something I can't make out.

A beat later Shep's deep voice rumbles through the phone. "Sorry you're going through all this, man. But Kirby's tougher than she looks. You know that."

"No one's very tough when they're unconscious and pumped full of drugs," I say with a sigh. "But thanks. And thanks for helping us get some answers. I'm going out of my mind over here."

"I can imagine. Which is why I think it's time to send out the Colin signal. Get your fans on the case. But this time, instead of tracking you down at your hotel or the club—"

"I ask them to help find Kirby." I complete his thought, hope lighting in my chest only for reality to shut the party down a second later. "But the police warned me not to talk about what happened. They said that if I did, I might make it harder for them to find Kirby, and I could be charged with interfering with their investigation."

"But you're talking to me," he points out, "and Bridget."

"I am." I chew the inside of my lip as an idea sparks in my mind. "And I wouldn't have to talk much. Might be better if I don't talk. At least not at first. The fans pay closer attention when I sing."

"Brilliant," Shep says. "Get some footage to me in the next hour, and I'll make sure it's leaked to every gossip site and news outlet and front and center on our website."

"I won't need an hour." I spin on my heel, heading for the bedroom where I left the guitar Kirby had sent over last night. "I've already got a bunch of melodies bubbling on the backburner. Some lyrics, too. It won't take long to throw something together with a request to help look for Kirby at the end. And if the police decide to come after me, then let them come."

"Just share when she went missing and where, and the police won't have a leg to stand on. It's not like you're sharing secret details of the investigation. You're just asking for help finding your friend."

"She's more than my friend," I confess, lifting the guitar case onto the bed and flipping open the latches.

"I know that, man," he rumbles. "Known for a while. Just not sure what took you so long."

"I was an idiot."

Shep starts to say something comforting, but I cut him off. "And I'm still an idiot. I didn't tell her how I feel. I was waiting for the perfect moment, and now..."

"There will still be a perfect moment," he assures me.

"And I bet Kirby has a pretty good idea how you feel. I mean, yeah, you're an idiot. Her, not so much."

"I hope you're right," I agree, jaw tight. "I'll have the song to you in twenty minutes tops. Tell Bridget again I'm sorry, will you?"

"I will, but she isn't blaming you. You didn't make your ex fall off her rocker. I'm just glad she's not pregnant. That would have been a hot mess to deal with for the rest of your kid's life."

"Agreed." I swing the guitar into my lap as I sit down on the edge of the bed. "If Kirby doesn't want to be with me or make babies, I'm getting a vasectomy and heading any future hot messes off at the pass."

"You're twenty-nine, dude. Might be a little early to make that kind of decision."

"I'm almost thirty, and it's not too early. If I can't have kids with Kirby, I don't want kids. She's the only person I want that kind of life with." The only person I want any kind of forever with.

I end the call and tune my guitar. Kirby is my true north, my home base, the only person who knows me inside and out and likes me just the way I am. And I feel the same way about her.

Letting all of that move my hands, I start to strum, finding the melody, the chorus, and then the bridge before taking a breath and singing straight from the heart.

CHAPTER TWENTY-THREE
Kirby

a girl trekking down a deserted road, wearing a party dress and coffin lining wrapped around her feet, holding a faded vintage umbrella like a parasol —that's not something you see every day. I'd probably laugh if I saw me.

I focus on the ridiculousness of my predicament, brainstorming more and more absurd ways the character of the Stranded Girl could have ended up in a coffin in the middle of nowhere. Anything to distract myself from my dangerously parched throat and the way my head is starting to spin a little more with each mile that passes by beneath my makeshift shoes.

If I don't get water soon, I'm going to pass out.

And if I pass out, and no one happens to drive by, see me, and decide to have mercy on my unconscious self, then I might not be leaving this desert as a girl.

I might be leaving it as a corpse, one Colin will most likely have to identify at the morgue, which will break his heart into thousands of irreparable pieces. If I die because he talked me into staying in Vegas, where his ex-girlfriend drugged me and threw me into a coffin, thereby making him an indirect contributor to my death by exposure, he will never forgive himself.

And I will never forgive myself for failing him by being a weakling who couldn't keep walking for ten miles. The sign at the first crossroads I came to at the end of the junkyard's access road said ten miles to Coyote Springs, with a little gas station symbol underneath it. In less than ten miles now, I will reach a gas station where they will have a bathroom and a faucet that I will be able to stick my mouth under and drink until I don't feel like my throat is being turned inside out by murderous dust bunnies.

In less than ten miles, I will reach a phone and sturdy desert folk who will take matters in hand and fetch me a pair of flip-flops to wear while I call the police and Colin and my sister and finally my real estate agent, to tell her that I'm not going to be listing my house after all. If Colin doesn't want to be in love, then I'm going back to my cats, who will help mend my broken heart with rough tongue kisses and lots of snuggles and cat hair stuck to every item of clothing I own, and I am never leaving home again. I just have to get there.

Have to keep...

Going...

One foot in front of the other...

Keep...

Going...

Keep...

I stumble, the world goes fuzzy, and the next time I blink, I'm on my hands and knees with my forehead in the gravel beside the poorly-paved stretch of road.

Not stumbled, genius. You passed out, my inner voice

helpfully tells me. *And you're probably going to pass out again, and the next time you might not wake up, and then we'll both be dead!*

"Not helping, jerk," I croak.

Not trying to, psycho.

"Relax." I collect my umbrella from the ground beside me, grateful it didn't blow away while I was out.

I can't relax, I'm freaking out! Are those buzzards up there? Buzzards! Already circling! Waiting for us to die so they can pick our bones clean!

"Getting hysterical is only going to make things worse," I say, standing and shuffling forward on wobbly knees. "We have to remain calm."

Quit walking like that! You're getting gravel in between our toes!

"Dirt don't hurt."

But it feels weird, and I don't like it, and I want to go home, and oh my God, I'm going to scream. Ahhhhhhhh! Ahhhhh! Ahhhhh!

I wince at the wail of my inner voice losing her shit in my head, wondering if this is what it's like to experience a mental breakdown. First you start talking to the voice in your head, then the voice has a meltdown, and then all you hear is wailing between your ears until it finally drives you completely around the bend.

"Around the bend," I mutter, heart lurching as I realize the wailing isn't inside my head, after all.

It's coming from the road! It's the wail of an ambulance, complete with flashing red lights and a serious dust cloud kicking up behind the wheels, meaning whoever's driving is in one hell of a hurry to get where they're going.

"To get to us," I tell the inner voice. "We're saved!"

Saved! Oh my God, we're saved. I hope they have water.

"Water and an IV, I bet," I say, lifting an arm over my head and waving it back and forth. There's no way they'll be able to miss me—I'm the only thing on the road to the storage yard, where they've surely been sent to hunt for me—but I'm so excited to see them I can't help myself.

I'm already composing my thank you for rescue, and wondering if there's a chance Colin was allowed to ride along to come get me—God, I want to see him so badly, to let him know that I love him and that I never want to come back to Vegas *ever* again—when the ambulance cuts left, and the lights skitter across the desert toward the mountains.

"No," I mutter in disbelief before adding in a croak-screech. "No! I'm here! I'm right here!" I wave my umbrella and my arm, making giant swoops through the air, but the vehicle doesn't slow.

It continues to race away, leaving me to eat its dust.

The gravel cloud reaches me about thirty seconds later, whipping into my face and arms on a sudden breeze. I shift the umbrella in front of me to blunt the worst of it and squeeze my eyes shut while my soul folds itself into misery-shaped origami. This is so much worse —to be so close to salvation only to have the life preserver jerked away at the last moment.

"I'm so thirsty. If I were adrift in the ocean, I would drink it," I say, voice thick with the tears I'm too dried out to shed. "Even though I would know I shouldn't."

And then you would die, the inner voice says, quieter now, her hysteria vanishing along with the last of her hope.

"No." I clench my jaw and stand up straight, moving

the umbrella back into sun-blocking position above my head. "We're not giving up hope. We're too close. We have to be almost to the gas station by now. One foot in front of the other. We've got this. No quitting because quitting is for quitters who quit."

The inner voice doesn't dignify my lame-ass pep talk with a response, but she doesn't start bellyaching again, either. And as I trudge on, aiming my pitiful self forward, gaze skimming back and forth over the horizon for some sign of civilization, my heartbeat remains steady.

I'm going to get there. I have too much left to do to check out now.

I have stories to tell and adventures to take and a beautiful best friend who needs to know that I love him, even if he doesn't love me back.

I'm thinking of Colin, of his smile and his laugh and how good his hands feel on me, how perfectly right, when a pale-blue spike separates itself from the horizon.

Pulse leaping, I squint and shift my umbrella to block out more of the sun, bringing a roundish shape shimmering into focus beneath the spike.

A sign! It's a sign!

I'm almost there! The next mile passes faster than any of the distance before, proving that hope has a power all of its own. Finally, I reach the cracked parking lot of Coyote Feed and Fuel, where a single battered white pickup truck is parked outside. When I see the *Open* sign flashing in the window, my soul soars.

A minute later, I stumble inside, bell ringing overhead as blessed coolness envelopes me. A sob of relief gathers in my chest, about to be born into the world, when I hear his voice. *Colin's voice*. Singing a song I've never heard before.

At first, I'm certain I'm losing it—I'm hallucinating this gas station and everything in it—but then I recognize the melody. It's the same one Colin was fiddling around with while I was putting my makeup on last night.

It's real. Colin is really singing a song. About missing his only one.

My hands start trembling first, and then my arms, and by the time I shuffle over to get a view of the television mounted on the wall above three faded yellow diner-style booths, I'm shaking all over. And then I see his face, looking so exhausted I know he must have been up all night worrying about me, and I start to cry, my shoulders shaking and my face scrunched as the last of the liquid left in my body oozes out to stick to my lashes.

Because the lyrics are exactly what I've always wanted to hear. That he's looking for the one who got away, the girl he didn't get a chance to love the way he wanted to love her, the person who is now and has always been his only one.

His only one. My only one.

Thank God.

And then he speaks directly into the camera, banishing any shred of doubt.

"I'm asking for your help guys, to find my only one," he says, as the screen cuts to a shot of me, laughing on the boat last summer, my hair wild around my face. "Kirby Veronica Lawrence went missing from the Cairo casino carnival display last night around three a.m. She's five foot three, slim, blond hair and blue eyes, last seen wearing a short, sparkly midnight blue dress and heels. If anyone has seen her, please call the number at the bottom of the screen or post on the message board we've set up on the Lips on Fire site." Colin's face fills the screen again, making me sob even harder with a strange, elated sort of sadness as he adds, "Let's find her, guys. She means the world to me, and I'd really appreciate your help."

I press a hand to my chest, trying to pull myself together as the bored-looking attendant leaning against the wall of cigarettes behind the counter fluffs her ball of heavily-sprayed brown hair and asks, "You all right, kid?"

I point to the television. "That's my friend. He's looking for me."

She frowns, glancing back and forth between the television and me twice before something clicks behind her eyes. "Oh my God, you're the one? From the song? Girl, you look like hell. You must have been through something."

I nod, face scrunching again, but before I can start sobbing or attempt to explain myself, she hurries around the counter, wiping her hands on the thighs of her skin-tight faded blue jeans. "Here sweetheart, you sit down." She reaches for me, taking me by an elbow and guiding me to one of the booths with a hand on my back. "Those motherfuckers. They've got no decency. Trafficking women right and left. You're lucky you got out alive."

I start to tell her that I wasn't trafficked, just thrown away in a coffin by a crazy woman, but she shushes me with a wave of her hand.

"Save your strength, honey, you're safe now. Let's get you something to drink. You look parched." She wiggles over to the wall of soda dispensers next to the pizza-to-go window before glancing over her shoulder. "Sprite? Lemonade?"

"Water," I croak. "Just water, please. No ice."

"Water coming right up." She grabs a cup, filling it with a rush of cool, clear goodness that summons a rabid wolf spirit to life inside of me. If I had the energy, I would race across the room, shove her out of the way, and stick my mouth directly beneath the dispenser. But now that I'm finally safe, my adrenaline and fear-powered strength has abruptly abandoned me.

I'm so weak I can barely pull a napkin free of the dispenser to wipe the dust from my face without shaking.

"Should have offered you water in the first place," she says, setting it down in front of me and watching with thinly disguised fascination/disgust as I grab the cup with both hands and guzzle like a savage. I'm probably going to make myself sick, but I don't care. If I puke it up, then I'll fill the cup and try again. I have returned to the land of milk and honey, where water is just a button-push away, and I intend to take full advantage of this blessed miracle.

I'm never going to take water for granted again.

Sweet, sacred, beautiful water...

I finish drinking and slam the cup back down onto the table with a satisfied huff.

"More?" she asks.

"Yes, please," I say, holding it out to her with an already less trembly hand.

"Okay, I'll get you some, but you should take it slow, kid, or you'll bring it back up again." She takes the cup, keeping me in her sight as she backs toward the machine. "So how long were you out in the desert? I'm Patty, by the way."

"Kirby," I say. "And a few hours, I think. Since I woke up, anyway." I glance toward the checkout counter. "Do you have a phone? I should call my friend and let him know that I'm okay. I hate to see him so worried."

"So that rock star guy is your friend?" she asks, pressing the cup against the dispenser again. "Like, for real?"

"For real." I'm trying to remain patient. I get why she's interested. I bet they don't get a lot of juicy drama out here in the middle of nowhere.

"Like...your boyfriend, too, though, right?" She jabs a thumb toward the television, where the local news has moved on to a story about a bed bug epidemic at some of the less savory casinos, confirming that I want out of here. Yesterday. "That was a pretty romantic song to write for a friend."

"Yeah. He must have written it after he realized I was missing." My heart attempts a giddy River Dance in my chest before realizing it's too weak for giddy and settling for disco-fingers instead. "That's the first time I've ever heard it."

Patty presses a hand to her chest and sighs. "Wow. That's special. I mean, not worth getting kidnapped by human traffickers for or anything, but special." She starts toward me with the water refill, but pauses halfway across the scratched black-and-white tile, motioning toward me with her free hand. "But you're okay, right? They didn't like...hurt you, hurt you? Did they?"

I shake my head. "No, I wasn't hurt. And I wasn't taken by human traffickers. It was..." I trail off, too desperate for more water and access to the phone to get into the sensational details right now. I've known Patty all of five minutes, but I can already tell she's like a dog with a bone with juicy gossip. "It's a long story. Bottom line is that my friend has no idea where I am, and I should call him." I point toward the counter again. "So could I? Use your phone?"

"Duh. The phone." Patty thunks her forehead with the heel of her hand. "Of course. Sorry. I'm working a double. Been on since midnight."

I make a sympathetic face as she sets the water down in front of me. "I'm sorry. That's a long stretch."

She grins. "Yeah, but I don't mind. My ex has my kid Sunday through Tuesday, so I like to work extra these days, save up my time off for my little guy. He's two and so fucking cute, you wouldn't believe it. I'll show you a picture when I get back. Going to have to let you use my cell to call. The landline here is a piece of shit. Our credit card machine is out more than it's in service. I keep telling the owner to get a chip reader so we can run shit on our cells when it's down, but he won't listen. Cheapest bastard you'll ever meet, which you probably will."

She glances at the clock on the wall beneath the television. "He'll be in any second. Comes to pick up the cash himself because he's a lunatic who doesn't trust the armored van service. He'd rather tote around a bunch of money in his stupid Subaru." Patty rolls her eyes and points toward the front door. "If he comes in while I'm gone, tell him I'm taking a leak and don't ask for the phone when I get back, okay? I'll have to explain it to him first, or he'll flip out on me for having it out of my locker." She taps her head. "Not quite right up here, if you know what I mean. Or maybe he's just old and set in his ways. People get like that sometimes as they age. Rigid, you know? Like they can't handle things changing anymore."

I nod, fighting the urge to beg Patty to get the phone already. After prolonged exposure to Bridget's best friend, Theodora, I thought I was used to chatterboxes —the girl couldn't shut up to save her life and talks through movies like it's her job to offer a running commentary—but Patty is giving her a serious run for her money.

"But change is the only thing you can count on," Patty says, pointing at me. "Take that to the bank, right? I mean, you didn't expect to be hanging out with me when you woke up this morning. You gotta take what life dishes out and roll with the punches, ya know?" Her finger slides to the right. "Grab yourself something from the bakery case if you want. My treat. Going to get the phone now. I know I talk too much."

I smile, but don't disagree with her. "Thank you. I'll take you up on that."

Patty gives me a thumbs-up before doing a quick one-eighty and wiggling back behind the counter, through a doorway that I guess leads to behind the scenes at the gas station. Her jeans are so tight she doesn't seem to be able to bend her knees fully, and I can't help thinking that she would have been out of luck if she'd woken up in a coffin and needed to climb a fence.

Though I suppose she could have taken her jeans off and gone over in her underwear. Patty strikes me as the kind who wouldn't hesitate to do what needs to be done, even if she has to do it in her skivvies.

I rise, carrying my water with me as I cross to the bakery case beside the checkout counter. There isn't much left this time of day, but what's there looks surprisingly delicious. The lone muffin has a sugar-crusted top and fresh raspberries poking through the yellow crust, and the cinnamon roll is not playing around. It's as big as my hand and drenched in icing.

Just looking at it is enough to make my belly snarl with sugar-rush anticipation.

The water is playing nice with my stomach—a little sloshy, but no nausea—so I figure there's no reason I can't add some cinnamon roll into the mix. I fetch the tongs from the holder and load the sinful treat onto a paper plate from the stack on top of the case.

I fully intend to sit down before I dig in, but as soon as the bun is in my hot little hands, all bets are off. Sliding the pastry until a gooey edge hangs off the side of the plate, I open wide and take a T-Rex-sized chomp. So when the bell tinkles over the door, signaling the arrival of another patron, my mouth is way too full to tell them that Patty will be back in a second.

I spin, holding up a hand with one finger raised, but the person who just walked in isn't a cranky old change-hating man coming to pick up a money drop.

It's Peter.

My ex.

This isn't good news for me. I know that even before he pulls the gun from his pocket and says, "Guess who's still getting emails every time you use your frequent flier account, babe?"

Not good at all.

CHAPTER TWENTY-FOUR

Colin

*W*ithin twenty minutes of the video going live, the message board gets enough traffic to crash the site, and my cell phone is ringing non-stop.

Shep had the hotline number forwarded to my cell first, then Bridget's, then his. But even with the three of us answering calls as fast as we can, soon fans are raging on social media about not being able to get through to me. Then other fans pile on the complainers—ripping them a new one for misuse of the hotline number and potentially putting a woman's life in danger with their immature behavior #GrowUp #BasicAF #LipsOnFire #FindKirby.

Soon the Find Kirby hashtag is trending, and random people are using the label to hawk their protein supplements and work-from-home schemes, and I'm feeling like a royal, Grade A idiot for thinking I could tame the dragon of social media.

The only good news is that if the Vegas cops have noticed what I'm up to and are calling to tell me to cut it out, they haven't been able to get through the bombardment.

Thankfully, my close friends are able to bypass the madness with a text message. Within ten minutes, I hear from the rest of the band, Cutter and Zack both texting to let me know they can be in Vegas by the end of the day if I need help searching for Kirby or just friends around for moral support. Shep offers to fly out with Bridget, as well, but I tell them all to hold off for now. If I know Kirby, as soon as she's safe and sound, she's going to want to be on the first plane back home. She loves a good adventure, but this hasn't been that. It's been a shit show, and I'm sure she can't wait to put Vegas in her rearview mirror.

I have to believe we—someone—will find her today. Any minute, in fact. The thought of her still missing by the time the others can get here, still missing when the sun goes down tonight, makes me sick to my stomach.

Though I'm sure the coffee I've been guzzling since five a.m. isn't helping the stomach situation.

Phone pinned between my ear and shoulder as I listen to yet another young girl tell me how much she loves my music in a breathless rush that makes me worry she might pass out before she finishes, I cross to the minibar and grab a roll of antacids from the top shelf. I pop two, chewing and swallowing before I interrupt as gently as possible. "Thanks so much, but have you seen a woman resembling Kirby Lawrence? This hotline is just for sharing news that might lead to her being brought home safe and sound."

"Oh, um, yeah," the girl says with a nervous laugh. "I do know a girl who looks like her. But she's in eleventh grade at my school. Is your friend in eleventh grade?'

"No, my friend isn't in eleventh grade," I say, just barely keeping the anger from my voice. This is just a dumb kid being dumb. She has no idea what it feels like to worry that something terrible might have happened—or is currently happening—to the person you love most in the world. "Thanks for the tip, but I need to move on to the next call."

But when I tap the red button and my cell immediately starts buzzing again, I don't answer.

I'm so frustrated I'm afraid I'll lose my shit on the next caller.

I collapse back onto the couch, staring out at the skyline as Murder leaps onto the cushions beside me with a plaintive meow. "I know," I say. "I miss her, too."

Murder meows again, cocking his head as he steps closer. Tentatively, I reach out, slowly bringing my fingers to his neck and working them into the fur beneath his collar, the way I've seen Kirby do a hundred times. After only a moment, a soothing rumble fills the air, and Murder curls onto the couch beside me, one paw resting on my thigh in a way that seems to say, *I'm here, dude. You've got this. Keep answering the phone. We've got to find Kirby.*

I don't know if this truce is permanent or if Murder has simply decided to play nice until his favorite human returns, but the fact that he isn't trying to bite my hand off or separate my balls from my body is comforting.

And he's right. I have to keep trying. I've answered a hundred useless calls, but the hundred and first might be the one we've been waiting for.

I take a deep breath, but before I can hit the answer button, a text pops through from a number I don't recognize. I pull up my messages, nearly jumping out of my skin when I see Kirby's face staring back at me from the screen. I surge to my feet, sending Murder leaping to the floor with a yowl as I pace away from the couch, enlarging the shot.

Kirby's face is streaked with dirt, her hair is a windswept mess, and her shoulders are sunburned, but she's wearing the dress she was wearing last night, and she's alive.

But scared. Or angry? Angry and scared?

I'm staring into her wide blue eyes, trying to read her mind, when the second text comes through—*If you want to see your fuck buddy again, meet us at the Pancake House by the airport in thirty minutes. Come alone. That includes the cat. Leave it in your room. If you call your friends or the police, I'll know, and we'll be gone. As soon as I have confirmation that you've received this message, I'm destroying the phone. You won't be able to contact me again.*

Heart pulsing in my throat, I reply, *Who is this? Regina, if this is you, we can put this behind us and talk as long as you want to talk. Just let Kirby go.*

Bubbles fill the screen and then, *Right. How stupid do you think I am, dipshit? I'm using a burner phone, but I'm going to reveal my identity because you asked? Fuck you, asshole.*

Jaw clenched, I scan the text, something pinging in my gut. This could be my ex, but my intuition is screaming that it's someone else. *Fine,* I type back. *Then just let me talk to her. Let me hear her voice so I know that she's all right.*

A middle finger emoji pops up, followed by, *Pancake House. Thirty minutes. You'd better get going, hotshot. Even without traffic, it's going to take you twenty minutes to get across town. I'd hate to have to do something awful to your best buddy because you can't stop being a pompous dick for five minutes and follow directions.*

I bite my lip hard enough to taste blood. *Don't you dare hurt her. She's innocent. Kirby's one of the most good-hearted people in the world. Whatever beef you've got with me, she's not part of it.*

A laughing emoji and another middle finger are my only response. And when I try to send another message —*Seriously. Don't touch her. I'm on my way*—it fails to deliver.

The bastard clearly wasn't kidding about trashing the phone.

It's a man who's got Kirby. I'm almost sure of it. The tone of the texts screams smug, pissed-off, entitled dickwad.

The suspicion alone is enough to make my vision haze over with red. Some piece of shit has his hands on Kirby, threatening her, maybe even hurting her, and I don't even fucking know why. He didn't ask me to bring money for a ransom. But maybe he's planning to swap my life for Kirby's and escort me on a tour of Vegas's ATMs at gunpoint before shooting me in the head and leaving my body in the desert to rot.

But if that's what has to happen to keep Kirby safe, I'll do it. I'll turn myself over to this motherfucker in a heartbeat.

"Hang in there, Larry, I'm coming," I mutter as I order a car, which promises to be here in three minutes —just enough time to get down to the lobby and plenty of time to get across town.

I grab my room key, wallet, and, at the last minute, the wine opener from the mini bar, tucking it into the back pocket of my jeans. It's not much as far as weapons go, but at least it's something, an ace up my sleeve if I end up alone with this asshole and he drops his guard.

As I hurry for the door, Murder leaps up onto the back of the couch with a fretful meow.

I pause, stomach clenching. "I'll be home soon, buddy. But if I'm not, you take good care of her, okay? Love her extra hard."

The cat's eyes narrow, but he doesn't hiss at me. And maybe it's just that I've been up all night and am going loopy from lack of sleep, but I would almost swear he understands.

"Losing it, Donovan," I mutter, closing the door behind me and sprinting for the elevator. I suck in deep breaths, willing oxygen to my brain. I can't afford to be loopy and exhausted. I need all my wits about me to get Kirby to safety.

And to hopefully figure out why my not-quite-right-dar is insisting there's something I'm missing in those text messages.

I step into the elevator, pulling up the thread again and scrolling through as I zip toward the ground floor. But aside from sending my blood pressure spiking again, the second read-through accomplishes nothing. I probably just need to give my subconscious a chance to marinate on the problem.

But I don't have time.

"Come on, brain. Come on." I read it through again, but still nothing new, and then the doors ding open in the lobby and I'm on the move, darting around the crowd by the check-in desk and out into the noon heat where the car is already waiting to whisk me across town.

Hopefully I'll be seeing Kirby in twenty-five minutes or less.

The thought should be comforting, but it's not. Nothing is going to be comforting or right until I know she's safe.

I get to the Pancake House with time to spare and have just stepped out of the car and watched it drive away when it hits me—the wallpaper.

The fucking wallpaper in the shot the dickwad sent me.

It's the same as the wallpaper in the hallway outside our suite. He was at the fucking hotel with Kirby and just sent me on a wild goose chase. "Wait! Wait!" I sprint after the departing car, chasing it down the street.

I catch it just before it pulls back onto the strip and call the police as we're zipping back the way we came. But when I finally get through to whoever's answering the phones, they refuse to connect me with the officers handling the Kirby Lawrence case.

"I can take a message," she says, sounding pissed. "But they're too busy fielding calls from reporters right now to deal with any more drama. Some rock star decided to take justice into his own hands and set off a public relations nightmare down here."

"No, the nightmare is that you aren't listening to me," I snap. "Someone has Kirby somewhere at the Legacy hotel. He just sent me a message. He's threatening to hurt her. You have to send someone over to—"

"I'll relay the message as soon as I can, sir. Now I need to free up this line."

And then she hangs up on me, and my head almost explodes.

"Shit, that's messed up," the spiky-haired Asian kid

driving the car says, speeding faster. "I'll get you there, dude. I know a shortcut."

"The faster, the better, man, thanks," I say, holding on tight to the oh-shit handle as he puts the pedal to the metal.

CHAPTER TWENTY-FIVE
Kirby

I want to shout—*Colin, I'm here! Right here! Down the hall by the ice machine!*—but Peter has a gun pressed into my back, and I'm not 100 percent sure that's he's bluffing about putting it to use.

I'm *mostly* sure. Sure enough that I no longer want to wet my pants as he jabs the barrel into my spine and says, "He's gone. Get moving," but not sure enough to risk my life.

Or Colin's.

But seriously, Peter can't really be going to all this trouble to get custody of a cat. Can he? Even as a person who loves cats with an affection bordering on worship, I can't imagine myself going to these lengths.

"Can we please talk about this?" I ask, violating the "Keep your mouth shut" order he enforced on the drive back into town. "There's no reason things have to end like this, Peter."

"They're not ending like this," he says, mocking my voice in a way that hurts. I was vulnerable with this man. I loved him, opened up to him—maybe not as much or in the way that he wanted, but he's still able to hit me in places where I have my armor up with most people. "We ended a long time ago. This is just how we tie up loose ends. Now move. I want to have plenty of time to get gone before your boyfriend comes back."

"He's not my boyfriend," I grumble.

"Spare me."

"He's not," I insist. Because he's not, and because a perverse part of me wants to fight back, even if it's only verbal resistance.

"Shut up and move." He jabs the gun into my back hard enough to make my pulse spike.

"Fine, I'm moving." I step out into the quiet hallway with Peter close behind me, praying that someone will open the door to their room, sense that something not-right is going on, and call security.

Or better yet, the police.

But the floor remains still and silent save for the soft hum of the air conditioning rushing from vents in the ceiling and a rattle from the ice machine behind us. This entire level is composed of suites, which means fewer rooms and fewer guests. I have no idea how much Colin is paying for our suite, but it's enough that we have to swipe our key against a sensor to get the elevator to stop here, and I haven't seen another soul in this hallway since we checked in.

We might be the only people renting a suite, for all I know.

Which begs the question—"How did you get a key that stops on this floor, anyway?"

"I'm not hideous, Kirby. Some women actually think I'm attractive and are willing to help a cute guy locked out of his rock star buddy's room. And what part of shut up don't you understand? You didn't use to be this obtuse."

I roll my eyes. *Obtuse.* I'm a professional writer and even I don't throw around words like "obtuse" in casual conversation. Or in high-stress situations.

Like say, in the middle of a kidnapping, for example.

"But you were always a pretentious, pseudo-intellectual," I mutter, unable to help myself. It's not a nice thing to say—I get that—but I'm still shocked when Peter fists his hand in my hair and tugs it back, summoning a cry from my sun-cracked lips.

"Shut. The fuck. Up. Kirby," he growls softly into my ear. "Or you're going to be sorry."

I'm already sorry. So, so sorry that I stayed with Peter for so long, even when I knew it wasn't going to work out. But this time, I wisely keep my mouth shut. I just nod as best I'm able with his fingers tangled in my hair, and thankfully, he sets me free. "To the room. When we get there, I want you to go in and sit on your hands on the couch. Don't touch the cat. Do you hear me?"

I nod again to show that I've heard him but stay quiet, saving my resistance for when it will matter. I have to be more careful.

This isn't the Peter I knew, the intense, often insecure but thoughtful boyfriend who always let me have the salmon sashimi from a combo plate, while he took the icky tuna, and drove my car to the shop for an oil change when I was too mired in deadlines to commit to an hour at the dealership. This isn't my partner or my friend.

This is an angry man in the middle of an emotional meltdown, possibly even a psychotic break.

Possibly *a psychotic break? What's* possible *about it, Kirby? He followed you to Vegas and is holding a gun on you so he can steal your cat. What's* not *psycho about that?*

In the wake of my second kidnapping—or my first, if the coffin removal turns out to be an accident and not something Regina planned; so many mysteries to solve, so little time—the inner voice has reverted to sarcasm and general freaking out. None of which is helping me remain calm or figure out a way to escape Peter before he completes his cat-napping.

The only comforting thing about the situation is that Colin is moving away from danger and won't be caught in the crossfire.

Now, if I can just figure out a way to convince Peter to stop being crazy without getting killed in the process. I know Colin would tell me to let my ex take Murder—assure my own safety first, and then we can track down the guy who stole my baby—but I don't know if I can do it. I wouldn't put it past Peter to do something horrible to Murder, just to get revenge, and if my cat ends up paying for my wretched taste in men, I'll never forgive myself.

Imagining any innocent animal being tortured or killed guts me, but the thought of Murder's wickedly clever green eyes closing forever because I didn't fight hard enough to save him is devastating. Devastating enough to ensure that by the time Peter opens the door to the suite, I'm trembling again.

And then Murder races up to me with an excited, "Meow," and it's all I can do not to bend down and scoop his precious body into my arms.

But I remember Peter's directions, so I cross directly to the couch and sit down on my hands. Murder, not a cat to be denied his welcome-home snuggles, follows, but before he can hop up onto the cushion beside me, Peter scoops him up in one big hand, keeping the gun trained on me with the other.

Murder mewls in confusion, but he doesn't struggle or bite a chunk out of Peter. They were good buddies for a long time. Peter has been the provider of enough treats and catnip-flavored toys that when he lifts Murder to his lips and murmurs, "How's my big boy?" against his head, the cat begins to purr.

But I don't blame him. Murder is smart, but he's still a cat, and cats don't understand guns. He has no clue that the silver thing Peter is holding in his hand could kill me. If Peter were yelling at me or pulling my hair in front of Murder, however, it would be a different story.

The thought gives me the spark of an idea.

If I can get Peter mad enough to hurt me, but not mad enough to kill me, maybe Murder will get scared and run and hide somewhere Peter can't reach.

And then I'll...

I'm not sure what happens after that part of the plan, but it will come to me as soon as Murder is out of imminent danger. I'm quick on my feet, and I've written enough suspenseful "get away from the bad guy" scenes to have a few tricks up my sleeve.

The balcony for example...

There's another balcony right below us. One that sticks out farther than ours to make enough space for the lap pool that runs along the entire edge. If I can get out there and work up the guts to jump before Peter works up the guts to shoot me, there's a chance I can get away from him before he gets away with Murder.

I chuckle a little hysterically, and Peter shoots me a

narrow look, his hazel eyes bloodshot in his sunburned face. "What's so funny?"

"Nothing," I say before deciding this actually might be a way to break the ice and adding, "I was just thinking that you're going to get away with Murder." I pause for a response, but Peter's expression remains flat and irritable, so I gesture toward the cat. "You know, his name is Murder, and you're getting..." I wave a hand because that's not going anywhere. "Never mind. Bad joke."

"Awful," Peter agrees. "But I'm glad you think ruining a man's life is funny."

I sigh, shaking my head. "How did I ruin your life, Peter? *You* left *me*, remember?"

"Because I was tired of playing the fool." He cradles Murder closer, turning to murmur against his neck, "Did you know that, Murder? That your daddy is a fool? But your mommy's a cheating whore, so... Could be worse."

My jaw drops. "Peter! What are you talking about? I never cheated on you. Not once. That emotional affair bullshit is—"

"I'm not talking about the emotional affair," he spits. "I'm talking about you getting it hard from behind while he pulls your fucking hair."

"What are you..." My eyes go wide, and my stomach sinks as I connect the dots. P. Eater. Pumpkin Eater. Peter the Pumpkin Eater. "You're the one who rented the drone. You were filming us."

CHAPTER TWENTY-SIX

Kirby

I recoil against the couch, horrified and feeling more violated than ever. A stranger filming us was bad enough, but knowing it was Peter...

Peter controlling the drone.

Peter watching me and Colin naked and...

"Why?" I ask, throat tight. "Why would you do that?"

"I was trying to get footage of Murder in here alone," he says, having the grace to look at least a little ashamed of himself. "So I could prove that you'd violated the hotel's terms of service and convince them to let me take him with me. You're not supposed to leave an animal unattended, not even for thirty minutes, but I knew you would. I knew you'd care more about going out and partying with that rock star sack of shit than you would about Murder's well-being. Unfortunately, instead of what I was looking for, I got an eyeful of you fucking the man you swore to me you'd never fucked. *Swore* to me, Kirby," he says, his voice rising. "In that innocent, but kind of pissed off voice of yours that made me feel like *I* was the crazy one. But it was you. All along. Lying like a fucking sociopath."

"Peter, I didn't—"

"Don't lie to me," he shouts, making Murder squirm in his arms.

I'm making progress on plan "Mad, but not too mad," without even trying. Now to kick it up a notch.

"Please," I say, lifting my hands, fingers spread wide, "just calm down and try to think rationally." There's nothing Peter hates more than being told to calm down.

"Fuck you, Kirby," he says, but not as loudly as before. "You don't get to punch my buttons anymore. I'm free. And soon, Murder will be, too."

"But he doesn't want to be free from me," I say, trying another tack. "Murder loves me, and he knows that I wasn't with Colin while you and I were together."

"Stop," Peter growls through clenched teeth.

"Yesterday was the first time," I insist. "What you filmed with the drone. That was the first time we were ever together."

"It sure looked like it," he says in a cold, quiet voice that's scarier than the yelling. "The way you moved together—completely at ease and in sync like you were speaking a language only the two of you would ever understand." He sighs, his expression turning haunted. I can't help a stab of empathy, no matter how much I hate him right now.

"I'm sorry," I whisper gently. "I'm sorry you had to see that, and I'm sorry I didn't love you the way you needed to be loved. But I swear to you, Peter, that was the first time I ever had sex with Colin. I didn't lie to you or cheat on you."

"I don't believe you," he says softly, his gaze fixed on

the city outside the windows as he absentmindedly strokes Murder's back.

"It's still the truth," I say, inspiration striking. "Ask Bridget! You know there's nothing I don't share with her. Call her, ask her about Colin and me. She'll tell you that we hadn't even kissed until a couple of days ago."

"Bridget's a sweet kid, but she can't be trusted. She'd lie for you," he says, lips curving slightly as his eyes slide back to my face. "But maybe I will give her a call, once I'm settled in Mexico, see if she wants to fly down for a visit. Get to know each other better. I always thought she was the better-looking sister." He motions toward me with the gun, tipping the barrel up and down in a way that makes my pulse stutter. "Nice long legs, prettier face. Or maybe it just looks prettier because she's a brunette and not so damned pale. And every other word out of her mouth isn't a lie."

"I'm sure she'll be into that," I say flatly, "flying down to spend time with a loser who went so psycho over a perfectly normal breakup that he had to kidnap her sister and steal her cat."

He straightens his gun arm, leveling the barrel at my chest with a smile so chilling it makes my heart gallop. "Not if she doesn't know. If I kill you, no one will ever know who took Murder."

I shake my head, still struggling to wrap my mind around the fact that the guy pointing a gun at me is the same one who used to think I was cute when I woke up fuzzy-headed in the night and ran into the closet door trying to get to the bathroom. The one who was so patient with me when I took six more months to get around to "I love you," after he'd already said the words a dozen times. The man who told me he'd never let me down the way my parents had.

"They'll probably think it's that crazy fan who kept sending those threatening letters to your agent," he continues, smile widening. "The ones sent from a mental institution in upstate New York. I wasn't supposed to be able to send letters, but my friend Bruce snuck them out for me. Did you know that I was in the loony bin, Kirby? Did you even stop for a second to wonder where I went when you kicked me out of our house and left me with nothing?"

Face going hot and tears burning the backs of my eyes, I whisper, "It's *my* house, Peter. And I didn't kick you out. I gave you a month to get your stuff together while I stayed with my sister. And you have a job and money of your own, I never—"

"But not the kind of money I would have had if I'd stayed with the firm instead of giving everything up for you."

"I never asked you to do that," I say, fighting the urge to start crying. I don't want him to know how much he's scaring me, but the longer he holds that gun on me, the more worried I am that he's actually going to use it. "Please, Peter, I—"

"But I knew I had to," he cuts in. "I knew if I didn't leave Boston, you'd never be mine. You'd find someone closer, more convenient, and I'd lose my chance. And then I lost it anyway. Lost everything, even my sanity. I was so devastated by what you did to me that I tried to hurt myself, Kirby. I was in there for thirty days afterward. Thirty fucking days and you never called to check on me. Not once. And you're the one who said you wanted to stay friends." His lip curls. "Some fucking friend you are."

He cradles a once-again squirming Murder closer to his chest. My cat isn't used to being held for so long, and he's getting antsy. But maybe he can also tell that Peter isn't quite right. Instead of getting his claws involved for a warning dig into Peter's arm, the way he usually would when detained against his will, Murder draws his neck into his shoulders and goes still, eyeing me with a *"what's going on here?"* expression that I answer with a rush of breath and a shake of my head.

I don't know what's going on here.

But I know that if I want to live through it, I'm going to have to do something.

I lift my hands by my sides again in surrender. "You're right. I've been a bad friend to you, and I'm sorry." I take a deep breath and let it out slowly. "And I think you need Murder with you more than I need him with me."

"I'm taking him because I'm a better father," Peter snaps, rolling his eyes. "Not because I'm some sad sack who needs my pet as a security blanket."

"Okay. So you can take him. I won't fight you. I just want to say goodbye and help you get his things together."

"I can get his things," Peter says, but he lets the gun fall back to his side, giving me hope that I can get him to drop his guard long enough for it to make a difference.

"I know, but I don't want to forget anything, and I won't remember where I put it all if I don't go into the bedroom myself and check." I motion toward the second bedroom as I rise oh-so-slowly from the couch. "Can I please go in and get his toys and food and everything you'll need for the trip? I have a crate, too, if you're flying."

"Ah, ah, ah," he says, smirking at me over Murder's head. "Don't try to get sneaky and figure out where I'm going or how I'm getting there. I'm going to vanish south of the border. That's all you need to know." He pauses before nodding toward the bedroom. "But go ahead. Get his things. Just remember that I'll be right behind you, and I have a gun."

"I know." I walk out around the couch, arms still lifted on either side of my head. "It would be kind of hard to forget. It's been scaring me half to death since you showed up at the gas station."

He steps back, putting more space between us as I pass by, clearly trusting me about as much as I trust him. "You're not acting scared. Haven't seen you ball up on the ground yet."

I pause, hurt by his words at first, and then... inspired by them. I stand up straighter, feeling strangely proud of myself. "You're right. I mean, I am really scared, but I'm not losing it. I'm not having an episode. I'm...okay."

"Probably because you don't think I'll hurt you," he says, his voice gentling. "And I won't, Kirby. I don't want to, anyway. But if you pull something or try to stop me from taking Murder, I can't promise I won't use this." He lifts the gun a few inches away from his thigh before letting it drop again, his haunted eyes fixed on my face. "I don't have anything left to lose. I've lost my career and the woman I loved, the woman I thought was going to be my family, and all the people who were important to me because they were important to you. Like Bridget and your friends from Hidden Kill Bay. After I left, I was so fucking lonely, I even started missing Theodora, even though she—"

"Never shuts up," I finish, feeling for him even as I wish I could lock him in a cage and throw away the key.

"Yeah," he says with a sad smile, one that contains a hint of the man I used to know.

It's sad that he felt so lost, but it's not my fault. I don't owe him a solution to his problems, just like I didn't owe him happily ever after on his terms. And I certainly don't owe him my life or my cat.

If he hadn't been so damned stubborn and jealous, we'd probably still be together. I cared about him, and I don't like change—I don't have time for it with deadlines moving closer together every year and worrying about my sister like she's a baby bird still vulnerable in my nest. If he hadn't grown increasingly obsessed with my relationship with Colin, and with controlling who I could see and how late I could stay out to see them, I would have settled for happy enough. I would have made a life with Peter and done my best to forget that the man I loved most of all was beyond my reach.

But Colin wasn't beyond my reach; we just hadn't found our moment yet. And now we have. Now I know that he loves me as much as I love him, and I owe that, at least in part, to Peter. His crazy set me free.

And maybe it wasn't so crazy, after all.

And maybe admitting that might help my case more than my denials have so far.

"Peter, when we were together, I thought you were out of line, saying I was having an emotional affair," I say softly. "But now I think I can see where you were coming from. I didn't want to admit my feelings for Colin, so I denied them, even to myself. And that wasn't fair, but I swear I wasn't intentionally lying or trying to deceive you." I shrug and shake my head. "I was just mixed up and struggling and trying to find happiness like everyone else. And for a long time, I was really happy with you."

He swallows. "I was happy with you, too."

"And maybe that's enough, huh?" I ask, taking a careful step closer. "To know we had something special and good, even if it didn't end the way either of us would have liked. To know that we tried together, and we learned from each other, and that our next relationship is going to be better because of it?"

I know it was the wrong thing to say as soon as it's out of my mouth, but there's no sucking it back in.

"Your next relationship with your fuck buddy?" Peter sneers. "Great, Kirby, I'm so happy I could make things easier for that piece of—"

"Peter please, I—"

"Back on the couch!" he shouts.

"No, please, I just—"

"The couch," he bellows, summoning a howl from Murder before they both abruptly go silent in the wake of a sudden banging on the door.

CHAPTER TWENTY-SEVEN

Kirby

*W*e all freeze, exchanging wide-eyed glances for a beat before Murder wrenches free with a full-body twist, my lips part, and Peter jabs the gun my way with an urgent hiss. "Keep your mouth shut."

"Hello? Who's in there?" Regina's voice filters through the door, flooding me with twin rivers of relief and disappointment.

Relief that it's not Colin, and he's still safe.

Disappointment that it's not Colin, and I'm still alone with Peter, and rescue is nowhere on the horizon, and now this.

Regina certainly won't be any help. If Peter lets her in, she'd probably hold the gun on me for him. Or find another coffin to throw me in.

"Who's there?" Regina repeats plaintively. "I know it's not Colin. Colin doesn't yell like that. Not even at me. Kirby? Are you okay?"

Peter's eyes blaze and his grip tightens on the gun as he mouths, "Don't say a word."

I widen my eyes meaningfully and spread my fingers in the universal sign for "but she heard us yelling," a fact Regina confirms when she says, "I heard Kirby's voice, and I heard a man shouting. If someone doesn't come answer the door and let me see that Kirby's okay, I'm going to call hotel security."

Eyes squeezing closed with a silent curse, Peter huffs and puffs, his face going red with rage before he finally forces his arm back to his side with an obvious effort. "Go," he whispers, jerking his head toward the door. "Get rid of her. Don't let her inside. Don't let her know anything's wrong."

I nod my agreement and call out, "Just a second Regina, I'll be right there, everything's fine," before slipping around the couch and padding toward the door with Peter close behind me.

When we reach the hallway leading to the second bedroom, Peter tucks himself against the wall by the bathroom, out of sight of the front door. "Don't try to run. I'll be after you in two seconds, and I swear I'll shoot you both. If you want your friend to leave here alive, get rid of her."

"What am I supposed to tell her?" I whisper back. "She heard us yelling, and she knows Colin's voice."

Peter's lips curve in a hard smile. "I'm sure you'll figure something out. You're a good little liar."

Clenching my jaw against the smart-ass response trying to springboard off my tongue and punch him between his bloodshot eyes, I cross to the door, catching sight of my reflection in the mirror above the entry table on my way past. I look like a shipwreck survivor—dirty and dusty, with tear tracks on my cheeks and a rat's nest of blond hair perched on my head like the world's nastiest toupee. There's no way in hell that Regina is going to believe everything's okay in here, no matter how hard I lie.

I'm going to have to make a break for it. To trust that Murder is hiding under the bed and will be safe until I get back with help.

And I'm going to have to keep Regina alive while I'm at it because two wrongs don't make a right, and she might be pregnant, and I'm not a monster person. But I don't have to be sweet about it, that's for damned sure.

Anxiety vultures flapping frantic wings in my chest, I reach for the handle and open the door. Regina's eyes widen, and her jaw drops, confirming I look like something the cat declined to drag in because it was just too fucking gross.

"Oh my God," she murmurs, hand flying to cover her perfectly glossed lips. "Oh my God, Kirby, I'm so sorry. I didn't—"

"Save it," I snap, adrenaline humming as I mentally calculate the distance between the door and the emergency staircase by the elevator, our best chance at getting out of the line of fire before Peter bursts into the hallway behind us.

"No, seriously," she says, threading her fingers together. "I never meant for you to get dumped in the desert or hurt. I just wanted you asleep and out of the way so I could talk to Colin. And then you wandered into the exhibit and—"

"Seriously, Regina, save it," I say, starting to worry that she won't listen when I tell her to run. And if she doesn't listen, she could die.

"And the coffin was right there, and I couldn't resist,"

she barrels on, oblivious. "But I was going to tell Colin where you were, I promise."

"Regina, what if I told you I would forgive you if you would do one thing for me?" I ask, crossing my fingers that she's smart enough to get the message hidden in what I'm about to say.

Her eyes narrow skeptically. "I'd say...good. Because I really *am* sorry."

"I'd like my stuffed panda back," I say, pushing on before she can speak. "The really big one that I was carrying when you drugged me. I won it at one of the carnival games at the Circus casino."

She's still frowning as her lips part on a, "But I—"

"I know you liked it, but it's the first time I've ever won anything," I cut in, eyes widening and nostrils flaring as I silently will her to read between the lines. "So if you could go get that for me and bring it back later tonight that would be great."

Her gaze cuts over my shoulder and back to my face, suspicion blooming in her eyes. "What time?" she asks before mouthing, "Are you okay?"

I answer by mouthing "No, help me," before adding in my normal voice, "Any time after six and before ten." I point at her then jab my finger down the hall. "I'm going to take a shower and a nap and rest up from being stranded in the desert without water for hours first."

"Okay." She nods her head meaningfully as she backs away. "I'll go get that and bring it back to you, and then we'll be best friends again," she says, clearly trying to play the tricky lie game but sucking at it. "Like we've been for years."

I flare my nostrils again, warning her to get out of here and get help, but it's too late. I feel Peter moving behind me a beat before I hear his footsteps on the tile. "Run!" I shout to Regina, slamming the door closed before I spin and dive for Peter's knees.

He isn't expecting to be tackled and goes down hard, knocking his skull on the tile with a nasty sounding *thud* that's quickly drowned out by the boom of the gun going off in the close space.

I scream, running frantic hands over my chest and stomach as I roll across the carpet toward the couch. But I'm not shot. No holes, no blood, just my heart lunging out of the starting gate as I jump to my feet and sprint for the balcony.

I'm wrenching open the door when the second gunshot rips through the air, shattering the glass in the picture window above the Jacuzzi, not two feet from where I stand. I scream again but ignore my gut-level instinct to drop and ball up like a startled hedgehog.

There's nowhere to hide and nowhere to run. I've got to jump, and I've got to do it fast before Peter calms down and his aim improves.

I take the last three steps to the edge of the balcony, brace my hands on the railing and go for it—up and over.

And then I'm falling through the hot desert air, nerve endings sizzling with terror as I pray I haven't overshot the jump, that I'm going to land on the balcony below and not keep falling until I end up splattered across the pavement.

The sting on the bottom of my wrapped feet as I hit the surface of the lap pool and the water envelopes me in a full-body hug is one of the best things I've felt in my entire life. Even the slight ouch when my knees collide with the bottom of the pool—it's shallower than it looked from up above—is a blessing.

I'm alive. I'm alive and away from Peter and everything is going to be okay!

My celebration lasts all of the five seconds it takes to emerge from the water with a gasp to see Peter plummeting through the air and crashing into the pool beside me.

CHAPTER TWENTY-EIGHT
Colin

I explode from the elevator to the sound of a gunshot and the sight of Regina running down the hall toward me, her eyes electric with fear. "Colin! He's got a gun! He shot her! I think he shot her!" she screams, making my stomach plummet and my heart rip down the center.

I run harder, sprinting around Regina as she calls out, "Don't go in there! I'm going for help! We need help!"

But I can't wait. Kirby's in trouble and I need to get to her—now.

The second gunshot comes as I'm fumbling my key card from my pocket. I hear Kirby scream, and it's all I can do not to start kicking the fucking door down. "I'm coming, Kirby!" I shout, finally smashing the key against the sensor. The second it turns green I slam inside, just in time to see Kirby jump off the balcony.

Jump.

Off the fucking balcony.

While a man with a gun runs after her through a shattered window.

My soul flattens inside me like a crushed beer can, but there's no time to think about what's happening to Kirby on the other side of that fall—did she land on the balcony beneath us? Jump too far and take everything that's good in the world with her?

The man with the gun is on the move, almost as if he—

"Fuck!" I launch into motion, already knowing I'm going to be too late. I'm fast on my feet, but not fast enough to reach Kirby's attacker before he follows her over.

The man with the dark brown hair makes the jump, and I catch a glimpse of his profile silhouetted against the desert sky. It's only visible a second, maybe two, before he plummets out of sight, but it's long enough for me to peg him.

It's Peter, Kirby's ex. The man who followed us to Vegas and filmed us and is now trying to kill the woman he used to cuddle on his lap at barbeques with a smug-ass grin on his face like he knew how much I hated seeing his hands all over her and was doing it just to fuck with me.

I didn't realize back then I was jealous. I just thought Kirby deserved better than a dude-bro with a bad haircut who looked like he'd taken a dump in his pants when he wore khakis, and he *always* wore khakis. But now I know I wanted to rip off his arms because he was with the woman I love.

My girl. My Kirby.

My favorite human, who I would never hurt, no matter how badly things ended between us because real love doesn't work that way. Real love lets go; it doesn't snuff out.

That creep never loved her, and if he hurts a single hair on her head, I'm going to take him apart, piece by piece, and feed him to Murder for breakfast.

I'm going over—it's not even a conscious decision, just something that has to be done to get to Kirby, so I do it. I reach the edge, swing my legs over and follow them down into the lap pool.

The fall is brief but insane, time seeming to slow as my nervous system registers with a jolt the fact that I've just jumped off a fifteenth floor balcony and my brain takes stock of the situation below—Peter breaking the surface of the water and Kirby climbing out of the pool —and then I hit.

I bend my knees, absorbing the impact and push to the surface as fast as I can, lunging for Peter. But I'm still wearing my dress shoes from last night and they slip on the slick pool bottom. My fingers barely graze his shoulder, and he turns, registering my face with a look of rage so intense it takes my breath away.

And then his hand wraps around my neck, forcing me back under, and I really wish I'd held on to that last gasp of air.

I punch him in the junk—there's no honor in a lap pool fight with a psychopath—but the water slows me down, blunting the force of the blow. Peter doesn't let go, simply shifts away and brings both hands to wrap around my throat. I see the gun float to the bottom and reach for it, but it's too far away, and Peter's hands are quickly making the world go fuzzy around the edges.

I realize I'm in deep shit and might actually die here, drowned in three feet of water by a coward who wears pooped-himself khakis, when Peter abruptly lets go.

I surface with a gasp to the sound of a flock of birds

being ground up in a blender. I swipe my hand across my eyes and blink, bringing the frenzy of black on Peter's head into focus.

It's Murder, all teeth and claws and pissed-off bared fangs, doing his best to fuck Peter up.

I have never loved an animal as much as I love that crazy cat right now.

Holding my breath, I duck under the water, grabbing the gun before I hurry to the edge and roll out of the pool onto the sun-warmed stones of a balcony even bigger than ours. A moment later, a soggy Kirby emerges from inside, followed by a flock of women in red hats carrying folded chairs, a flagpole, and other makeshift weapons.

"Colin!" Kirby hurls herself into my arms, hugging me tight before pulling back to peer up at me with worried eyes. "You're okay? Are you okay?" Her hands skim over my chest and stomach, where my shirt is plastered to the skin beneath.

"I'm fine, and I've got his gun. It's you I'm worried about," I say, my voice breaking as I add, "Did he hurt you? Are you—"

"I'm fine," she says, lips quirking as she glances over her shoulder. "And the Madams of Mayhem have already called the police and security. They should be here any minute."

"And we'll keep this shit for brains in check until they get here," says a buxom little woman brandishing a stapler.

"Looks like the cat's doing a good job on his own," another woman adds, laughing. "Come over here, Mr. Kitty. We'll finish him off for you."

"Murder, baby, come here," Kirby says, moving out of

my arms.

I grab her wrist lightly. "No, let me. I don't want you anywhere near that asshole." I hand her the gun and approach the pool just as Peter gets a hold of Murder and hurls him into the air. I lean in, catching the churning fur ball right before he hits the water, fully expecting to be clawed to death for my efforts.

But to my shock, after his initial twitch of surprise at being snatched away from danger, Murder stills, shooting me a relatively chill look before turning to hiss in Peter's direction.

"I agree." I stroke a soothing hand down Murder's back. "He should have his eyes clawed out and fed to the birds. Good work, buddy."

"I'm going to kill you," Peter growls, starting for the edge of the pool only to be stopped by a flying folding chair that hits him on the shoulder. "Ow!"

One of those women has excellent aim. Her upper body strength isn't too shabby, either.

"Stay where you are, asshole." A tall woman with dark brown curls poking out from beneath the rim of her red bowler hat points a menacing finger his way. "You're done hurting people today."

"Or cats," Kirby adds as she gathers Murder into her arms and moves into mine, leaning against my chest as hotel security rushes out onto the balcony, followed seconds later by the police.

We turn over Peter's weapon while the police pull him out of the pool and take him into custody, still fuming and cussing and hurling enough threats Kirby's way that a cop feels compelled to assure us that he won't be out on the streets anytime soon. "We'll hold him until the bail hearing. It'll be at least a week," he says, glancing between Kirby and me. "I know you two have been through a lot, but we'd love for you to come down to the station and give your statement. And hopefully introduce what you're wearing into evidence."

Kirby nods. "Sure. Can we grab something to change into from our room first? I've been wearing this dress for way too long, and I'd love some real shoes."

I glance down to see soggy fabric wrapped around her feet and shake my head. What a fucking night.

"Sure thing," the policeman says. "I'll have a squad car waiting for you downstairs. Just come on out whenever you're ready."

"Thanks. We appreciate it." I turn to ask Kirby if she needs a doctor for her feet or anything else, but before I can speak, Regina rushes onto the balcony with a dramatic cry of relief.

"There you are!" She throws her arms around me, Kirby, and Murder. "I'm so glad you're all okay! I was so scared. That guy is fucking crazy."

"Whereas drugging me and pushing me into a coffin where I almost died is perfectly sane," Kirby says dryly while Murder issues a warning rumble that Regina thankfully takes seriously, stepping back.

"I explained that." Regina lifts her hands in surrender. "It was an accident, and I really am sorry." She shoots a glance toward where the two remaining policemen are roping off the area around the lap pool with crime scene tape before adding in a whisper, "Please don't press charges. I'll never do anything awful to anyone ever again, and I'll leave you and Colin alone, I promise."

Kirby shoots me a searching look, and I shake my

head, answering her unspoken question. "She's not pregnant. There's no baby, mine or anyone else's."

"I was on uppers and downers at the same time," Regina says with a shrug, as if that explains everything. "The combo makes stupid things seem like a good idea. So I won't take those anymore, either. At least, not at the same time."

Kirby arches a dubious brow, but when she sighs, I can tell she's going to let Regina off the hook.

"The police already know what she did," I cut in. "The casino security system got it all on tape. All you have to do is say you want to press charges and they'll put the ball in motion. There's no reason she should get away with what she did to you."

"I know," Kirby says, her tired eyes finding mine. "But I have enough drama on my plate right now. And I believe that she's sorry." Her lips curve into a hard grin. "And I don't plan on coming back to Vegas. Ever again. So I doubt our paths will cross."

"Oh, but you've got to come back, sweetheart," one of the red-hatted women says, clearly having no issue with eavesdropping. "We want you to be our keynote speaker at next year's 'Death in the Desert' conference."

"We're aspiring mystery writers," the one with the stapler explains with a giddy giggle. "And this is just about the most exciting thing that could have happened to us. A famous writer *and* an attempted murder, right on our balcony in the middle of the annual meeting. Seriously. We couldn't have asked for a better ending to our conference."

"Glad we could oblige," Kirby says. "But I'm going to have to say no. Unless you're interested in having your conference in Hidden Kill Bay next year. I do own a bed and breakfast with a pool house you could use as a meeting room."

The red hats explode in titters of excitement, already making plans as Kirby turns to Regina and says, "Goodbye."

"So we're good?" Regina asks.

"No, we're not good," Kirby says with an incredulous laugh. "I never want to see you again, and if I do, I'm going to sic my attack cat on you. But I'm not going to press charges, so scram while the scramming's good. And lose Colin's number while you're at it."

"Okay, okay, glad you guys aren't dead," Regina says, before fleeing back into the meeting room and the hotel beyond.

Kirby nods after her, hugging Murder closer with one arm. "You ready to get out of here? Pack up so we can leave as soon as we're done at the police station?"

"Yes, but I have to do one thing first." I thread my fingers lightly into her damp hair and pull her close. And then I kiss her, slow and gentle, but with an intensity that leaves us both breathless by the time I pull back to whisper, "I love you," for the first time. "And not just as a friend."

Her lips tremble into a smile. "I know. I heard your song. At a gas station. Before Peter got to me."

I exhale. "How the hell did he find you anyway?"

"A combination of a frequent flier account email mix-up and being really handy with a police scanner. Turns out he's actually an excellent private detective."

"I want to snap his head off his body," I growl. "When I heard that gun go off, I—"

"It's okay," she says, rubbing her hand back and forth on my chest. "It's over now. We're safe, Peter and Regina are out of the picture, and you're back in the song-writing groove." She beams up at me. "I love my song, Colin. So much."

I gather her closer. "Enough to forgive me for being too dumb to realize I've been in love with you forever?"

"Well, I was dumb, too," she says, leaning into me as Murder grumbles in irritation between us. "Hush, baby, I need to tell Colin how stupid we both were."

"And that you love me, too?" I ask, even though I'm pretty sure...

Mostly sure...

Still, I cross my fingers behind her back and hold my breath, waiting for that sparkle in her eyes to find its way into words.

"When I woke up in that coffin and thought I was dead, that was my only regret," she says, brushing my wet hair from my forehead. "That I didn't get a chance to tell you that I love you." She drops her voice, adding in a wicked whisper, "Or do all the things we did in the mirror room at least twenty more times."

"There's so much more fun to be had, baby." I hug her closer. "I promise, I'm going to get you so addicted to mind-blowing sex that you'll never be able to walk away from me."

"I'm not going anywhere. Ever," she says, lips curving. "Except home. With you, where I expect your clothes to be in my closet by the end of the week."

I smile. "Yes, ma'am." And then I kiss her again and again, until Murder squirms free with a disgusted yowl, but that doesn't stop us. Neither do the titters from the mystery writers or the clicking sounds as they snap pictures.

For once, I don't mind the invasion of privacy.

I want a picture to remember this day, the first day of the rest of my life with my best friend. My Larry.

"Can I still call you Larry now that we're gross in love?" I ask when we come up for air.

"You'd better," she says, grabbing my face and pulling me down for another kiss.

"You're very forceful today," I say, smiling against her lips. "I dig it."

"Waking up in a coffin will do that to a girl," she murmurs back. "Now, shut up and kiss me like you mean it."

So I do.

For a long, long time.

EPILOGUE

Kirby

Two months later...

September in Maine is proof that the universe loves us and wants us to be happy. And the Hidden Kill Bay Claw Down Lobster Fest, which turns our sleepy town into a madhouse for one weekend every September, is proof that the cockroaches of the sea are delicious and worth leaving home for.

It is literally the first time Colin and I have been out of my house (or the recording studio he and Shep built behind it) for the past two months.

But why bother leaving the house when there's so much fun to be had inside it?

In the bedroom, in particular?

And in the shower, and on the kitchen table, and in front of the fireplace, and out in the garden in the dark before the raccoons showed up and scared us half to death.

Damn raccoons. But the running inside naked and

celebrating our escape up against the wall by the laundry room was hot...

"You know the worst part of being out in the world again?" I ask as Colin and I stroll through downtown toward the marina on a crisply gorgeous fall day, with Murder on his leash in front of us and the smell of steamed lobster already teasing my nostrils.

"You're not naked?" Colin says, copping a feel of my ass as we stop at the corner, waiting for the crosswalk light to change.

"I was going to say that *you're* not naked." I lift my face to his, welcoming the kiss he presses to my lips with a smile. "But yes. I like it when I'm naked, too. When our nakedness is mutual, if you will."

"Oh, I will," he says, arm going around my waist.

"So...you want to grab some chardonnay at Square Liquor, I'll grab a couple to-go plates from the festival, and we can meet up in my bedroom in fifteen? Twenty-five if Theodora isn't too busy to talk my leg off at her table? I would skip it, but she's my honorary little sister and this is her first year qualifying for a chef's table so..."

Colin wrinkles his nose. "Nah, let's go. Walk around. See the sights."

"What sights?" I ask as he takes my hand, starting across the street as the light changes. "We grew up here. We know the sights."

"The ocean is different every day. And the trees are killer this year. Look at all that red and gold. Gorgeous."

I shoot a skeptical glance his way. "As gorgeous as my boobs?"

"Not even close," he says without missing a beat, "but your boobs will still be attached to the rest of your smoking-hot body after we eat lobster and get a little sun. You're starting to turn translucent again, Spooky, and Murder is clearly in the mood for a walk."

Murder is, indeed, pulling at his harness, dragging us inexorably toward the marina, but that probably has more to do with the smell of food than any great longing for physical activity. Murder's been even lazier the past two months than we have, which is understandable considering he's fixed, and even if he weren't, there are no lady cats in my house.

"Okay, then we'll walk and eat lobster," I say, though I can't help feeling that something is off with Colin. "Should I be worried that this is the first time in two months that you haven't jumped at the chance to see my boobs?"

Laughing, he leans down to kiss my forehead. "No. You shouldn't. I'm still entirely under your thrall and committed to fucking you stupid every night."

"Good." I smile, pleased. "I like being fucked stupid. It's so relaxing. I never realized it before, but stupid people totally have it made."

"I imagine truly stupid people aren't very relaxed. They're probably stressed out from trying to understand shit and being thwarted by their lack of brains, you know?"

I hum, pondering this as we cut across the square to the marina parking lot where, to my surprise, I see the Lips on Fire tour bus parked at the end of a long line of chartered buses that have come bearing tourists.

I point at the sleek black vehicle. "What's up with that? It's still a month until you leave."

A month, thirty whole days, which is not even close to long enough.

I don't know what I'm going to do with myself when

Colin leaves in October, but I realize he has to go. My Only One has been in the top ten Billboard Charts since he released the recording a week after we got back from Vegas, and advance sales of the new album are strong and steady, but touring is how musicians make money these days. And it's what he and the rest of the band love—making music for their fans, taking their show on the road, living like nomads with nothing to worry about but whether their instruments are in tune and where the cool bars are in any given city.

"We're getting the couch and chairs reupholstered and making our sleeping berths soundproof. Everyone's finally had enough of Cutter's snoring." Colin nods toward the bus. "The marina rented us a parking spot until it's done."

I frown. "But you could have parked it at my place. It would fit in the driveway." I cock my head, mentally measuring. "I think."

"Then you'd have nowhere to park, and between the recording studio and my basketball hoop, I've already taken over most of your back yard."

"*Our* back yard," I correct him. "I want you to feel as at home there as I do."

"I do. And I don't want a tour bus in my driveway, reminding me of things I don't want to think about just yet."

I sigh. "Yeah. Me, either, I guess."

We fall silent as we cross the parking lot, pausing only once for Murder to sniff an empty beer bottle he decides isn't as interesting as the food smells up ahead, before we step onto the dockside path.

About ten years ago, the city widened the beachside walkway to nearly fifteen feet across, but there's still barely room for us to blend in with the rest of the foot traffic. The Claw Down is as hopping as ever.

Before he can get freaked out by all the stranger feet, I pick Murder up, holding him close as we turn left onto the pier, now lined on both sides with makeshift cook stations and lobster-themed decorations. Even the boats moored on the docks farther down are flying festive flags, including one skull and lobster claw pirate banner that is so perfect it would usually make me smile.

But thinking about Colin far away from me for weeks on end without time to fly back for a visit has spawned a black hole in my stomach, and it's doing its best to suck all the joy and light deep down inside it. But the black hole doesn't get to win. If I learned nothing else from the insanity in Vegas, it's that you have to relish the good times so you're ready to hold on through the bad.

"Lobster ravioli, lobster fritters, or lobster stew?" I ask in an upbeat voice, determined not to get mopey until that bus actually pulls out of town. "What first?"

"I was thinking we could hit Theodora's table," Colin says. "Show our support, get our hands on some of that grilled lobster with coconut curry before she runs out."

I nod seriously. "That shit is so good. I've been craving it since she made it for Bridget and me a few weeks ago while you were recording."

"I know." He squeezes my hand, exhaling in a rush. "You talked about it for three days straight. So let's go get some."

"Sounds good." I let him lead the way down to Theodora's station.

She's one of the few female chefs with a featured

dish, and her wild raven curls and bright red chef's jacket stand out in the crowd.

Her parents ran the only Indian restaurant in town for twenty years before they retired to Florida a while back. Theodora grew up waiting tables and helping out in the kitchen, a combination that made her fluent in Hindi, English, and Spanish, and which she credits for her gift of gab.

She insists she talks all the time because she spent so much of her life helping her Hindi-speaking parents communicate with the English-speaking servers and getting everyone on the same page with the mostly Spanish-speaking kitchen crew. I, however, believe she was born chattering and never stopped. Sometimes her bubbly stream of consciousness makes people underestimate her, but Theo is a force to be reckoned with—in or out of the kitchen.

As we take our place at the back of the line, I watch her breezing around her little kingdom, holding forth with a steady stream of criticism and encouragement as she keeps the yumminess rolling out, and I feel a surge of pride. She's all grown up, our Theo, as is the cute brunette with the braids working one of the two cash registers while Shep mans the other, enjoying the relative anonymity that comes with being a band's drummer instead of its lead singer.

Bridget spots me, and I wave. But instead of the grin I'm expecting, my sister goes pale and drops her blue eyes back to the register.

I frown, nudging Colin in the ribs. "Hey, was Bridget okay when you dropped the new linens by the B&B yesterday?"

"Yeah, she was fine. Why?" Colin asks.

I shake my head and scratch Murder's neck thoughtfully, summoning a purr from his chest. "I don't know. She's acting weird."

"Probably just busy," he says, dismissing my worry in a way that's a little odd, too. But before I can ponder it further, Bridget is flapping an arm behind her like she's having a seizure, and Theo is suddenly not talking.

Not talking, but she is hurrying around to the back of the cook station and then scurrying back.

Something is definitely up, and I intend to get to the bottom of it before Bridget and Theo have a lapse in judgment. Ninety percent of the time, they're trustworthy mid-twentysomethings with their heads on straight.

But every once in a while, they pull a Kirby, giving in to sudden, out-of-character impulsivity that ends in disaster.

"You two are not going to hike the Appalachian Trail," I say as we step up to Bridget's register, pointing a warning at her. "You're not in good enough shape, and it's way too late in the year to start. You'll freeze to death. And need I mention that neither of you has ever backpacked in your life?"

"I know," Bridget says with a sharp exhalation. "You guys want two plates, right?"

"Yeah, two specials," Colin says.

"Do you know?" I press, because the thought of her and Theo following through with their latest crazy plan scares me half to death. "Because you could die out there, Bridget. You could freeze. Or starve. Or get eaten by bears. Or wolves."

"I know, Kirby. I hear you, I promise." She sighs, gaze still fixed on her money drawer.

"Or get really bad poison ivy or hypothermia or infected blisters or—"

"I said I know." She looks up, the shine in her eyes making my heart flutter into full-on helicopter sister mode.

"What's wrong," I whisper, leaning in. "Why are you crying?"

"I'm not crying," she whispers, blinking faster as she shoots a panicked look Shep's way. "I've just got smoke in my eyes."

"The smoke is super bad," Theo says, dropping two claw-filled plates off personally and giving Bridget's arm an encouraging squeeze. "Hi, Kirby and Colin. Bye, Kirby and Colin."

And with that, she disappears, sending my internal alert level from Code Yellow to full-on Imminent-Danger Red. "What's going on?" I demand as Shep shifts over to stand beside Bridget. "That's officially the fewest words I've ever heard her speak at one time. By several hundred thousand."

"She's just slammed." Shep casts a worried glance down at Bridge before he adds, "And Bridget's upset because we...had a fight. Right, Bridget?"

She turns round eyes his way, hesitating a moment before she nods too fast. "Yes. We did. You were really awful."

"A total jerk," he agrees. "Can you ever forgive me?"

"I don't know." Bridget lifts her nose with a sniff. "Probably not. I am really, really disappointed in you, Shepherd."

"What did you do?" I ask Shep, who avoids my gaze. I look back to my sister. "What did he do? I've known him practically since he was born, Bridge, and I don't think I've ever seen him be a jerk."

"Gotta keep the line moving," Theo says, poking her head in quickly, her eyes also refusing to meet mine as she says, "We'll all talk later. Bye, Kirby and Colin."

Colin gathers our plates, shooting a hard look Shep's way. "Yes. We'll all talk later. Come on, Kirby."

"Call me if you need me," I tell Bridget as I move away.

She smiles, but I can tell she's still sad. Or mad. Or something. "I'm fine. Go on. Just...be nice, okay?"

I frown, but before I can demand she explain what the hell is going on, Colin has his arm around me, dragging me away.

"No, I have to go back," I say, getting more upset with every step we take from my sister. "Something is seriously up with her. I know when she's about to act out. Remember that time I woke up and found a note saying she'd run away to join the circus?"

"She was thirteen," he reminds me as he sets our plates on one of the bar tables scattered throughout the center of the pier.

"That time. There have been others." I try to head back the way we came, only to have him to take hold of my upper arms and bend down until his face is in front of mine.

"Eat your lobster," he insists.

"I'm not hungry anymore," I insist back.

"Yes, you are, Larry. Now eat some fucking lobster before this surprise gets any worse."

"Surprise?" Their weird behavior clicks, clues now obvious, banking my raging sisterly protectiveness. "That's why you're all being freaks except Murder?"

"That's why we're all being freaks except Murder." He nods toward the plates. "So. Lobster?"

Setting my cat down, I move carefully around Colin, approaching the plates with a mixture of curiosity and trepidation. Why make such a big deal out of this unless it's a big deal?

Maybe...a very big deal?

Is that why Bridget was being weird? Because she knows *I'm* weird and that I've never had any inclination to get married? Like, none at all? Is she terrified that I'm going to break Colin's heart by telling him I don't want to get hitched?!

I would *never* break Colin's heart. I love him to the moon and back. I love him down to his cells and the code of his DNA. When I die, I want to be burned and stored on a shelf until Colin is ashes, too, and then I want us to be mixed together in a dusty cocktail and made into something creepy like a cremains statue so that our children can be horrified by how weird and in love their parents were.

I want to have babies with this man, desperately loved babies that will be half him and half me and all beautiful because they will have been made out of the strongest love I've ever known.

Pure, wild, soul-stirring, bone-melting, heart-healing love. The kind of love that I already know is forever— with or without a ring.

Though I'd honestly prefer without. I don't want the law involved. I just want his promise and his time and his hand in mine.

Pulse speeding up, I search the plates for something sparkly, panicking a little until I spot the flat gray key clenched in one claw. My breath rushes out, "A key."

"A key," Colin says, smiling widely. "You should've seen your face." He nudges my shoulder. "You thought it was a ring, didn't you?"

I punch him in the arm. "Maybe. And you knew I would. You were deliberately fucking with me."

"Maybe a little," he admits, "but if I'd known it would upset Bridge so much, I would have told her not to worry."

"She'll be okay," I say. "As soon as she knows we're okay."

"I hope we'll be more than okay." He takes the key between two long, elegant fingers. Fingers that know exactly how to touch me and are attached to a heart that knows just how to love me, a fact he proves as he says, "This key fits in the lock of the new writer's lair the contractors just added to the back of the tour bus. It's just a little box, but it's got a door you can shut, a window where you can watch the world go by, and one of those fancy chairs you like. And the desk is the same height as the one you have now. I had it built special so it would feel just like home." He searches my face, excitement and nerves mixing in his expression. "The guys in the band are all psyched about it, and I hope you will be, too."

Tears sting the back of my eyes as I realize what this means. "You want me to come with you? On tour?"

"I want you to come with me everywhere." He brushes my hair from my face, curling his fingers around the back of my neck in that way that makes me go boneless every time. "I don't want to be away from you, Larry. Not any more than I have to be, not until death does us part."

"Me, either," I say, echoing the vow. "Until death

does us part." I press up onto tiptoe, sealing the promise with a kiss that I feel everywhere. "I choose you, Colin Donovan."

"And I choose you, Kirby Lawrence," he whispers against my lips. "You'll always be my only one."

I pull back with a grin and tears in my eyes. "So that's all the married we need, right?"

"All the married we need," he says, hugging me closer with a laugh. "I know marriage isn't your jam, Larry. And I don't need a piece of paper. I just need you." He glances up at the sky with an adorably shy grin as he adds, "And maybe some really cute kids with your baby blues someday. But it's cool, too, if you don't want kids."

"Yes, to babies," I say, smiling so hard my jaw starts to hurt. "But I want them to have your eyes. Your eyes are the best."

"See," Shep says, making both Colin and I jump and pull apart. We turn to see him standing behind us, a beaming Bridget by his side. "I told you it was going to be fine."

"He doesn't want to get married," I assure Bridget. "Just to be together forever." I hold up the key. "I'm going to write my next book from a lair in the back of the tour bus."

"So you said yes?" she asks.

I nod, deciding to give her romantic heart what it wants. "I said yes."

"I'm so happy!" Bridget's eyes begin to shine again. "I thought you were going to say no, and Colin was going to cry, and everything was going to be awful. I'm so glad you're going to be together forever!"

"Aw, come here, Bridge." I pull her into my arms as

she continues to sniffle with happiness, and Shep and Colin go in for a bro hug.

When I finally have her settled, Shep and Bridge return to their stations, and Colin takes me out to the tour bus to show me my new digs. "You sneaky bastard," I say, laughing as I soak in the amazingness of my cozy new lair. "That's why you had the tour bus parked by the pier."

"Guilty," he says, shutting the door behind us, locking Murder on the other side. "And because I wanted to do this." He reaches for me, lifting me into his arms and guiding my legs around his waist as he slams me against the wall.

We kiss like we haven't tasted each other in months —wild and hungry—as he fumbles my panties to one side beneath my skirt and I rip open his fly. And then we come together, and it's magic and home and beauty and play and love, all of it dancing between us, creating a bubble of unshakable joy that nothing can break.

Because he's mine, and I'm his, and we're going to be banging best friends forever.

"Forever," I whisper against his warm neck as we catch our breath.

"And ever," he agrees, setting me down and helping pull my clothes into place. "Now can we get lobster to take home so I can eat it off your tits?"

I wrinkle my nose. "Lobster is a gross thing to eat off of someone's tits."

"Not *someone's* tits," he corrects, pretending to be scandalized. "*Your* tits, Larry. And everything is delicious and sexy when eaten off of your tits."

I bite my lip. "Fine. You can eat lobster off my tits. But I'm licking cocktail sauce off your dick after."

"That's gross." He kisses my cheek. "And I would expect nothing less. I love you a ridiculous amount, you know that?"

"Does this mean you intend to bang me stupid after we're done playing with lobster and sauces?" I ask, wrapping my arms around his waist.

"The very stupidest," he promises.

And then we collect our fur baby, buy an obscene amount of lobster, and Colin takes me home where he proves he's a man of his word.

Ready for more red HOT friends-to-lovers rom com?
Keep reading for a sneak peek of HOT AS PUCK.
Available Now!

Or pre-order BANG THEORY now.

TELL LILI YOUR FAVORITE PART!

I love reading your thoughts about the books and your review matters. Reviews help readers find new-to-them authors to enjoy. So if you could take a moment to leave a review letting me know your favorite part of the story —nothing fancy required, even a sentence or two would be wonderful—I would be deeply grateful.

Thank you and happy reading!

SNEAK PEEK

The NHL's biggest bad boy is about to fall for the virgin next door...

I am the world's biggest dating failure. We're talking my last date went home with our waitress kind of failure.

But I have an ace in the back pocket of my mom jeans— my sexy-as-sin best friend, NHL superstar forward, Justin Cruise.

Justin owes me favors dating back to seventh grade, long before he became a hotshot with a world famous...stick. So in return for my undying platonic loyalty, all I want is an easy-peasy crash course on how to be a sex goddess.

How hard can it be?

* * *

I have never been so hard in my life.

The things I want to do to my sweet, kindergarten-teaching, mitten-crocheting best friend Libby Collins are ten different kinds of wrong. Maybe twenty.

But I'm a firm believer in teaching by example, and by the end of our first lesson, we've graduated to a *hands on* approach to her sexual education: my hands all over her, her hands all over me, and her hot mouth melting beneath mine as I prove to her there isn't a damned thing wrong with the way she kisses.

Give me a month, and I'll transform Libby from wall flower to wall banger, and ensure she's confident enough to seduce any guy she wants.

Problem is... the only guy I want her seducing is me.

Hot as Puck is a sexy, flirty, friends-to-lovers Standalone romantic comedy from *USA Today* Bestseller Lili Valente.

Please enjoy this excerpt from
HOT AS PUCK
Available Now!

Justin

This is it, the night I'll look back on in fifty or sixty years and stab a finger at as the moment my life changed forever. Somewhere out there, in the throng of people wiggling to the club beat pulsing across the Portland skyline from the most exclusive rooftop lounge in the city, is the woman I'm going to marry.

Next summer.

In eight short months.

Because I'm dying to settle down, develop a food-baby where my six-pack used to be, spend Friday nights on the couch in my give-up-on-life sweatpants arguing about what to watch on Netflix and picking out names for the five or six kids my wife and I will bang out as quickly as possible to ensure we'll have an army of small people to share in the grinding monotony of our wedded bliss.

Ha. Right.

Or rather *no*. Hell no. Fuck no, with a side of "what kind of reality-altering drugs have you been huffing in the bathroom?"

Sylvia is out of her goddamned mind! I'm twenty-eight years old—tonight, happy fucking birthday to me—and at the top of my game. I have zero interest in a long-term commitment to anything but my team.

The Portland Badgers are riding a ten-game winning streak, thanks largely to the fact that I bust my ass in the gym every other morning so I can bust my ass on the ice every time Nowicki spaces-out eighteen minutes into the period and forgets what his stick is for. That rookie's untreated ADHD is a pain in my ass, but the rest of the forwards and I are taking up the slack and then some. I'm averaging over a point a game, leading the league in goals, and on my way to an elite season. Maybe even an Art Ross Trophy-winning season, though I don't like to count my eggs before they've been scrambled, smothered in cheese and hot sauce, and wrapped in a burrito.

God, a burrito sounds good. I'm so fucking hungry. I would kill for Mexican right now, or at least something cooked and wrapped in something other than seaweed.

Nearly three thousand dollars in hor d'oeuvres are being passed around this party on shiny silver platters, and there's not a damned thing I want to eat.

I let Sylvia—who has very firm opinions about many, many things—handle ordering the food, and apparently she thought sushi, sushi, more sushi, and some weird, rock-hard, low-fat cookies that taste like vanilla-flavored air were all anyone would want to shove in their pie-hole tonight. Just like she thought I should get down on one knee and put a ring on her finger in time to plan a block-buster summer wedding or she would need to "explore her other options."

Explore her other fucking options. What the fuck? Who says something like that to a guy they swear they're desperately in love with? If she were really that gone on me, wouldn't I be the *only* option? The only person in the entire world that she could even remotely consider spending the rest of her life with?

I kind of want to hate Sylvia—what sort of person tries to blackmail you into proposing to them on *your* birthday? She should have at least waited until *her* birthday next month—but I just keep thinking about how lonely my bed is going to be tonight. Sylvia is clearly deeply deluded about how far along we are in the evolution of our relationship, but she's also very pretty, gives the best head I've ever had, bar none, and smells really, really nice.

I have a thing about the way a woman smells. Not her perfume or her soap or her body lotion, but *her*. The woman herself. Her base note, the scent that rises from her skin when she's lying in the sun or kissing me after a run or just hasn't showered in a while.

Yes, with the right woman, I enjoy logging some

quality bedroom time while she's a little bit dirty. Don't fucking judge me! It's my birthday!

Anyway... No one smells as good as Sylvia does at the end of a long day on my boat, with sweat, sea salt, and sunscreen dried on her skin. Making love to her on the deck this past summer, with her long legs wrapped around my waist as I did my best to take home the trophy for most orgasms delivered in a single afternoon, I was convinced I'd finally met someone I could stick with for longer than a season.

But it's not going to happen. It's only October and I've just told Sylvia she's coo-coo for Cocoa Puffs and that I'll have her shit packed up and sent to her office tomorrow afternoon.

And then she said that I was an emotionally unavailable jerk who is incapable of sustaining an adult relationship. And then I said that she's a blackmailing, birthday-ruining, manipulative, sushi-obsessed control freak who should try to choke down a carb once in a while because it might make her more fun to be around on pizza night or donut morning or any other day of the goddamned week involving carbs because a life without carbs is a stupid life. And then she flipped me off and told me to "have a nice long, lonely existence, asshole," before knocking over a tray of champagne glasses on her way to the elevator at the other end of the roof.

The only good news? Very few of my guests seemed to notice our fight or Sylvia's dramatic exit.

It's nine-thirty, we've all been drinking since six, and most of my nearest and dearest are feeling no pain. I should be feeling no pain, too. I'm on my third tumbler of GlenDronach, haven't eaten anything since lunch because the food at my party is unacceptable—if Sylvia and I were really meant to be, she would have realized I hated sushi two months ago—and haven't drunk anything more serious than a beer since before the preseason.

But somehow, I'm stone-cold sober.

Sober and tired of celebrating, and wishing I could slip out and grab a deep-dish pizza from Dove Vivi. The cornmeal crust thing they've done to their pies is addictive, and I'm pretty sure there's nothing in the world fresh mozzarella, house-made bacon, and a hearty slathering of pesto can't fix.

Portland is home to some of the best eats in the world. It's also home to more strip clubs per capita than any other city in the nation. If I weren't committed to being a good host, I could have pizza in my belly and boobs in my face in under an hour. But I'm not the kind to ghost on my guests. I leave that for weirdos like my team captain, Brendan, who consistently vanishes from bars and clubs without warning, and clearly has issues with saying good-bye.

Not that I can blame him. After six years as a happily married man, going back to hitting the scene solo can't be easy.

I'm just glad to see him finally out and about again. After Maryanne's death, he shut down so hard a lot of us on the team were worried there might come a day when we'd show up for practice and learn Brendan wasn't coming back to the ice, either because he'd lost the will to play, or because he'd lost the will to live.

That's how much you should love the woman you're going to marry. You should love her so much that if she were taken away from you it would feel like your rib cage had been cracked open and some sadistic son of a bitch was cutting away tiny pieces of your heart, slathering them in salt, and eating them right in front of you.

I've never felt anything close to that. For Sylvia or any other girl I've dated.

So maybe Sylvia is right. Maybe I'm going to spend the rest of my life solo, with my loneliness occasionally broken by short-term relationships with various hot pieces of ass.

"Poor me," I say, lips curving in a hard grin.

Seriously, cry me a river, right? I've got a multi-million-dollar contract, a stunning loft with one-hundred and eighty degree views of the city, and my health, which is not something I'm stupid enough to take for granted. I was born with the kind of face that not even a black eye from scrumming with those douchebags from L.A. can wreck, and a body that performs—on the ice and in the bedroom. I should be laughing all the way to the dance floor, where I know of at least six or seven unattached hotties, any one of which would be happy to ease my birthday breakup pain by riding my cock all night long.

What do I want instead?

Pizza. My pajamas. And a crochet hook with an endless supply of yarn.

Nothing calms me down like hooking on a granny square until I've got one big enough to cover my entire damned bed. I've graduated to more complex projects since those early days learning how to hook so I wouldn't go crazy while I was stuck in bed with mono for three months, but sometimes mindless repetition is the only cure for what ails me.

And yes, I like to crochet. Again, I'll ask that you not fucking judge me, because it's my birthday, because my charity, Hookers for the Homeless, has provided over two thousand caps, gloves, and scarves to people in need, and because my Instagram account—Hockey Hooker—has over a million followers. Clearly, the women of the world have no problem with a man who enjoys handicrafts. Though, the fact that my first post was a body shot of me wearing nothing but a Santa Hat I'd crocheted over my cock probably didn't hurt.

I have no shame when it comes to selfies with my latest project. My friend Laura—childhood partner in crime and current public relations master for the Badgers—says she approves of my social media efforts to promote good will for the team. Her little sister and my crochet guru, Libby, thinks it's great that I'm using my yarn addiction to raise awareness of the homeless crisis. But let's get real. I started posing semi-nude for the tail and the attention.

I'm usually a big fan of tail and attention.

But now, as Laura and Libby climb the steps leading up to the patio from the dance floor, clearly intending to wish me a warm, bubbly, old-friends happy birthday, I wish I had an excuse not to talk to either one of them. Laura because she's insane when she's drunk—once she's had a few, the usually level-headed La can't be trusted not to embarrass herself and everyone around her—and Libs because I'm incapable of hiding anything from that girl.

Ever since thirteen-year-old Libs spent months teaching me how to crochet when I was housebound my sophomore year of high school—keeping me company and furthering my yarn-based education while we watched 80s movies and debated important things like whether *Better*

Off Dead or *Just One of the Guys* was the superior underrated teen flick of that particular decade—I've had a chink in my armor where the youngest Collins sibling is concerned.

She sees through me. Every damned time.

When I had a shitty first half of my first season with the Badgers five years ago, Libby was the one who noticed I was being eaten alive by self-doubt and talked me back from the edge. When my charity was getting audited by the IRS, Libby realized I wasn't nearly as chill about the whole thing as I was pretending to be and sent me a knight's helmet she'd crocheted and a note promising that everything would work out. And when Sylvia and I had a pregnancy scare last summer, Libby was the only person I told.

Hearing Libs say that I could absolutely handle being a dad had made me a little less terrified. Not that I'd believed her, but hearing that trying your best and loving your kid is all that really matters from a woman who spends every day with a classroom full of rug-rats was comforting.

But I don't want to be comforted right now. I want to get through the rest of this party and then hide out at home and lick my breakup wounds in private. So I plaster on a smile and hope it's too dark for Libby to see how shitty I feel.

"Hello, birthday boy!" Laura throws her long arms around me, hugging me hard enough to make my breath rush out with an *oof* as she crushes my ribs, reminding me she's also freakishly strong when she's three sheets to the wind. "I love you, Justin. I'm so glad we're still best friends. Let's go do happy-birthday shots on the roof to celebrate!"

"We're already on the roof." I grunt again as she hugs me even tighter.

"Yes, we are, and as high up as anyone needs to be right now," Libby agrees, meeting my pained gaze over her sister's shoulder, her brown eyes anxious. Clearly, she's also aware that her big sis has entered the bad-decision-making portion of the evening and should be monitored closely until she's home in bed.

"No, the real roof, the one through the locked door behind the DJ booth." Laura points a wobbly hand toward the stairwell on the other side of the dance floor, then twists her long red hair into a knot on top of her head. "I've been practicing my lock-picking skills so I'll be ready when I quit PR to become a spy."

"As one does," I observe dryly.

"Exactly!" Laura jabs a bony finger into the center of my chest. "See, you get it. So let's do this. We'll break the lock, climb the stairs, and be the highest things in downtown. Get shots and meet me there. Or maybe we should stick with martinis." She moans happily as she wiggles her fingers in the general direction of the bar. "Those Thai basil martinis are so amazing! Perfect with the sushi. Like, seriously brilliant. Sylvia did a bang-up job with the catering, Jus. Especially for a woman who looks like she hasn't eaten since last Christmas."

"Laura, hush," Libby whispers, nudging her sister in the ribs with her elbow.

Laura bares her teeth in an "oh shit" grimace before smacking herself on the forehead. "Fuck, I'm sorry. I forgot about the storming out and knocking over a tray of drinks on her way out of the party thing. Are you two okay?"

"We're fine," I say, cursing silently. So much for

avoiding this particular conversation. "She just decided it wasn't working for her. It's no big deal."

"But breaking up on your birthday sucks." Laura's lips turn down hard at the edges. "And I thought she was one of the nice ones. I mean, I didn't know her that well, but she seemed nice."

"She was nice." I take another too big drink of my scotch. "And now she's gone. But she hadn't even unpacked her boxes yet, so it shouldn't take long to move them all out."

"That's right. I forgot you two had moved in together. Bet that makes you want to keep drinking, huh?" Laura reaches back, putting an arm around Libby, hugging her much shorter sister closer as she not-so-subtly tries to steal Libby's martini.

Libby, who I suddenly realize is looking very un-Libby-like in a tight black tank top and a pair of leather pants that cling to her curvy thighs, huffs and swats Laura's hand away. "Enough! Stop using displays of affection to try to steal my drink."

"Why? It worked last time," Laura says, grinning wickedly.

"Well, it's not going to work this time. I'm keeping my martini." Libby narrows her eyes, which are ringed in heavy black liner and some silver glittery stuff that emphasizes how enormous they are. It's a look that's way more rock-star than kindergarten teacher and also decidedly...odd. For her, anyway.

I can't remember the last time I saw Libby wearing makeup or tight clothing. She's a "layers of linen draped around her until she looks like an adorable bag lady or a hippie pirate" kind of girl. I'm used to the Libby who wears ruffly dresses, clogs, and crocheted sweaters, and totes her knitting bag with her everywhere she goes.

This new look is so unexpected that I'm distracted long enough for Laura to snatch my scotch right out of my hand.

"Hey, give that back," I say, scowling as she dances out of reach. "It's an open bar, psycho. Go get your own scotch."

"But it's more fun to steal yours," Laura says. And then, with the gleeful giggle of a woman who is going to be very hungover tomorrow morning, she turns and flees into the throng of dancers writhing to the music, tossing, "Come get me when it's time to break and enter! You know you want to," over her shoulder.

Libby sighs heavily, and I turn back to see her watching me with that same anxious expression, making my heart lurch. "I don't want to talk about Sylvia," I say, cutting her off before she can ask.

"Okay," she says, letting me off the hook far more easily than I expect her to. "But can we talk about something else? Something kind of...private?"

"Um, sure." I do a quick scan of our immediate surroundings. Aside from a couple making out in the shadows about ten feet away, we're alone. Everyone else is either out on the dance floor, queued up at the bar, or lounging on the couches near the fire pit on the other side of the patio, soaking in the view of the city.

"Thanks." Libby smiles nervously as she lifts her glass. "Just let me down a little more liquid courage first."

"All right," I say, wondering who this woman is and what she's done with my sweet, rarely drinks more than one drink, doesn't own a stitch of black clothing, would never leave the house without putting on a bra Libby.

I really don't think she's wearing a bra under that lacy shirt. And I really can't stop staring, trying to solve the bra or no-bra mystery, and I'm swiftly becoming way too fixated on Libby's breasts for my personal comfort.

"Maybe I should get a drink, too." I start for the bar, needing a moment to pull myself together, when Libby puts a hand on my arm.

"I'm sorry," she says, but I have no idea what she's apologizing for, only that her touch feels different than it did before. As different as the Libby I've known since she was a kid is from this seriously sexy woman standing in front of me.

HOT AS PUCK is Available Now!

BONUS SNEAK PEEK!

Bang Theory, Shep and Bridget's story, is out 11/04/19!

Bang Theory is a laugh out loud, friends-to-lovers comedy featuring a girl with zero game and a guy with all the right night moves...

Bridget's positive her best friend—bearded dreamboat and drummer for one of rock's hottest bands, Shep—can help her solve the How To Become A Sex Goddess equation. Shep's positive that giving the girl he's secretly in love with lessons in seduction is going to kill him.

But what a way to go...

Pre-order BANG THEORY now!

ABOUT THE AUTHOR

Author of over forty novels, *USA Today* Bestseller Lili Valente writes everything from steamy suspense to laugh-out-loud romantic comedies. A die-hard romantic and optimist at heart, she can't resist a story where love wins big. Because love should always win.

When she's not writing, Lili enjoys adventuring with her two sons, climbing on rocks, swimming too far from shore, and asking "why" an incorrigible number of times per day. A former yoga teacher, actor, and dancer, she is also very bendy and good at pretending innocence when caught investigating off-limits places.

You can currently find Lili in the mid-South, valiantly trying to resist the lure of all the places left to explore.

Find Lili at www.lilivalente.com

ALSO BY LILI VALENTE

Red HOT Laugh-out-Loud Rom Coms

The Bangover

Bang Theory

The Hunter Brothers

The Baby Maker

The Troublemaker

The Heartbreaker

The Panty Melter

The Bad Motherpuckers Series (Standalones)

Hot as Puck

Sexy Motherpucker

Puck-Aholic

Puck me Baby

Pucked Up Love

Puck Buddies

Sexy Flirty Dirty Romantic Comedies (Standalones)

Magnificent Bastard

Spectacular Rascal

Incredible You

Meant for You

The Master Me Series

(Red HOT erotic Standalone novellas)

Snowbound with the Billionaire

Snowed in with the Boss

Masquerade with the Master

Bought by the Billionaire Series

(HOT novellas, must be read in order)

Dark Domination

Deep Domination

Desperate Domination

Divine Domination

Kidnapped by the Billionaire Series

(HOT novellas, must be read in order)

Filthy Wicked Love

Crazy Beautiful Love

One More Shameless Night

Under His Command Series

(HOT novellas, must be read in order)

Controlling her Pleasure

Commanding her Trust

Claiming her Heart

To the Bone Series

(Sexy Romantic Suspense, must be read in order)

A Love so Dangerous

A Love so Deadly

A Love so Deep

Fight for You Series

(Emotional New Adult Romantic Suspense.

Must be read in order.)

Run with Me

Fight for You

Lover's Leap Series

A Naughty Little Christmas

The Bad Boy's Temptation

The Lonesome Point Series

(Sexy Cowboys written with Jessie Evans)

Leather and Lace

Saddles and Sin

Diamonds and Dust

12 Dates of Christmas

Glitter and Grit

Sunny with a Chance of True Love

Chaps and Chance

Ropes and Revenge

8 Second Angel

Co-written Standalones

The V Card (co-written with Lauren Blakely)

Falling for the Boss (co-written with Sylvia Pierce)

The Happy Cat Series

(co-written with Pippa Grant)

Hosed

Hammered

Hitched

Humbugged